Since You've Been Gone

SINCE YOU'VE BEEN GONE

A MAGNOLIA SOUND NOVEL

SAMANTHA CHASE

PRAISE FOR SAMANTHA CHASE

"If you can't get enough of stories that get inside your heart and soul and stay there long after you've read the last page, then Samantha Chase is for you!"

-NY Times & USA Today Bestselling Author **Melanie Shawn**

"A fun, flirty, sweet romance filled with romance and character growth and a perfect happily ever after."

-NY Times & USA Today Bestselling Author **Carly Phillips**

"Samantha Chase writes my kind of happily ever after!"

-NY Times & USA Today Bestselling Author **Erin Nicholas**

"The openness between the lovers is refreshing, and their interactions are a balanced blend of sweet and spice. The planets may not have aligned, but the elements of this winning romance are definitely in sync."

- **Publishers Weekly, STARRED review**

"A true romantic delight, A Sky Full of Stars is one of the top gems of romance this year."

- **Night Owl Reviews, TOP PICK**

"Great writing, a winsome ensemble, and the perfect blend of heart and sass."

To all the animal lovers out there...

Remember This:
"Saving one animal will not change the world, but surely for
that one animal, the world will change forever."
Please support your local animal rescue.

To my dear friend Christine and the wonderful staff of our
local rescue,
SAVING GRACE,
this one's for you.
https://savinggracenc.org/

1

"Damn. That is one *fine*-looking man."

"Ew, Mom! Stop it!"

"What? What did I say?"

Emma Ryan stared in wide-eyed horror as her mother continued to gaze at the shirtless man on her cellphone screen.

"What are you even watching? And why?"

Without tearing her eyes away from the screen, Christine Ryan-Foster dropped a bombshell. "Do you remember Garrett Coleman?" she asked, and before Emma could say a word, she continued. "He's a veterinarian now–like we all knew he would be–and he did this video at a shelter up in Maryland and it went viral." She hummed with approval. "And I can totally see why."

A shudder of revulsion rocked Emma. "He's my age, Mom. He's young enough to be your son! Stop it! Stop it right now!"

There was a host of other reasons why this was disturbing to her, but she wasn't about to voice any of them right now.

"Oh, hush. There's nothing wrong with a little harmless looking. And it's for a good cause."

Rolling her eyes, Emma walked around to the opposite side of their kitchen table and sat down. "Now this I've got to hear."

It took a solid minute for her mother to put her phone down and look at her. "Garrett's working with the shelter in the video, and, every week, he does a post showing him doing something incredibly sweet to help a scared animal."

Well...that didn't sound like anything that would have her mother thinking sexy thoughts. So maybe when she said he was fine, she meant that he was a good person.

"Oh, well...good for him. And I'm glad you're looking at him as a good person instead of..."

"And he is always shirtless," Christine interrupted with a grin. "Mmm, mmm, mmm...*fine*."

Yeah, that time there was definitely a tone that made it abundantly clear that fine meant sexy.

With a loud sigh, Emma rested her head in her hands. "And the good cause?"

"Well, his videos have brought a lot of attention to the plight at the shelter and people have been lining up to adopt! Since his first video a month ago, almost all of their animals have been adopted!" She looked at her daughter and smiled. "Almost one hundred pets found their forever home because of him. Don't you think that's amazing?"

There was no way she couldn't agree because it *was* amazing. With a nod, she straightened in her seat. "Good for him and good for the shelter. It's very cool."

And so totally Garrett.

He was one of the good guys–always happy, always friendly, always ready to lend a hand.

Or give you the shirt off his back.

Literally.

*Don't ask to see the video. Do **not** ask to see the video...*

"I wish you two still kept in touch," her mother said, interrupting her thoughts again.

"Why?"

"Honestly? We could use a little help like this for Happy Tails. We've got more dogs here now than we ever have before, and...I don't know." She let out a long breath. "I'm exhausted, Em. It's a lot of work to rescue these dogs and try to find them homes. Plus the expense of feeding and getting medical care for all of them is so high"

"Doc MacEntyre has always had a soft spot for us. I'm sure he can handle a few more dogs this month."

"Doc MacEntyre is talking retirement and hasn't found anyone to take over his practice."

"What?!" Emma cried. "When did this happen?"

Her mother shrugged. "He's been talking about it for a while, but when he was here last week, he told me he had another three months before he was closing up shop."

For a moment, she had no idea what to say. Her lips were moving, but no sound was coming out.

"Em? You okay?"

"I...I...I guess I had no idea all this was going on. What are you going to do? Have you reached out to other vets?"

"Of course, but none of them can offer what Doc did. And none of them were willing to come here and make an afternoon of it once a week." She sighed. "So I've got the team working on making calls and trying to raise some money so maybe we can stock up on medical supplies before his office closes."

"How's that going? Last I heard, Georgia Bishop was handling that sort of thing."

"She is, and she's really good at it, but..." She shrugged.

"But what?" For a moment, she didn't think her mother was going to answer her. Then Emma looked at her–really looked at her–and noticed how tired she looked. "Mom? Is everything okay?"

"We didn't want to burden you," she began, but her voice cracked.

Reaching out, Emma placed her hand on top of her mother's. "Mom? Come on, you know you can tell me anything."

This time when Christine looked up at her, there were tears in her eyes. "Ed's got to have back surgery. We can't put it off any longer, and...and I just don't know how we're going to handle everything. He won't be able to work or help with all the animals and now without a vet..." When she started to cry, Emma squeezed her hand.

"It's going to be okay, Mom. You know you have a ton of people who are more than willing to help. What can I do? Just tell me. I can get Ryleigh, Madison, and Wyatt to school in the mornings before I go to work, and you know they can help around here too."

Groaning, Christine shook her head. "Your sisters are a mess. You remember what it was like when you were their age. The last thing they want to do is get dirty or break a sweat. All they want is to hang out with their friends, and your brother has football practice. If we want him to get a scholarship for college, he really needs to be focused on that." She shook her head again. "I don't know how I'm going to handle it all. I don't want to ask Georgia to do more fundraisers, but it's what we really need. Then I saw Garrett's videos and thought..."

But she didn't finish.

Which was fine with Emma because she knew exactly where her mother was going with her train of thought.

If Garrett could do some of those videos for Happy Tails, it would be a great help.

Not that there was anything she could do about it. As it was, it sounded like her plate just got a lot fuller. Helping out with her siblings wasn't really a hardship–and she enjoyed having the time to bond with them. With Emma being twenty-six and her siblings ranging from ten to fifteen, there typically wasn't a whole lot that they did together. Maybe while her stepfather was recovering, she could spend some quality time with them.

And maybe find a way to add more hours to a day.

Squeezing her mother's hand again, she forced herself to smile. "It's all going to be okay. I can help make calls and pitch in wherever you need me, okay?"

Christine gave her a slight nod. "I do have one...other bit of bad news."

Oh, good grief...

"Axel is back."

"What do you mean he's back?"

Another nod was her mother's response before letting out a weary sigh. "The foster family brought him back and said he was too difficult and even said he was unlovable."

Emma jumped to her feet in outrage. "Excuse me?! Unlovable? That's insane! Axel is one of the sweetest and most lovable dogs we've ever had here! And did they call him difficult because of his little gimpy leg?" She began to pace as she let out a growl of frustration. "I hope you revoked their foster care status because anyone who would bring that sweet boy back is just insane!"

Standing, Christine walked over to make herself a cup of coffee. "You know these things happen sometimes. Not every dog is a good fit for every home. It's sad, and I hate when it happens, but...it happens."

While it was true, it was the third time it happened for Axel, and it broke Emma's heart. "I just don't understand how no one could want him. He's a sweet puppy. His leg really doesn't hold him back much anymore, and if people were just a little patient..."

This time her mother turned and gave her a sardonic smile. "Em...come on. You know I love all animals, but Axel can be a little..."

"Okay, he can be a little rambunctious, but he's a puppy! He's supposed to be like that!"

"Normally, I would agree, but in Axel's case, he's only happily rambunctious when he's with you. The foster family said he was a little vicious and almost openly hostile toward them."

"Openly hostile? Come on, Mom, even you have to admit that's a little dramatic. He was just nervous, that's all."

"Emma," Christine said with exasperation. "Axel is going to be a difficult dog to place because there's only one person he's bonded with, and that's you."

She groaned again because it was true, and in a perfect world, she'd take him home with her and give him all the love and acceptance he could ever need. Unfortunately, her condo didn't allow pets, so unless she was willing to either move back home or find someplace else that would probably cost more money, her hands were tied.

"I'm not trying to make you feel bad, sweetheart," her mother said, interrupting her thoughts. "But I wanted you to be prepared in case you went out to the barn and saw him."

"That's exactly what I'm going to do. I'm going to go out and see him and make sure he knows how awesome he is and try to undo the trauma the foster people caused!" She walked over to the refrigerator and grabbed a bottle of water before heading for the door.

"He's not traumatized..."

"Says you," Emma murmured before walking out the door.

Stalking across the yard, she tried to force herself to calm down. Axel noticed when she was upset, and honestly, so did the other dogs. No need to get everyone all worked up just because she was ticked off.

The property was massive, and just six months ago, they were able to purchase some of the surrounding property so they could expand. Happy Tails–and their family home– now sat on close to five acres and it made her smile when she looked around. Her mother and stepfather accomplished so much in the last eighteen years. They had met at a volunteer event for an animal shelter, bonded over their love of dogs, and had been together ever since. It was a really sweet story, but to see what they accomplished over the years and how many dogs they saved and found homes for was just short of astonishing.

So why couldn't they find a home for Axel?

As if sensing her thoughts, the tiny Border Jack mix spotted her and came running over. Emma immediately crouched down and held out her arms for him. He was all of eleven pounds of short brown fur, but he had enough speed and enthusiasm for a team of horses.

Especially when he jumped into her arms and knocked her over, happily licking her face.

"Easy, boy," she laughed, hugging him close. A few other dogs ran over to investigate and she found herself surrounded by a small herd, all vying for her attention. Luckily, most lost interest after a few minutes and she was able to get to her feet with Axel in her arms. His tail was wagging like crazy as she walked around to the small picnic area they had set up for families to come and meet with the dogs.

Once she was seated, she looked down at him and smiled. "I'm glad you're back," she said quietly. "That family didn't deserve you, and I promise we're going to find you the best home in the world." She kissed his head. "I wish it were with me, but...unless you've got some ideas for me to make more money, I'm afraid I'm stuck living where I'm at."

Her divorce three years ago pretty much bankrupted her–mainly because her useless ex emptied their bank account and ran up their credit cards before taking off. She'd been working as hard as she could to rebuild her credit and her life, but it was taking a lot of time and energy. She was exhausted and miserable and wished something would go her way for once.

"If things don't get better, buddy, I'm going to be living in the barn with you."

Axel's response was to lick her cheek.

Looking around, Emma saw the improvements that had been made and knew all the fundraising was definitely a blessing, but right now she was a little hyper-focused on everything they were going to need in the next few months and how it was going to happen.

Reaching into her pocket, she pulled out her phone and let out a long breath.

Just look at the video...

Glancing at Axel, she said, "No one can know that I'm doing this. It has to be our little secret."

This time he licked her eye.

Gross...

With a quick look over her shoulder to make sure no

one else was around, Emma swiped the phone screen and pulled up her Instagram account. A minute later, she found one of Garrett's videos and couldn't help but smile.

And not just because he looked amazing without a shirt.

He was sitting in a cage at the animal shelter beside a terrified-looking beagle. Garrett was eating popcorn out of a stainless-steel bowl that was identical to the bowl of food in front of the dog. The whole time he was talking softly to the poor little thing and encouraging it to eat. It took a solid five minutes for the dog to slowly inch forward and sniff the food and then another few before he started to eat.

"Damn," she murmured as she reached up to wipe tears away.

Before she knew it, she was on to another video of him–shirtless again–playing guitar to a Golden Retriever whose owner had passed away. Apparently the poor dog had been forgotten, and when he was finally rescued, he was under-weight and malnourished.

She cried some more.

Next thing she knew, she'd watched half a dozen videos of Garrett being ridiculously loving and patient and nurturing to different traumatized animals. She'd clicked the heart icon under each and every one of them, but it wasn't until the last one where he was pulling an elderly dog along on a wagon in a park because the poor thing had been hit by a car and lost use of his back legs that she finally had to comment.

"I always knew you'd do amazing things @GarrettCole-manVet. Glad to see you're still sweet too."

Yeah, it was cheesy, and he probably never read all the comments from his adoring fans, but it made her feel better to say something.

If she were the braver sort, she'd message him and ask for his help, but...she wasn't.

For a few more minutes, she looked at pictures of him and sighed–sandy brown hair that always looked a little messy and a cropped beard looked good on him. Emma always thought he was cute, but as he got older and matured, he'd turned into a ridiculously good-looking guy. He was so good-looking that she tended to revert to her stuttering ways because she'd get nervous around him. It was crazy because they were friends– good friends–but there had been a time when she felt like it was weird. Garrett was confident and popular, while she was always quiet and shy. Their friendship didn't make sense, and she was the envy of many, many girls because she never had to work for his attention. They were just friends.

Just. Friends.

Every once in a while, she used to dream about what it would be like if they were more than friends. It was silly and always just a fleeting sort of thought, and she certainly never did anything about it. Then, at seventeen, she started dating Steve March and...

Yeah, she didn't want her thoughts to even go there. She wasted far too many years on that relationship and now look where she was.

She looked down at Axel, who was curled up in a ball and sleeping in her lap, with a sigh. She smiled and gently pet him. "We'll get through this, sweet boy. Somehow, we'll find a way for everything to work out."

Garrett Coleman knew he'd met the girl of his dreams when he was eight years old.

He just never told her.

Staring down at his phone, he couldn't help the stupid smile on his face. Emmaline Ryan had commented on one of his videos and it was crazy how happy that made him.

His first thought was to send her a message and see how she was doing, but...he didn't want to seem overly anxious. His second thought was to try to see if anyone he knew had her phone number so he could call her, but...that seemed a little stalkerish.

With a sigh, he leaned back on his sofa and tried not to be such an idiot about the whole thing. It was one comment on one video. For all he knew, she was just being nice and wasn't looking to actually talk with him.

Well, that's a depressing thought...

Before he could do anything else, his phone rang, and it was stupid how he could feel disappointed that it wasn't an incoming call from Emma.

Instead, it was his older brother Austin.

"Hey!" he said as he answered. "What's up?"

"Is this the Hot Doc? Mr. Sexy Vet? The social media sensation known for..."

The groan was out before he could stop it. All those damn titles people had given him on social media were killing him. "For the love of it, Austin. Give me a break."

"Damn, you're no fun. What are you doing this weekend?"

"I'm fine, thanks for asking," he said with a small laugh. "And how are you? How's Mia?"

Luckily, his brother took the hint. "Sorry. We're doing well. Great, actually. Mia's been in her writing cave for the last few weeks trying to finish up a book, and I've been busy getting plans finalized for the house."

"That's awesome! Although...I thought the plans were already finalized."

"I had to tweak a few things and get permits filed, nothing crazy. It was more time-consuming than anything else." He paused. "So listen, we're breaking ground on the property this weekend, and I kind of had this idea of all of us being there for it. Mom's already planning on making a big picnic lunch for everyone, and Jackson's on a short leave and said he'd be here, so...I don't know. I just thought it would be cool if you were here too and we'd do this together."

For a moment, Garrett was speechless. Austin wasn't usually the type who embraced a lot of family togetherness, but ever since he moved back to Magnolia Sound and fell in love with Mia Kingsley, he'd changed.

For the better.

"Um...yeah!" he finally said. "That sounds great! I'll see about making it a long weekend and getting Friday and Monday off. The drive should only take a little over three hours, so..."

"Wait," Austin interrupted. "I thought you were up in Maryland."

"Nope, I'm in Norfolk now."

"When did that happen?"

"A few weeks ago. I'm sort of traveling around a bit and working with different offices and trying to figure out where I want to settle at. I've had a lot of amazing offers, but it's hard to commit when I know nothing about the area, you know?"

"Yeah, I do. So what kind of offers? Partnerships or just joining the staff?"

"Mostly just joining the staff, but I did meet with a clinic up in Delaware that I could possibly become a partner in after the first year. It's a huge practice–well-established–and they're looking to expand. The area is beautiful, the housing market is great, and I have some friends who live locally. The salary is phenomenal, and, really, there's no downside to it."

"Then why not just accept it? What's holding you back?"

Good question...

With a shrug, he replied, "I'm not sure. You know I like to be thorough. Cover all bases. Do enough research to make sure I'm making the right decision."

"Overthinking. The word you're looking for is over-thinking."

"It's not..."

"That's exactly what it is, and one of these days all that overthinking is going to cost you. Hell, you could miss out on a great position because you're trying out all these other places when you probably already know some of them aren't going to be a good fit!"

"I won't know until I go and check it out," he reasoned.

"Garrett, listen to me," Austin countered. "I'm older than you."

"Barely..."

"Still talking!" his brother shouted, effectively shutting Garrett up. "I'm older and I've known you your whole life and you have a tendency to overthink and be overly cautious and you can't tell me that's never come back to bite you in the ass!"

"Okay, maybe it has a time or two, but..."

"But nothing! If this job in Delaware is as great as you think it is, then trust your gut and go for it!"

"They gave me until the end of the month to make a decision."

He heard his brother sigh before he asked, "Yes, but do you really *need* until the end of the month?"

Garrett knew he didn't, but he also knew he'd made some commitments and didn't want to let anyone down, so...

"I do," he said. "I've made arrangements to visit clinics to help out and I'm not going to let anyone down. It's just not who I am. I'm a man of my word and so..."

"So you're going to overthink and be thorough and just be you," Austin said wearily.

"No one's asking you to do it. There's no need to sound so put out."

It took a minute, but Austin finally conceded. "You're right, you're right. I would get pissy if anyone tried to tell me how to live my life, so who am I to try to do that to you? Sorry."

"Wow, Mia has really worked wonders on you," he said with a small laugh.

"What's that supposed to mean?"

"You've mellowed, and it's kind of awesome and freaky at the same time. Now I *have* to come home so I can witness it in person!"

"Garrett..."

"No, no...don't say anything and ruin it! If I can get the time off, I'll most likely drive down Thursday night and stay at Mom's."

"Um...just make sure you let her know that first. Don't surprise her."

"Okay, but...why?"

"She's dating."

"Dating?"

"Yeah. As in, she has a boyfriend."

For a minute, Garrett had no idea how to react to that news. "So that means…"

Austin growled. "Just make sure you call so you don't show up while she and her boyfriend are maybe…having a date night at home! Jeez, do I need to paint you a picture?"

He shuddered. "Please don't."

And then he shuddered again.

"Maybe I should just stay with you," he mentioned, thinking it was possibly the safer option.

"No. Every night is date night at home for us and you'd be in the way," Austin teased.

"TMI, brother. T-M-I."

"Just call Mom and give her the heads-up. I'm sure it will be fine."

"So who's the guy? Have you met him?"

"Yeah. Dominic Jones. He owns Jones Automotive on the north side of town. He's Scarlett's dad."

"Oh, wow…I had no idea he and Mom were…I mean… when did this start?"

"Garrett, breathe. It's not a big deal, and you can't be all weird about it when you're here. Mom's really happy, and Dom's a good guy, so…relax, okay?"

Raking a hand through his hair, he nodded. "Yeah. I'm good. I swear. I just wasn't expecting that."

"It's not like she was going to stay single forever." Austin paused. "Or so everyone keeps telling me."

"Okay, so then I'm not the only one a little unnerved by this announcement." Relief washed over him. "What does Jackson think?"

"He really didn't seem to have an opinion. All he said was 'cool,' so…there's that."

"How did he end up being the most chill out of the three of us?" Garrett mused.

"Beats me. Although, personally, I think he wasn't really paying attention so I'm not sure we could say with any certainty how chill he is."

"Sounds about right. I haven't talked to him in a while. Is he doing okay?"

"He's contemplating whether he's going to re-up with the Marines and if he doesn't, does he want to come back to Magnolia Sound? Plus, he's getting deployed in a few weeks, so he's got more important things on his mind rather than whether or not Mom has a boyfriend."

They were both quiet for a minute before Garrett asked, "Do you think he'll move back home? Really?"

"There was a time when I thought I wouldn't, but now that I'm here, I couldn't imagine living anywhere else. It's been nice reconnecting with everyone." He paused. "Did you reach out to any clinics around here, by chance?"

"Seriously?" Garrett said with a gruff laugh.

"What's wrong with the clinics around here? If any of us were going to move back home after college, I figured it would be you."

"Why?"

"I don't know. You had a really tight group of friends you were always with–some of whom still live here–and I guess I just thought you were more of a small-town guy."

There was a time when Garrett would have agreed, and there definitely had been a time when he truly believed he'd move back to Magnolia.

But then...he'd missed his opportunity and lost the girl he was always too cautious about asking out, and the thought of living in the same town with her and her husband was beyond unappealing.

"She's divorced now, you know," Austin said, interrupting his thoughts.

"Who?" And yeah, it was stupid to pretend he had no idea who his brother was referring to.

"Emmaline."

There were only a handful of people who called her that–most called her Emma–but Garrett has always preferred her full name. He sighed. "That's ancient history, man. And besides, it's safe to say that ship has sailed."

She did comment on your video...

"I'm just saying...you never liked to talk about it, but you talked about it enough that I knew why you stayed away. That reason is gone now. Maybe when you come home this weekend, you should stop in at Happy Tails..." Austin paused and chuckled. "I sound ridiculous saying that name. Anyway, I'm sure she'd be happy to see you." Another pause. "You know, stopping in to catch up with an old friend. No big deal."

The idea had merit, but...Garrett wasn't sure he could do it. A comment on social media was one thing.

He had a feeling if he went and saw Emma face-to-face, he'd be that same nervous kid he'd been since the third grade.

"You're overthinking it, G," Austin said, once again interrupting his thoughts.

"I'm not."

"You are!"

"I'm not!"

"Okay then, tough guy. I *dare* you to go and see Emmaline," his brother challenged.

With a groan, he raked a hand through his hair again. "Dude, we're adults. Daring me is ridiculous."

"How about I make it interesting?"

Oh, God...

"We can bet money on it. I'm sure Jackson would love to get in on it too."

"No...don't involve him. He gloats worse than you." And yeah, he was practically whining.

"Fine. No Jackson. But what do you say to a hundred bucks?"

I can lose a hundred bucks and still be okay...

"Or..." Austin went on. "If you go and see her, then I'll donate the money to the animal charity of your choice."

"You should be doing that anyway."

"But if you don't go and see her..."

Here it comes...

"You owe me a week of labor on the new house."

"Wait, so you donate a measly hundred bucks if I win, but then I owe you forty hours of hard labor if I lose? How is that fair?"

Austin laughed. "Fine. You can name the amount–within reason. What do you say?"

It went without saying that Garrett was going to help with the house no matter what. Once things hit a point where the main construction was done, he knew they'd all be pitching in with painting and landscaping and whatever else needed to be done. It was technically a no-brainer. He could skip out on seeing Emma and be no worse for the wear.

"Garrett?"

Or...he could go and see her and put his mind at ease that she was doing okay and move on with his life.

Decisions...decisions...

"Garrett!" his brother snapped.

"Yeah, sure. I'm in."

2

"I can't do it. I don't want to."

Emma smiled. "How about this–you read these three pages to me, and tomorrow we'll see if your mom will bring you to the barn so you can read to one of the puppies. What do you think?"

Five-year-old Callie Wells looked up at her with wonder. "Really? I can read to the puppies?"

"If you finish this assignment and read these pages to me, I will talk to your mother and we'll make all the arrangements."

Then she silently prayed that Mrs. Wells would be agreeable.

In her career as a speech therapist, Emma worked with the surrounding school districts on an as-needed basis and then tutored on the side. Some afternoons, she met with clients at their homes; other times–like today–they were at the library. She'd heard about programs where students read to dogs as a way of feeling less intimidated about reading and she'd tried it a few times with great success. It was time to see if it could work for Callie too.

Beside her, the little girl began to hesitantly read. "The c...c...at...cat..." Pausing, she looked up at Emma apologetically. "I'm sorry I'm not so good at this."

Emma reached over and gave her small hand a gentle squeeze. "I think you're very good at this," she told her, and with a smile, she encouraged her to keep reading.

When their session ended twenty minutes later, she talked to Callie's mother about the possibility of doing a tutoring session at the barn and she was completely on board!

"Does Callie have any allergies? Has she ever been around dogs?" Emma asked, knowing she would need to sign a consent form and a release form that Happy Tails used when people came to inquire about fostering or adopting one of the dogs.

"We have a Chihuahua at home. His name is Pickles," Mrs. Wells explained.

"Maybe tonight you could have Callie read to him? You know, as practice?"

"Oh, I'm not sure that's a good idea."

"How come?"

"Pickles is a little...ornery. He's my husband's dog, and he's ten years old. I think Callie overwhelms him."

With a smile, Emma held up her hand. "Say no more. We'll wait until tomorrow and I'll be sure to pick out one of the more mature and patient dogs to sit with us."

"Thanks, Emma. We'll see you tomorrow."

Once they were gone, Emma gathered her things and put the books they'd used back on the shelves. Then she wandered around and picked up a few books for herself before going to the checkout desk. "Hey, Shelby," she said softly, mindful of not talking too loudly.

"Hey, Emma! How did your session go today?"

"We're making progress, but tomorrow we're going to go over to Happy Tails and try reading to the dogs. I'm hoping that will make Callie feel a little more at ease."

"Oh, what a great idea!" Shelby looked around and seemed to be figuring something out in her head. After a minute, she turned back. "Okay, this is totally off the top of my head, but...what about bringing a few dogs here once a month for an after-school sort of thing? We can let the kids take turns reading to them! What do you think? Am I crazy?"

"Are you kidding? I think it's wonderful! Of course, I'd have to talk it over with my mom and see about getting volunteers to come with us to help with the dogs, and I'm sure you'll need to talk to someone about the legalities and insurance and all that other stuff that probably needs to be dealt with."

Shelby's smile fell. "Darn. I hadn't thought of that. I just know we have a few kids that come here after school because they don't have anywhere else to go and I thought it could be something fun for them."

And that gave Emma an idea.

What if she went to the high school and proposed an after-school program with students volunteering at Happy Tails? They could possibly get some sort of school credit for it, and her mother would get some extra help while Ed was recovering! It was a win-win situation!

Feeling very excited over the idea, she quickly explained it to Shelby as she checked out her books. "Please don't think I'm rude, but I'd love to go and run this idea by my mother and see what she thinks. Then I'll go to the school tomorrow and..."

Shelby laughed softly. "Emma, it's okay. Go. Go and

take care of things. I'll talk to you next week and we'll see if the idea for the library is even viable."

"Thanks, Shelby! Have a good night!"

The sun was already starting to go down and when she looked at her phone, she saw it was after five. It meant her mother was probably cooking dinner and trying to get everyone to do their homework and chores. And as much as she wouldn't mind dinner with the family, it had been a long day and she really just wanted to grab some takeout and head home. She'd call after dinner and run the idea by her then.

Feeling a little better now that she had a plan, Emma considered her options. Chinese takeout was really what she wanted, but she also needed to do a little grocery shopping. "Okay, I can call in the order while I'm shopping and pick it up on the way home. No big deal." And again, now that she had a plan, she got in her car and drove the short distance through town and parked in front of the Publix. As soon as she opened the car door, the smell of pizza hit her and she wondered if maybe she wanted that instead of the Chinese food.

Too many decisions...

While she thought it over, she shopped for her groceries.

Or...tried to.

The bakery was closest to the entrance, and suddenly all thoughts of dinner were gone and replaced by whether she could simply skip it and just have cake. Or cookies. Or brownies. Heck, she was an adult; she could have all three if she wanted to!

And right now, with so many delicious options, she seriously wanted to.

She was so busy strolling and staring down at the baked goods that she didn't notice the people around her.

Particularly the guy she just rammed with her shopping cart.

"Oh, my goodness!" she said as her hand flew to her mouth. "I'm *so* sorry!" Feeling completely horrified that she'd been so clumsy, Emma took a step around her cart to make sure the guy in question was alright.

He turned around before she got to him and she completely froze.

"Garrett?" she whispered.

His smile was lethal–dimples and all–and she wasn't sure if she should laugh, cry, or hug him. "Hey, Emmaline," he replied quietly. "Fancy running into you here." And yeah, he was making fun of her in the sweetest way and she instantly relaxed.

She hesitated and forced herself not to run over and hug him. They weren't kids anymore, and since she could still picture him without his shirt on in all those videos, she had a feeling no matter how innocent she might think a hug would be, her mind would immediately go to all kinds of not-so-innocent thoughts.

So she stayed where she was and smiled at him. "I...I didn't know you were in town. Are you here to see your brother? I heard he recently got engaged."

He nodded but didn't say anything, so Emma just let herself look at him–and tried not to fan herself. Garrett Coleman had always been handsome; even as far back as the third grade, she thought him to be the most handsome boy in school.

And to be honest, the videos did *not* do him justice because up close and in person, he was damn beautiful.

She felt herself blush as she took a small step back and cleared her throat. "So...um...how...how have you been?"

Great. After all these years of not stuttering, you choose now to start again?

"I'm doing well, thanks. How about you? How have you been?"

Her first instinct was to tell him the truth–that she was exhausted and stressed and almost in dire need of a miracle–but now wasn't the time for that. Instead, she gave the polite answer.

"Yeah, I'm doing good, too. Keeping busy," she said with a practiced smile. He was studying her just as closely as she was studying him, and she wished they had met up at any other time or place–preferably after she had about sixteen hours of sleep and fresh makeup on rather than at the end of the day when she most definitely looked tired. There were so many things she wanted to ask him, but all she could do was nod to the marble pound cake in his hands. "Good choice. It's one of my favorites, too."

"My mom's a little partial to it and I didn't want to go home empty-handed," he explained.

"That's very sweet of you."

"Well, I'd hate to prove you wrong," he said, his smile going from charming to a little shy.

"Um...wh...what do you mean?"

She could have sworn he muttered a curse as he looked away, but when he faced her again, he took a step closer. "You know...your comment on Instagram the other day. You said you were glad to see I was still sweet."

O-kay...where was a sinkhole when you needed it most?

Why couldn't lightning strike her down?

Anything to avoid this awkward exchange!

"Oh, well...yeah. Your videos are amazing," she forced

herself to say. "It looks like you've helped a lot of scared animals, Garrett. That's pretty incredible."

Wait...was he blushing now?

With a slight shrug, he took another step closer and Emma felt ready to sway toward him and give him that hug she was fighting. "You know I've always enjoyed working with animals. Goes back to the times I used to come over and help out at the barn. Your stepdad was always so cool and really helped me figure out what I wanted to do. He encouraged me a lot."

"Really? Ed did? Why didn't you ever tell me?"

Another shrug. "I don't know. I sort of felt like it was this cool thing between Ed and me. It was nice to have someone take an interest in me and what I wanted to do, considering my own father never did."

"Wow," she replied quietly. "I bet he'd love to know that."

"He follows me on social media and we've messaged back and forth a lot over the years. I think I've thanked him like a thousand times, but...it still doesn't feel like enough. I mean, how do you truly thank someone for making such a strong and positive impact in your life?"

And she knew he wasn't just saying it because Ed was her stepfather. He was saying it because it was true. Ed was genuinely one of a kind. He married Emma's mom when Emma turned nine and he always treated her like she was his own daughter. When her mother got pregnant with their first child, Emma feared that she would be tossed aside. After all, she was just a stepchild.

But she never was.

They'd been one big family of equals and it warmed her heart to know that Ed had also shown that kind of love and acceptance to Garrett.

"He's truly a great guy and you're so lucky to have him as a stepdad."

Emma nodded. She thought back to how long she and Garret had known each other. The two of them had initially bonded in Mrs. Reed's third-grade class over their speech and reading habits, the fact that both their dads weren't in their lives, and eventually, their love of animals. Garrett Coleman had been one of her best friends and it just hit her how much she'd missed him.

So she gave in and did the one thing she told herself she shouldn't.

She hugged him.

———————

Garrett didn't respond for all of three seconds, but then he gave in and wrapped his arms around Emma, hugging her back.

She was a little thinner than he remembered, and she felt delicate and fragile in his arms. Her long hair was pulled back in a ponytail and smelled like wildflowers, and it was all he could do not to inhale deeply.

Five minutes after seeing her again and you're already playing with fire. Awesome.

When she pulled back and smiled at him, he blurted out the first thing that came to his mind. "Have dinner with me."

Her whiskey-colored eyes went wide. "What?"

Nodding, he repeated himself. "Have dinner with me."

Now she completely stepped out of his embrace and looked mildly uncomfortable.

Way to go, dummy.

"I mean...you know...we can just go and grab some pizza

and catch up," he stammered, trying to erase that wary look off her face. "If you're busy…"

"No," she quickly interrupted. "It's not that. I j…just thought you w…were going to your mom's." She nodded toward the pound cake.

Damn. He'd forgotten about that.

"Oh, she's not expecting me until later tonight. I was going to surprise her, but…"

"But…?"

Yeah, either he was going to come off as sounding like a crappy son or cheesy.

He opted for both.

"Like I said, she's not expecting me, and I'd really like to visit with you for a little while. It's been too long since we've hung out."

Thankfully, that put a smile back on her face. "Well…I was planning on just grabbing some takeout after I shopped, but I guess I can shop afterward, so…"

Don't appear too anxious…

Carefully, he placed the pound cake back on the shelf and smiled at her. "Then let's go!"

It was a little crazy how excited he was about this and how it was a genuine effort not to let it show and scare her off.

Together they put her cart back and walked down to Michael's Italian Restaurant while they made small talk about shops they passed along the way. Garrett held the door open for her and was pleased when they were seated right away. "I thought there'd be more of a wait," he commented once they were situated.

"It's still kind of early." Then she laughed.

"What?" he asked, unable to hide his own amusement. "What's so funny?"

"It's like we're one of those old couples who come in for the early bird menu!" She laughed again, and once he looked around, he realized she was right. They were the youngest people in there.

And when she noticed him looking around, she did the same and laughed harder.

Then they were the ones being looked at.

"Okay, okay, okay," he said, his voice getting quieter with each word. Reaching across the table, he gently grabbed her hand as they took a few minutes to collect themselves. "I think we're a little too rowdy for this crowd."

With her free hand, she wiped at her eyes and nodded. "Oh, my goodness. I don't know why I thought that was so funny, but...it was!" Letting out a long breath, she straightened in her seat. "Sorry about that."

"Nothing to apologize for. I thought it was funny too." He looked down at how her hand was still in his and wondered if he should let it go or...just keep holding it.

Emma slowly pulled her hand free and he did his best not to take offense.

"So," he said, "what's been going on in your life?" Because he and Ed kept in touch, Garrett probably knew more about her than she realized, but there was no way he would let on. "Where are you working?"

"Well, I'm a speech therapist now," she began. "I work with the elementary schools in the county as well as tutor after school."

"That's great, Em. And speaking as your first student, I can say with great certainty that you're a great teacher."

She looked at him funny for a moment. "What do you mean?"

"If you remember correctly, it was back in Mrs. Reed's class that we were reading buddies and you helped me learn how to read. You were an awesome teacher back then, and you tutored me quite a bit through middle school and high school, so…" He grinned. "You were a great help to me and I know I wouldn't be where I am today if it weren't for you."

Her cheeks turned the sweetest shade of pink as she looked away. "Somehow, I doubt that."

"It's true!" He waited until she was looking at him again. "I was a terrible reader and had a short attention span. As I got older, I had a hard time keeping up with what was being taught and couldn't take notes because of it. You were there to help me out more times than you probably signed on for, and…I don't know." He shrugged. "I don't think I ever thanked you for it, so…thank you."

She was still blushing but she gave him a small smile. "And you're a veterinarian. Tell me about that."

Now it was his turn to blush because he knew she'd seen his videos.

Honestly, it started out as a dare from one of the lab techs at the clinic where he was working. One of those, "Hey, let's make a video to draw some attention to these poor dogs," and Garrett had agreed to be the face on the camera.

He still wasn't sure who dared him to take his shirt off or why that became the ongoing theme of the videos, but they were working, so he kept doing it that way.

With a nod, he told her about college and veterinary school and how he was currently looking for a clinic to call home and all the ones he had scheduled to work with for the rest of the month.

"Wow! You're certainly in high demand," she said with a small laugh. "Good for you! Have you picked a favorite yet?"

"There is one up in Delaware that I'm leaning toward,

but...I don't know. I need to meet with them all and get a feel of the area so I know I'm making an informed decision. I have until the end of the month to let my top choice know my decision."

Her shoulders sagged a little as she said, "Oh."

"What? What's the matter?" It seemed like an odd reaction to his news, but for the life of him, Garrett had no idea why she seemed disappointed.

"It's nothing," she murmured and picked up a menu. "What do you like on your pizza? I'm totally a pepperoni and mushroom girl, but if there's something else you'd prefer..."

"Em?"

"Or maybe we should get the Sicilian with the fresh mozzarella and basil. It's very yummy." Her face was buried behind the menu and Garrett reached over to pluck it out of her hands. Her eyes went wide as she tried to snag it back.

But he held it just out of her grasp.

"First, I happen to like both those options, so whichever you prefer, that's what we'll get. And second, why did you seem disappointed about my decision at the end of the month?"

"It...it just seems like you're rushing, that's all. I mean... wh...what if something else comes along next month? What if you haven't explored all...all the options?"

He hated that he was making her stutter. She didn't do it much–only when she was nervous, it seemed–and the last thing he wanted to do was make her uncomfortable.

"Believe me, I've been looking at all my options for the last two months and this is what I've narrowed it down to. They're all great clinics and I'm sure I'll be happy no matter which one I choose."

"How come none of them are in North Carolina?" she asked, her voice slightly tentative.

There was no way he could explain to her why he'd made that decision initially, but he had to say something. "I guess I wanted to see what else was out there. I grew up here and never traveled anywhere else until I left for college. Plus, there really wasn't anything for me here," he admitted.

"Your mother's still here and I know you have other family here in town. Plus, I thought I heard somewhere that your older brother lives here now. I would think they all count as something here for you." There was no condemnation in her tone, just genuine concern.

"Maybe," he said with a shrug. "I guess it's something to think about. I do have a lot of friends up North who have been like family to me. It would be hard to say goodbye to them."

"I imagine it would be." She paused and looked about to ask something when the waitress came over to take their order.

"Which are we getting?" he asked Emma.

"Hmm...they're both so good, but..."

Garrett held up a hand to stop her. Smiling up at the waitress, he said, "Can we get the Sicilian with the fresh mozzarella and basil and add pepperoni and mushrooms to it?"

"Oh, my goodness, Garrett!" Emma said with a laugh. "That's going to be too much!"

"Nah. There's no such thing as too much pizza. Trust me." Once the waitress got their drink order and was gone, he focused on where they were before. "What about you? What made you decide to come back to Magnolia after college?"

"My family," she said simply. "I couldn't imagine not living near them. My brother and sisters are a handful for Mom and Ed, and I like to help out whenever I can. Plus, I think I'd miss being away from Happy Tails. It's such a part of who I am that I don't know what I'd do without it."

"So you help out there a lot?"

She shrugged. "As much as I can with my work schedule." She paused for a moment. "Actually, tomorrow I'm bringing one of my students there to read to the dogs. She's a little shy, and I thought getting her to read to the animals might help. I've done it with a few other students with great results, so I'm hoping the same will happen for Callie."

"That sounds amazing! What a cool idea!"

"I'd like to take credit for it, but I can't. I've read studies on it, and it just so happens that I have access to a bunch of dogs in desperate need of love and attention. Too many of them, sadly."

"You've got a full house there, huh?"

"Right now, we've got more dogs than we ever have so Mom's a little frazzled." She paused and, again, she looked like she wanted to say more but changed her mind.

"I'd love to come by and see everyone if that's alright. Ed mentioned how they bought more land and are expanding. It's been so long since I've been there, and I guess now that I'm grown and a vet, I'm curious about the day-to-day of the place."

"They're really amazing at what they do. I wish more people were willing to do what Happy Tails does. Heck, it would be cool to see it as a franchise and locations saving dogs all over the country!"

The thought made him smile because he knew how much it was needed. He'd seen far too many animals who'd been neglected and in desperate need of care and a home.

Hence the videos.

"That would definitely be cool," he agreed. "I heard my aunt has been helping out with some fundraising." Pausing, he shook his head. "I thought Ed was joking when he told me, but then my mom and brother confirmed it. I can't even imagine how that happened."

"Oh, she's been incredible," Emma gushed. "I get that she's not the warm and fuzzy type, but she certainly knows how to get things done to raise money."

"Yup. Aunt Georgia's always been motivated where money's concerned," he murmured.

If Emma caught on to the sarcasm, she chose to say nothing. "Anyway, she's been a huge help to us. We've gotten some attention from the fundraisers and have been featured on the news and in the papers, so it's fair to say we've come a long way since you've been gone."

"Then I definitely want to come by and see it." He paused and tried to stop himself from coming off as too pushy. "Do you think it would be okay for me to come by tomorrow afternoon? I've got plans with my family for most of the weekend, but I have some time tomorrow if you think that would work."

"My tutoring session ends at 4:30," she said and then stopped herself. "I mean, you don't need me there to go over. Mom and Ed would be thrilled to see you no matter when you went over."

"Is Ed still working from home?"

She nodded. "He is. For the life of me, I still don't understand everything he does or how he's able to manage it all from home, but his laptop is never far from his side. Every once in a while, I'll find him in the barn with the dogs and he'll have his laptop with him and his headset on, talking to a client. It's amazing to watch."

"He's a good man, for sure."

Their waitress returned and put their drinks and pizza down and for the next several minutes, the conversation focused on their dinner and what other places Garrett wanted to eat at while he was home for the weekend.

Beyond that, there was never a lull, and even though it seemed like Emma kept directing them to neutral topics–mutual friends, places they were both familiar with–she seemed to shy away from anything overly personal. As much as Garrett wanted to ask more about her life–especially since her divorce–he knew he could bide his time. His plan was for them to finish their dinner and go back to the grocery store where they'd go their separate ways.

It was getting late and his mother was expecting him to show up sooner rather than later and as much as he hated to cut short this opportunity that landed in his lap, he wanted to be able to spend time with Emma without watching the clock.

But tomorrow, he hoped to show up at the barn and spend some time with her parents and then–somehow–get them to convince her to go out for a real dinner with him.

Like a date.

And it had nothing to do with his brother or their bet and everything to do with wanting more time with Emmaline Ryan before he had to head back to Virginia.

3

"I think he likes me, Miss Emma!" Callie said with a big smile the following afternoon. They had just finished reading to Opie, a small terrier who was happily trying to lick her face.

"I do too, Callie! And he's giving you kisses to say good job!"

"Yay!"

When Emma stood up, she noticed her mom talking with Mrs. Wells and...Garrett.

For a moment, she froze and wanted to quickly run and fix herself up a little, but...there was no way to do it without drawing way too much attention to herself. Instead, she smiled and gave a small wave before picking up Opie. "Your mom's here, Callie. Let's go tell her how much you read today!"

Taking the girl's hand, they walked over to join everyone, and as soon as they did, Callie started talking about how much fun she had reading to Opie. Emma caught Garrett's eye and smiled and immediately felt herself blush.

"Emma, we can't thank you enough," Mrs. Wells said. "I

think this was a great session for Callie and maybe we can do it again next week?"

"Um..." She looked to her mother to see if that was okay, and Christine nodded. "That sounds great."

"Tell you what," Christine interrupted, "why don't you and Callie come into the office with me and we'll look at the schedule together. Emma, why don't you show Garrett around? Ed won't be back for about an hour and he mentioned wanting to visit with him too."

"Oh, uh...sure. Great!" It wasn't until she and Garrett were alone that she spoke again. "So...um...you came."

His laugh was low and just a little gruff. "I told you I was going to."

It was true. After they'd finished dinner and walked back to the Publix so Emma could do her shopping, Garrett had said he'd see her tomorrow.

She just didn't think they'd be here at the barn at the same time for some reason.

"Who's this little guy?" he asked as he gently scratched the pup's ear.

"This is Opie. We rescued him from a hoarder last month." She gently scratched the dog's belly as she spoke. "He's very mellow and really good with kids. We're hoping he gets adopted at our next event."

"When's that going to be?"

"It was supposed to be next month, but we pushed it up to next weekend. Hopefully, we'll get a good turnout." Emma let out a wistful sigh. "I wish we'd find homes for all these little guys."

She instantly regretted her words because the last thing she wanted to do was ask him for his help. If her mother wanted to do it, then fine, but Emma was not about to put that kind of pressure on him.

Although...if she did happen to ask him, they could do a video right now, and...he'd have to take his shirt off, so maybe...

No! Bad Emma!

"How'd your session go?" he asked, breaking into her thoughts.

"Session? Oh, you mean with Callie?"

He nodded.

"It went really well. She was much more relaxed when she put her attention on Opie rather than worrying about me."

"Have you thought about offering this option to more of your students?"

"Not everyone needs this kind of thing."

Gently, he took the dog from her arms and snuggled with him–effectively making her ovaries want to explode. "Oh, come on, Em. Every kid could use this kind of thing." He nuzzled the little dog and was rewarded with puppy kisses. "And this is a great reward!"

She'd never been so jealous of an animal in her entire life.

Bad, bad Emma!

"It's something to think about, I guess."

He placed the puppy down and watched him scamper off. "So let's see all the new stuff," he said excitedly. "I already see how the barn's been expanded and rehabbed, and I noticed a couple of new buildings scattered around."

They walked out of the barn and Emma pointed out the new supply shed which was for the mowers and tools to maintain the grounds, and how the building beside it was for supplies for the animals. "We get a lot of donations from all over. Sometimes people don't want to send money, so they buy food and bowls and all kinds of supplies for us. It's amazing." She pointed to several areas with picnic tables and a few fenced-off areas where they held meet and greets for dogs and potential owners or foster families.

"They've done so much," he commented as they continued to walk. "What are those?"

Emma let out a small laugh. "Those are dog houses that have been donated by Scarlett Bishop. I don't know if you knew about these, but..."

Garrett stopped in his tracks. "I've only met her a handful of times, but...this is wild! How...I mean...when..." He walked over to them and inspected them. "These look like they're handmade!"

"They are! Scarlett's really talented. She's been making them and donating them to us for years!" She paused. "I don't remember you ever talking about Mason being your cousin back when we were in school. Were you guys close?"

He shrugged and continued to inspect the houses. "We were kind of the black sheep of the family. My Aunt Georgia never missed an opportunity to tell us how we didn't belong since my father wasn't around anymore." He made a sound of derision. "She's seriously the worst."

"Oh, um...I d...don't think sh...she's that bad," Emma stammered and mentally cursed herself. Garrett straightened and looked at her before she blurted out, "She's been handling all the fundraising for Happy Tails and has been a total blessing!"

All he did was arch one dark brow at her before moving away from the dog houses. He followed a gravel path that led back toward the fenced part of the property. Emma had to jog to catch up, and when they got to the gate, he paused and looked at her. "Anything back here?"

Nodding, Emma reached over and opened the gate. "Ed created some walking paths back here where we can work on training the dogs with leashes." They stepped through and she closed the gate behind them. "And there's another barn back here that isn't quite finished yet."

"What's it for?"

"Eventually, he'd like to have a complete clinic on site. It's a long way off, so for now, I think–once it's finished–they'll use it either for extra storage or office space. It's a bit far from the house and everything else, but he didn't want to take away from the open area the dogs use now. This is all out of the way so the construction didn't scare any of the animals."

"Damn, the man thinks of everything," he murmured.

"Except how to manage it all when he can't." The words were out before she even realized it, and Garrett stopped in his tracks beside her.

"What do you mean?"

"What? Oh, it's nothing," she replied quickly. "Look, there's the barn! I'm hoping they set up a loft in it. I think it would be awesome to be able to look down on everything and see what's going on, don't you?"

"Emmaline...?"

Ugh...she knew when he used her full name that he wasn't buying what she saying.

Drat.

With a sigh, she turned to face him. "Okay, here it is–Ed has to have back surgery. He's put it off for as long as he could and now...now it has to be done and my mother is freaking out because she doesn't know how she'll handle everything. We have volunteers, but...it's going to be rough."

"And you're blaming Ed for this?" he asked incredulously.

"No! That's not what I meant at all. I just..." She sighed loudly. "Actually, I blame both him and my mom because they knew he was going to need the surgery, and...maybe doing all this stuff back here could have waited! Why take on more projects and expansion when they knew he was going to need like...six months to fully recover?"

"Oh, damn, Em, I'm sorry. I didn't mean..."

But she wasn't paying attention. "Don't get me wrong, this is all going to be great down the road, but right now, it's just extra stuff to stress everyone out! I can't help out as much as they need because I'm already working all day with the schools and then tutoring four days a week just to keep my head above water! My siblings are too young to be of much help, and all the fundraising isn't going to put people here to take care of it all!"

Her breathing was ragged and Garrett stepped in to hug her and she let him.

And immediately regretted her little outburst.

Strong arms gently wrapped around her and she placed her head against his shoulder. "Sorry."

"You have nothing to apologize for. It sounds to me like you're dealing with a lot."

"Still, that was crappy of me to just spew all that at you."

He laughed softly, resting his head against hers. "What can I do to help?"

There was her opening.

It wouldn't be wrong if he was offering, right? She didn't have to feel bad about it if he was the one to put it out there. It was perfect. All she had to do was tell him what she was thinking, and at least some of her prayers would be answered.

Pulling back, Emma looked up at him and...

"You are very sweet for asking, but...it's all going to be okay."

Coward.

"Em, come on. There has to be something."

You could take off your shirt and promote Happy Tails and help us go viral…

"I appreciate that you want to help, Garrett. But you're only here for the weekend, and you've got enough on your own plate with your job search." She stepped out of his arms. "I think Ed is going to be thrilled that you cared enough to stop by and see him." Glancing toward the new barn, she smiled. "Come on. Let me show you the new space and then you can talk to him about it. He'll love that. Trust me." And before he could answer, she was walking away.

And kicking herself the entire time because she blew her chance.

Luckily Garrett didn't push, and they walked around the new barn as she yammered on about how she envisioned it while he patiently listened. If he heard the stutters or the stammers, he said nothing. And on the walk back to the main part of the property, he asked about the dogs and her favorite part of helping out. She was just about to answer when Axel came running toward her and leaped into her arms like they were going to do the lift from *Dirty Dancing.*

"There's my best boy!" she crooned as she snuggled him in close. "Were you good today?" His tail was going a mile a minute as he licked her face. "I know. I know, sweet boy. I missed you too!"

"Who is this little guy?" Garrett asked, moving in close and scratching Axel's head right before the dog let out a small, menacing growl.

"Oh, sorry. He's not great with new people," she said softly, doing her best to distract Axel. "He was just returned for the third time and it breaks my heart. I seem to be the only one he's bonded with."

"So why don't you adopt him?"

"My place doesn't allow pets, so..."

"That's too bad." Rather than ignore Axel or heed the dog's warning, Garrett continued to study him and carefully held out a hand to him to sniff. When the growling stopped and the sniffing started, Garrett started to talk to Axel in soothing tones until—much to Emma's amazement—he squirmed to get out of her arms and into Garrett's!

Traitor...

Garrett's smile was a mix of surprise and pleasure as he happily accepted the squirming dog. "Hey, buddy! See? I'm just here to hang out with a pretty girl, too."

And just like she'd been doing since running into him the night before, she blushed.

"Um...I see Ed's car in the driveway," she said, hoping to distract him from looking at her.

"What about...?"

"We can bring Axel with us. They're used to him being with me."

They had only walked half of the way to the house when Ed stepped outside and spotted them. His smile was wide as he jogged over and shook Garrett's hand. "Hey, Christine told me you were here and I couldn't believe it! How are you?"

"I'm doing great," Garrett replied. "I'm in town for the weekend and wanted to stop over and say hello and see all the improvements you've been telling me about. Everything looks great! Emma's been showing me around."

"Do you have dinner plans?" Ed asked. "We'd love it if you could stay."

"Oh, um..." He glanced at Emma and she had no idea

what to say or if he was looking at her for approval or to help him leave.

"You're staying too, aren't you, Em?" Ed asked. "Your mom made her famous chicken enchilada casserole and there's enough there to feed an army."

Dammit, that was one of her favorites. She smiled up at Garrett. "If you enjoy Mexican food, you'll love it. But if you have plans with your family..."

"I'm going to be with them all day tomorrow," he interrupted. "And I'd love to join you for dinner."

Okay, this wasn't quite what Garrett had in mind for his Friday night with Emma, but...there was still time to salvage it.

They were in the house and Emma had gone to help her sisters with their homework while he and Ed were in the living room catching up.

"So I hear you're finally going to have the back surgery."

Ed groaned as he leaned back in his recliner. "I put it off as long as I could. The timing sucks but that's no one's fault but my own."

"I don't think anyone really wants to have surgery of any kind. No one blames you for putting it off as long as you could."

"Yeah, but...it seems like everything's hitting the fan at once, and, honestly, I don't know how we're going to manage it all."

There was clearly more to this than what Emma let on, and Garrett wasn't sure how much he should pry, but...the curiosity was killing him. "It's going to be a long recovery, sure, but the new barn can wait. That's not too big of a deal."

"I wish it were just the barn," Ed murmured, scrubbing a hand over his face.

"Ed, what's going on?"

The older man let out a long breath. "We have more dogs on the property than we ever have before. Normally that sort of thing wouldn't bother me because that just means we've rescued more and that's what we're all about. But Doc MacEntyre is retiring and doesn't have anyone to take over his practice." Pausing, he shook his head. "We've reached out to other vets in the area and none of them are interested in working with us the way Doc does. There's no way we can handle transporting the animals back and forth to new clinics–especially not while I'm laid up recovering. I'm telling you, it's just a bit of a mess."

"Damn, Ed. I don't even know what to say."

But a thousand thoughts began swirling in his head.

What if he talked to some of the vets? Or what if he talked to Doc MacEntyre? What if he didn't go to Delaware or to the other places he was supposed to over the next month?

As much as his heart was saying yes, Garrett hated to let all those other clinics down. Even if he didn't accept the permanent position in Delaware, every place else was relying on him to come in and help them over the next several weeks. How would it look if he simply backed down?

"Bah, don't listen to me," Ed said after a moment. "I know it's all going to work out. It always does. The community has always supported us and sometimes help comes from the strangest places..."

"Yeah, I hear my Aunt Georgia has been helping out.."

"She is like a force of nature, I can tell you that." Then he stopped and laughed. "I forgot that she was your aunt."

"I'm sure she'd like to forget that too," Garrett replied, and he was only partially joking. "But at least she's doing something good for Happy Tails, and really, that's all that matters, right?"

They sat in companionable silence for a few minutes as Garrett looked around the room. There were many framed photos scattered around the room and he stood up and walked around looking at them. There were several family shots–including one from what looked like Emma's college graduation that made him smile. She seemed so happy–they all did. They were a happy family–a whole family. And he could admit to himself that he was envious.

Moving along, he saw photos of Ed and Christine with different dogs, then some of their younger kids. The last picture on the shelf made him stop.

Emma's wedding picture.

Granted, it was a shot of her alone, but it still was enough to make his heart kick hard in his chest. She was a beautiful bride. Before he knew what he was doing, he had the framed photo in his hand and was studying it and hating the reminder that she'd married that jackass.

Ed came up beside him and put his hand on Garrett's shoulder. "Emma keeps asking Christine to put that one away, but...it's a great picture of Emma and my wife reasons that since she's alone in it, there's no reason it can't stay out."

Unsure of what to say, Garrett simply nodded before gently placing the photo back in its place.

"You know," Ed said after a moment, "I do have a small favor to ask."

Garrett immediately turned. "Of course. Anything."

"I know I invited you for dinner, but..." He raked a hand through his hair and looked mildly uncomfortable before he continued. "It's not healthy for Emma to only spend time with us. She's been divorced for three years, and I swear I don't think she's gone out with her friends more than a handful of times."

That was...a little shocking, but Garrett kept that to himself.

"Please don't think poorly of me, but...would you consider maybe taking her out to a movie or dessert or...hell, even dinner? It breaks my heart to see her working so hard and never just going out and having any fun."

Garrett was pretty sure he was frowning. "So...wait. You want me to take Emma out? Like on a date?"

A nervous laugh was Ed's first response. "I know, I know...it's awkward. I'm sorry. Forget I said anything. I'll... I'll just go and see when dinner will be ready." He went to walk away, but Garrett stopped him.

"Believe it or not, I had hoped to ask her to have dinner with me tonight," he admitted. "We ran into each other last night at the Publix and grabbed some pizza, but I was kind of hoping to ask her out for something a little...you know... nicer tonight."

Ed's smile started small and then grew. "And then I went and invited you to dinner and..."

"Technically, I was still having dinner with her, so..."

They both chuckled at that, but Ed only shook his head. "You know what I'm saying, and I feel a little bad even having this conversation because Emma's a grown woman. It just breaks my heart that she doesn't go out and socialize more."

"Maybe she has her reasons," Garrett suggested, but he was really curious as to what those reasons could be.

"She's embarrassed," Ed said quietly. "Most of her friends are happily married and having babies, and it bothers her that...you know...her marriage ended quickly."

It made sense, but there was something Garrett had to know.

"Did he hurt her?" he asked, his voice so low and gruff that he wasn't sure Ed would even hear him.

"Not physically or I would have killed him myself. But he hurt her emotionally and financially. She works so damn hard, and...hell, you have no idea how much Christine and I wish we could help her, but she's determined to do it herself."

That sounded like the girl he knew–always independent–even when it wasn't good for her.

Before Garrett could comment or even ask how he was supposed to convince her to go out with him again tonight, Ed walked out of the room.

He walked around with nothing else to do, looked at a few more pictures, and then stood in front of a large bay window and looked out at the property. It was massive and doing so much to help rescue animals, which Garrett always wanted for himself. It had a lot to do with growing up and volunteering here, but it was also something that just spoke to his heart. Hell, if he had money to invest in anything, it would either go to Happy Tails or to start up a place just like it on his own.

But he didn't have money to invest. He was fortunate not to have any student loans to pay off, thanks to his great-grandfather, but he'd spent so much time doing internships and searching for the perfect job that he didn't have a lot in savings. And what he did have, he needed to live off of until he was earning a steady paycheck.

A few days ago he was feeling like a relative success, but now? Not so much.

Emma walked into the room a few minutes later, looking worried. "Everything okay?" he asked.

"Ed's not feeling well. He said his back is killing him and he needs to lie down. Mom's upset and fussing over him and is trying to get everyone to sleep out tonight." She was wringing her hands. "I'm supposed to tell you that dinner's off."

"Oh." And yeah, he was kind of impressed at the lengths Ed was going to just to make sure Emma went out with him.

"He said to apologize to you and that he hoped to get a rain check."

"Of course. No worries." Was he supposed to just ask her out right now? "So, um...what about you? What are your plans now?"

"I'll probably grab some Chinese or maybe sneak a portion of the casserole and take it home with me. What about you?"

He pretended to think about it for a moment. "Hey, do you remember that bistro down the coast a bit? Blue Fin something? Is that still there?"

She looked at him oddly. "Um...I think? It's been years since I've gone down that way. How come?"

"They used to have a fantastic menu. I remember going there a few times before I left for college and thought I'd check it out and see if it's as good as I remembered."

The fact was that he already knew it was still there and had it on good authority that the food was even better than it was years ago. It was something he'd asked Austin about earlier today before confirming a donation from his brother.

"Oh, well...you could probably just go online and check

it out. I'm sure your family will be glad to have some more time with you."

Shaking his head, he explained, "Nah. Mom's got a date, and Austin and Mia are gearing up for tomorrow. They're breaking ground on their new home and have some things planned. That's where I'll be all day, so it was kind of cool to have people to hang out with tonight." Pausing, he pretended to ponder some more. "Why don't you come with me?" he asked mildly.

Her eyes went wide. "But...we just had dinner together last night. There must be other people you'd like to visit with while you're home."

He shrugged. "Not really. Besides, I feel like we rushed through our pizza last night because we both had things to do. Tonight we can just relax and enjoy a good meal. Come on," he pled. "Don't make me eat by myself." Then, nudging her shoulder playfully with his, he added, "Please."

One small hand smoothed over her ponytail as Emma bit her lip. Garrett knew she was trying to come up with an excuse to keep her from going with him, but he was going to do his damnedest not to take no for an answer.

"I'll even let you beat me at a game of putt-putt," he teased, reminding her of all the times they used to play miniature golf and she'd beat him. Her laughter in response was spontaneous and lyrical and made him smile. "I'll even throw in some ice cream on the pier, Em. Come on..."

Clearly he'd worn her down because she rolled her eyes and smiled. "Okay, fine," she said with another laugh. "But I'd like to go home and change first. Can we meet up in an hour?"

"Just give me your address and I'll be there."

Five minutes later, Garrett watched her drive away before turning and heading back into the house. Both Ed and Christine were standing in the kitchen, smiling from ear to ear. "You're a little devious," he told Ed, even as he shook his hand to thank him.

"I can't take all the credit. Christine was the one who came up with the excuse. We're just glad Emma didn't offer to stay and help get her siblings out of the house."

He slid his hands into his pockets and wasn't sure what else to say.

"We're just happy she accepted your offer to go out," Christine said after a moment. "I think her friends would all love to see more of her, but she just won't reach out. She's always been shy, but...it kills me to see her shutting herself away like this." Reaching out, she squeezed Garrett's arm. "You were always such a good friend to her and we always appreciated that."

"It wasn't any hardship," he replied. "If it weren't for your daughter, I probably never would have graduated high school–let alone gotten into college. I hated how we lost touch once I left for college, but..."

"We know," Ed interrupted. "Steven monopolized her time and didn't like her socializing with anyone other than him. There were so many warning signs that we all missed."

"I wish I had been around more. Maybe if I had seen what was happening..."

"Don't think like that," Christine told him. "We've all said the same thing and there's nothing anyone can do. It's over and done with and I just want her to be happy now and to get her confidence back."

He nodded. "Well, I'm not sure how much help I'll be, but maybe tonight she'll see that going out with a friend isn't a bad thing." Then he hugged Christine and shook Ed's hand before wishing them both a good night.

Once he was outside and climbing into his car, he

wondered if he was doing the right thing. Was he going to be able to spend this time with Emma as just a friend, or was he going to put his foot in his mouth and say something to make her uncomfortable because he wasn't thinking of this as just a friends' night out?

"Only one way to find out," he murmured as he pulled away from the Fosters' home.

"And you can just stay there and think about what you did!" Emma yelled at the pile of discarded clothes in the corner of her closet. She knew she was losing it, but after trying on four different outfits and none of them looking good, she was growing frustrated. Garrett was due to pick her up in fifteen minutes and if she didn't find something to wear soon, she would have to fake a headache and cancel on him.

Not that it would be a big deal because...this wasn't a date.

If anything, he probably felt bad for her after her parents had to cancel dinner and was just looking to do something nice.

Because that's the kind of guy Garrett was.

The good guy. The nice guy. The friends-with-everybody guy.

"Add the guy who looks ridiculously hot without a shirt," she murmured as she pulled on a pair of black skinny jeans. As soon as they were zipped, she flipped through every item hanging in her closet until she found a coral off-the-shoulder blouse. "It's this or topless, and I believe if anyone's going to go around like that, it should be Garrett." Fortunately, when she looked in the mirror, Emma finally liked what she saw. "And we have a winner."

After that, she did a quick touch-up with her makeup and decided to leave her hair down. There were always hair clips and a few scrunchies in her purse, so she knew she'd be okay if her hair became an issue later. Once that was all done and decided, she had nothing to do but pace.

And wonder what they were possibly going to talk about.

Years ago when they were in school, it was never an issue. They usually talked about schoolwork and what assignments Garrett was struggling with. She used to worry about how he would do in college, but apparently he managed just fine on his own.

She thought about asking him about the videos tonight.

Specifically, him doing one for Happy Tails.

"Why am I making such a big deal out of this?" she quietly asked herself as she looked out the window to see if he was there yet. "He obviously makes them all the time. What's the harm in him doing one for a friend?"

Once she wrapped her head around it that way, Emma felt like maybe it wasn't going to be such a big deal.

Actually, going out with him tonight wasn't going to be a big deal either. They'd gone out together countless times without things being awkward, and clearly she was the only one making more out of it than she needed to. He was a good friend, and if any of her other friends had invited her out for dinner, she wouldn't give it a second thought.

It was all in the mindset, she reminded herself.

But when she opened the door five minutes later and he smiled at her, she knew her mindset was wrong.

None of her friends smiled at her with a sexy dimple.

None of her friends smelled so good that she wanted to lean in and inhale deeply.

But mostly, none of her friends were insanely good-looking males.

"Hey," Garrett said, his smile just as warm as it always was. "You ready to go?"

Was it wrong that her heart sort of skipped a beat at the sight of him or that for just the teeniest, tiniest of seconds she imagined that this was an actual date?

Nodding, Emma reached behind her for her purse and keys. "Yup. Ready," she murmured, stepping out and locking the door behind her. They walked out to his car, which was a very nice Nissan sedan. "Did you happen to go online and see if this place was still there?"

He waited until they were both seated in the car before answering. "It is. I called Austin and asked him about it, and he said it was and he and Mia were just there last week."

"So...Austin's marrying Mia Kingsley. That's pretty huge, huh?"

He glanced over at her with a grin. "You mean because she's a wildly famous author whose books are being made into movies?"

Emma nodded. "It's all everyone's been talking about around town. People are hoping she'll write something that takes place in a coastal town so that maybe they'll film something here."

That made him laugh. "Yeah, I'm not sure if that's something she's looking to do. From everything I've heard, the movies they're making are all based on her series set in Boston and there hasn't been talk of any additional ones."

"That must be so cool to create something like that. Has Austin been to the set?"

"He went with her once. They went up to Boston the first week of filming and he said it was a lot of standing around and waiting." He shook his head. "My brother is not known for his patience."

"What about Mia? How does she feel about all of it?"

"About my brother's lack of patience?" he teased, making Emma laugh.

"No, I mean about the movie. It must be weird seeing your story come to life like that and yet not be in control of it."

"That's almost exactly what she said. She can go to the set any time she wants, but she said she'd rather be home working on her next book. She's very practical. Have you met her?"

"Just briefly. She did a signing at the library and I went and waited in line for two hours and talked to her for all of a minute before I was ushered away to keep the line moving. But from the little I saw of her, she seems very sweet."

"She's amazing. Way too good for Austin, but…" Looking at her, he winked. "But seriously, she's great, and if you ever want to meet her, just let me know."

"Oh, my goodness. I would never ask that of you."

"Why not?"

She shrugged. "Because it's awkward, Garrett. I mean… I wouldn't use you like that."

He let out an almost mirthless laugh. "It's not that big of a deal, Em, and trust me, you wouldn't be the first."

"What do you mean?"

He let out a long breath. "I don't know…I mean, there's been a few people that have asked me to get them signed books from Mia or blatantly asked me to introduce them. Most of the time, it's not a big deal. I don't mind doing it for friends; it's the acquaintances that bug me."

"Wow, I had no idea. I'm so sorry. But it just reinforces what I'm saying, Garrett. I would never ask that of you." And she knew she should probably change the subject. "So you're here for the weekend. How often do you come back to visit?"

"I'm ashamed to admit that I don't come home very often. Mostly for weddings or random holidays. After I moved away, I kind of enjoyed my freedom." He shrugged. "Then I graduated and started doing internships and looking for jobs and coming back to Magnolia really wasn't on my radar–not even for a visit. Much to my mother's dismay."

"Oh, I'm sure. She must love when you're all home to visit."

"It doesn't happen often–Jackson's the hardest one to get home because he's been deployed and stationed all over the world–but it's nice when we all get to hang out."

"Someday, I hope it will be like that for my siblings and me. There's such an age gap that I sort of feel more like one of the parents than a sister."

Garrett reached over and took her hand in his, squeezing it, and Emma sort of froze. It was such an unexpected reaction that she didn't know what to do. Pulling her hand away would be rude, she thought, so she just figured she'd wait it out until he let her go.

And waited.

And waited...

"So tell me about Axel," he said. "What happened to his leg?"

"He was from a litter that had been dumped on the side of the road just outside of town. By the time we got them, we weren't sure if any of them would make it. Doc MacEntyre thinks Axel's leg broke when they were dumped, but we can't know for sure. Either way, it was hard to splint his little leg and keep him calm and stable." She sighed. "No one sees how sweet he is and I hate it."

He squeezed her hand again. "Someone will. I promise."

"Maybe. I don't know. We have this event coming up, but...we're rushing it, and I don't think it's going to be as successful as my mom needs it to be. I wish I knew more about social media marketing." She let out a small laugh. "Or any kind of marketing. I'm terrible with that sort of thing. Scarlett's been helping out with it a lot, but she does it as a volunteer and we hate asking more of her than she already does."

"Social media is definitely a big help, but..." He paused and shook his head. "I know it can be a good thing, but it's sort of a blessing and a curse, you know?"

"No, I...I don't."

"Okay, here's the thing–all those videos you've seen me do? They've done a lot of good for the shelters and the clinics. Adoption rates have skyrocketed."

She was ready to praise him for it when he dropped a bombshell.

"But I hate doing them," he said grimly.

"I don't understand. Why?"

"Do you know why I've gotten so many job offers? It's because of those videos. Do you know how many people take me seriously now? Not many."

"Oh, Garrett...I had no idea!"

He nodded. "My brothers make fun of me all the time. They call me "Hot Doc" or "Sexy Vet," and I know they're just teasing, but they're not the only ones calling me that." He shook his head again. "At first, it was fun and I liked the attention, but now it just feels wrong and I have no idea if people are offering me jobs because I'm good at what I do as a veterinarian or if it's because I look good with my shirt off."

Do **not** *comment on that...*

Unsure of what to do, she was the one to squeeze his hand. "I can't even imagine what that must feel like. But you have to believe that people want to hire you because you're a good doctor. There's no way they'd offer you a job because of some videos. That would be crazy!"

"I don't know, I thought so too. At first. Once they started going viral, it was like I was getting dozens of offers a week! The ones I have it narrowed down to now seem legit, but what if as soon as I'm there, they want me to start doing videos? No one's ever going to take me seriously if I keep doing them."

It was at that moment that Emma knew she was never going to ask him for his help.

At least not in that capacity.

Clearly it was a good thing that she was such a chicken about bringing it up sooner because that would have lumped her in with all the other people Garrett felt betrayed by.

"O-kay...so...maybe you have to make that clear from the get-go. When you show up at these places over the next few weeks, you tell them that before you even see your first pet–no videos. If they don't have a problem with it, then you know you can trust them, but if they push back even a little bit, then you know it's not the right place for you."

That seemed to make him relax because he let out a long breath and smiled at her. "Thanks, Emmaline. I needed that."

It felt like her cheeks were on fire and she was thankful

it was a little dim in the car. "You realize you're still the only person who calls me by my full name, right?"

His smile grew as he glanced at her. "Good. I like knowing I'm the only one. It's a beautiful name for a beautiful girl."

Oh, my...

Gently, Emma cleared her throat. "So, um...dinner? We should almost be there. I wonder if the menu is still the same!" Her words all sort of blurred together, but thankfully Garrett didn't comment on it.

"I checked it out online when I went home to change and it looks mostly the same, but there were definitely some new items on there too. If I remember correctly, you love shellfish–especially shrimp and lobster–but you're not a fan of anything with scales or tentacles."

She was pretty sure her jaw was currently in her lap because that was the most accurate description of her feelings on fish that she'd ever heard.

"I can't believe you remembered that," she whispered.

"We've known each other a long time," he reminded her. "And we spent countless hours with it being just the two of us." He gave her hand one more squeeze. "I remember everything."

For some reason, Emma wasn't sure whether to be comforted by his admission or a little scared.

Okay, maybe not scared, per se, but she was suddenly racking her brain for anything stupid she may have said or done in front of him in the last eighteen or so years.

"Doesn't look too crowded," Garrett said, effectively interrupting her thoughts. She looked up and saw they were pulling up to the restaurant, and that was when he finally released her hand.

And she missed the contact already.

Oh, girl...you are in trouble if a bit of handholding is getting to you like this.

It was only normal, she reminded herself. It had been three years since her divorce and she hadn't dated since.

And it had been almost a year *before* the divorce since she had a man show her any kindness or tenderness.

Or any skin-on-skin contact.

Yeah...I'm in big trouble.

Once they were parked, Garrett got out of the car, and before Emma even unbuckled herself, he was opening the door for her with the sweetest look on his face.

Great, he's a gentleman too...

And when he held out his hand to her and she rested hers in it?

She seriously began to wonder how much of this was Garrett just being a genuinely nice guy and how much of it was her simply being starved for affection.

Dinner was fantastic–the food was delicious, the service was excellent, and the atmosphere was great. There hadn't been a lull in the conversation, but he could tell that something was bothering Emma, and as they pulled back up to her condo, he argued with himself about whether or not he should say something.

"Thank you so much for dinner, Garrett," she said softly when they were at her front door. "Again."

"It was my pleasure." They stood there for a moment, and he wondered if she would invite him in, but again, he didn't want to push.

"Um..." Turning from him, she unlocked the door and opened it. When she turned, she gave him a shy smile. "I had a really good time tonight. This was a treat for me. It's been a long time since I've gone out for such a nice meal, so...thank you."

"You're very welcome." He glanced over her shoulder into her home, and when he saw her stiffen, he knew he had his answer. Leaning in, he placed a soft kiss on her cheek and desperately tried not to linger. When he straightened, he smiled down at her. "I'm not heading home until Monday. Do you think it would alright if I stopped back at the barn on Sunday?"

She nodded. "Uh...yeah. That...that should b...be fine."

"Will you be there?"

Another nod. "I try to go every Sunday to help out where I can, so..."

"Then I'll see you then." And as he took a step back, he fought the urge to lean in and kiss her again.

Even if it was only on the cheek.

A small wave was her only response when he said good-night, and as Garrett dragged himself back to his car, he realized how wrong he'd been to stay away for so long. Emma didn't go inside until he pulled away, and the sight of her standing all alone by the front door was going to haunt him.

Hell, just the sight of her, in general, was going to haunt him.

She was still the same beautiful girl he'd always known, but there was a sadness there now that had never been there before that just about gutted him. Emmaline was a shadow of her former self that just wasn't acceptable to him.

But he had no idea what to do about it.

It wasn't particularly late, but late enough that he didn't want to call Ed and talk to him or even call Austin. When he'd left his mother's earlier, she mentioned that she and

Dominic were going out and he had no idea if she'd be home when he got there.

And was it wrong that he hoped she was?

Relief washed over him a few minutes later when he pulled up to her house and saw the lights on and both her and Dom's cars were there. Garrett wasn't opposed to talking to both of them about his night and about the situation with Emma. Maybe he'd leave out his long-buried feelings, but he was open to getting advice anywhere he could get it.

"Garrett! You're home early!" his mother said as he walked in the door. She was smiling and didn't seem the least bit put out by his appearance, so he took it as a good sign. But then again, that was the way his mom was. Grace Coleman was always happy to see her kids–no matter how bratty they were or how long they'd stayed away.

"Hey, Mom. Hey, Dom," he said as he walked farther into the room. They were sitting on the couch watching TV. "What are we watching?" He sat down on the big oversized chair opposite them.

"It's a documentary on The Bee Gees. So much talent in that family and yet so much sadness," she explained before picking up the remote and pausing it. "How was your night?"

Here was his opening...

Leaning forward, he braced his elbows on his knees, clasped his hands, and let out a long breath. "Okay, so...Emmaline..."

"Should I be here for this?" Dominic asked, glancing between mother and son. "Because if you'd rather talk to your mom alone, Garrett, that's okay."

Grace laughed and hugged him before looking at Garrett. "Don't mind him. He's not a fan of talking about relationship stuff with his kids, even though they all swear he's one of the main reasons they're all happily married now." She smiled at Dom and kissed him on the cheek. "You're a good man and I believe you'll have some important insight into this situation. Remember I was telling you about it yesterday."

"Wait," Garrett interrupted. "You've already talked about this? How? Why? I mean…"

She shifted slightly to face him. "Sweetheart, you've had a crush on that girl since the third grade. I never understood why you never asked her out."

Groaning, his head fell into his hands. "Because we were friends, Mom. Emma's been one of my best friends and I never wanted to do anything to mess that up."

"Plus, she was your tutor for a while so that could have gotten messy," Grace commented.

"And then she started dating that weasel Steve," Dom chimed in, and Garrett looked up at him in shock. "What? That's what your mother called him."

"Mom, seriously?"

"Oh, please. Steve March was a jerk. You said it enough times back when you were in school, and his mother was a bully too. We worked on a few PTA projects together and I never liked her." Pausing, she shook her head. "I only saw Emma a few times after she got married and she never looked happy. Honestly, I was relieved when I heard she was getting divorced."

"Do you see her around town much?" he asked.

"Not really, but…her sisters and brother all come to my office to see Dr. Phillips. Christine and I talk a little bit when she's there, but it's really just small talk. It's not like Emma has a need to go to the pediatrician."

He nodded.

"If I may say something," Dominic said hesitantly–even raising his hand. "What are you hoping to gain here?"

Straightening, Garrett asked, "What do you mean?"

"Well, it seems to me that you're leaving here on Monday and heading back to Norfolk. And then after that, you're going to be traveling around before you ultimately decide to take the position with the clinic up in Delaware. I get that Emma's a good friend and you have feelings for her, but…I'm guessing she already has some self-esteem or abandonment issues. Why start up something with her if you're not going to be here?"

For a minute, Garrett could only stare. "Um…"

"I hate to say it, honey, but Dominic's got a point. I get it if you're approaching this as a concerned friend who just wants to see Emma be happy. But I have a feeling that's not your only motivation here."

Dammit, they were right. What was he thinking? And why was he trying so damn hard? Didn't he have enough on his plate right now with finding a job and moving and finding a place to live? Did he really want to take on some kind of relationship with Emma–any kind of relationship with Emma–when he wasn't going to be around after Monday?

"You're right," he said gruffly, staring down at his hands. "I guess…I guess I just got caught up in things after I saw her. The last thing she needs is someone else letting her down."

Before he knew it, his mother was sitting on the arm of his chair and hugging him. "I think it's incredibly sweet that you care about her, but…"

"I know, I know," he murmured. "It's too late. I missed my chance." And it hurt to admit it out loud.

"I wouldn't say you missed your chance," Dom said.

"Years ago? Sure. But just because things aren't falling into place right now doesn't mean they won't down the line."

"No, I think he's right," Grace replied. "How long is he supposed to pine for this girl without anything happening? What if he meets the woman who's meant to be his wife and he blows her off because he's too busy fixating on a relationship that's never going to go anywhere? How long is he supposed to wait?"

"Um..."

Before either he or Dominic could respond, his mother had his face in her hands and a fierce expression on her face. "Listen to me, Garrett, and I say this with love. Do *not* throw your life away on a relationship that's never going to be. Learn from my mistakes. You cannot make someone change, and you can't take it upon yourself to decide what their life should look like. You haven't talked to Emmaline in years, and then you come back and suddenly envision all the ways you think she needs to be living her life. That's not fair to her and it's not fair to you."

Beside them, Dominic stood before walking over and kissing Grace on the cheek. "I'm gonna go," he said solemnly. "Call me tomorrow if you have time after you go over and help Austin and Mia." Reaching out, he shook Garrett's hand. "Good to see you, Garrett."

"You're leaving?" Grace asked.

"I think it's best."

"Why?"

"Grace..."

She shot a worried look at Garrett and now he had no idea what he was supposed to do. Leave? Go to his room?

"Mom," he said quietly as he stood. "Talk to Dominic. I'll just...be in my room."

And yeah, it sounded utterly ridiculous for a grown

man to be making that statement, and yet here he was. With a slight nod to Dominic, he walked out of the room and kept going until he was back in his childhood bedroom and closing the door.

"Good job, genius. You ruined their date night and made a mess out of your relationship with Emmaline. Brilliant." With a loud sigh, he kicked off his shoes before stripping down to his boxers and pulling out a pair of athletic shorts to sleep in. There wasn't much he could do to pass the time, but he wasn't quite ready to call it a night. "Maybe I'll read or watch TV," he murmured and almost immediately opted for the television. If he picked up his phone to read, he'd be tempted to go on social media, and it still gave him a bit of anxiety.

Another sigh was out before he could stop it because it seemed crazy to refer to how he felt as anxiety, and yet...it was the only way he could describe it. All the attention he had gotten in the beginning was fantastic. He'd actually enjoyed it and felt really good about himself. But then things changed and it stopped being fun. Women groped him when he went out and they recognized him. His friends made all kinds of snarky comments and laughed at him. Hell, his own brothers called him names too.

He was a grown man and should be more than capable of ignoring all of them, but...it became apparent that no one was seeing him for who he was. No one looked at the applications of Garrett Coleman, veterinarian; they only saw Garrett Coleman, social media sensation who never wore a shirt.

And yeah, there was definitely a time at the beginning where that got him a lot of female attention and he found himself dating a different woman almost every night of the week. It was fun and he wasn't going to try to say it was a bad thing, but...it was shallow, and he was at a point in his life where he wanted to be done with that kind of relationship.

Okay, maybe that last part didn't come to him immediately, but it had certainly been on his mind a lot more lately.

Add Emma into the equation and it confused the hell out of him.

So now what?

In the distance, he heard the front door close and felt really bad about ruining his mother's date night. After not dating for so many years, she deserved to be happy.

This is why you shouldn't move home...

There was a soft knock on his bedroom door and he called out, "Come in."

"Hey. You okay?" she asked as she stepped into the room.

Garrett sat up on the bed and laughed softly. "That was going to be my line." His shoulders sagged. "Seriously, Mom, are you okay?"

Shrugging, she sat down beside him. "Dominic doesn't like it when I bring up your father like that. Even without naming him."

"I guess I understand it, but...we can't pretend that we aren't who we are because Cash Coleman walked out on us all those years ago."

"He's not asking me to pretend your father didn't exist, but he doesn't like it when I try to take the blame or put myself down for it." She paused. "I blame myself for not seeing your father for who he was before he left, but we were in love–or at least, I was–and there was nothing there to make me suspect that he'd walk away from his wife and three sons."

It wasn't something they liked to talk about–and certainly never one-on-one like this–but maybe it was time.

"Obviously, I was too young to really understand anything that was going on," he said quietly. "One day he was here, and the next, he was gone, but we kept waiting for him to come back, you know?"

Grace nodded. "I did too. And the few times he did get in touch, it was like talking to a stranger, yet I still kept telling myself he would change, that he was going to come back and be my husband and be a father to you and Austin and Jackson. But he never did."

"How did you get through it?" Turning his head, he studied his mother's profile. "How were you able to hold it together for all of us?"

She let out a small laugh. "I cried a lot after you boys went to bed. But then I'd wake up every morning and know that I had to be strong. My children needed me and I couldn't fall apart. Every once in a while, I'd get a random money order in the mail or just some cash with no return address, and I knew it was your father's sorry way of trying to do the right thing. Your great-grandfather was the real hero, though. He didn't support us–not outright–but he always made sure we never went without. Ezekiel Coleman was one in a million."

"Yeah, Pops was the best. I know I wouldn't be...well...I don't think I could have gone to college and done any of it without his help."

Beside him, his mother nodded. "He used to tell me that he saw so much potential in you boys and how he refused to let Cash rob you of it. He said your father robbed all of us of so much of our lives." She sniffled. "I hate saying that because he is still your dad and I shouldn't say bad things about him, but..."

Garrett took one of her hands in his. "You never said anything bad when we were growing up and you allowed us to form our own opinions and that was incredibly gracious of you. But the reality is that there aren't any nice things to say about him. There's no excuse for what he did to us or how he treated us–or should I say forgot about us–so you say whatever it is that you feel, Mom. You're entitled to."

"While I know that's true, I can't help but feel responsible for the way things went. If I never married Cash…"

"Then me and Austin and Jackson wouldn't be here," he reminded her. "And maybe that would have been better for everyone…"

"Never," she said, her hands both gripping his now, her tone and expression fierce. "The three of you are the best things to ever happen to me and it makes everything I went through worth it." Then she let out a long breath. "But I hate how you all had to suffer. So yes, occasionally I get down on myself about it and that's what bothers Dominic. He reminds me how your father made his decisions without any thought to us and how we were innocent victims." She shrugged. "I know he's right, but he also doesn't fully understand. His wife died young, and he was left to raise his four kids alone. Technically, we were both single parents who had to learn how to be both mother and father to our children with little or no notice. The only difference is that his wife couldn't come back. Your father could and chose not to."

"Damn, Mom."

"I know," she said sadly.

"I feel bad that I brought any of this up and ruined your night."

She was quiet for several moments before giving his hand a gentle squeeze. "All I was trying to say, Garrett, is to be careful. I know you always had feelings for Emmaline and no one's telling you not to. But you had feelings for a young girl many years ago. She's a grown woman now and before you go turning both your lives upside down, make sure you're seeing her for the woman she truly is and not the woman you built her up to be."

Wow.

That was something he hadn't considered.

As much as he'd enjoyed seeing her the last two evenings and catching up on each other's lives, was he seeing her in the right way?

He had a feeling he'd be thinking about that for a long time to come.

5

"Em! I'm taking the Wilsons into the office to do their adoption paperwork!" Christine called out on Sunday afternoon. "Can you please get the rest of these guys rounded up and into the barn? It looks like rain!"

"No problem!" Emma looked around the yard and counted ten dogs, including Axel. He was dancing around her legs and she loved it even though it broke her heart that no one picked him today. "They weren't the right family for you, but don't worry, we'll find them someday." With a sigh, she started walking across the yard. Most of the dogs were settled back in the big barn. This little group had been out scampering around because the Wilsons weren't sure which dog they wanted. It was nice that they were adopting an older dog–Biscuit was a seven-year-old Labrador–but she hated how the rest of these guys still needed to find their forever homes.

The sky was getting darker and she knew if she didn't move fast, they would get rained on. So she made a game of it–calling out to each of them and offering incentives to get back to the barn. It was exhausting and she was feeling a little sweaty when she spotted Garrett jogging her way.

Awesome.

Groaning inwardly because she knew she was a mess, she did her best to smile as he got closer. "Hey!"

"Hey, yourself," he said when he reached her side. "It looks like they're running you ragged out here."

"I'm trying to get the last of the dogs into the barn before the rain," she explained. Glancing around, she did a count again and... "Oh, no!"

"What? What's the matter?"

"I can't find Axel! He was running along with me just a minute ago!" She began to run around and the other nine dogs finally listened and followed her into the building. Once she had the gate secured to keep them inside, she began running around calling out to Axel. Garrett was doing the same and she spotted him in the far corner by the gate leading to the new area she had shown him the other day.

"The gate was partially open!" he called out to her and Emma's heart dropped. There was a lot of property back there and most of it wasn't fenced in. Axel was a small dog who could run quite fast when he wanted to–even with his bad leg. When she caught up to Garrett, they walked through the gate and locked it behind. They walked quickly down the path while calling out to Axel. "Has he ever taken off like this before?"

"Never. He's not like that." She looked around frantically. "Axel! Where are you? Let's go get a treat!" Then she wished she had thought to grab a handful of them back at the barn. When Garrett went to keep walking, she put her hand on his arm to stop him. "Shh...let's listen for him."

It didn't take long for them to realize they weren't

hearing anything that could remotely be the dog and started walking again. They checked out the few small buildings as they kept calling out to him, and with every minute that passed, Emma grew more and more upset.

"What if he ran through the woods and out to the street? What if a bigger animal caught him? He's just so little and...and..."

Garrett stopped and wrapped his arms around her. "It's going to be okay. We're going to find him. I don't think he could have gone that far."

The boom of thunder made them both jump and she could have sworn she heard him mutter a curse. It was only a matter of time before the rain...

Emma looked up and got a raindrop right in the eye.

Moving away from Garrett, she started walking again and calling out to Axel. Together they walked toward the new barn, and she had a feeling in another minute, they were going to need to take cover in there while praying this was going to be a short storm.

"Axel!" Garrett called out. "Come on, boy! Let's go home!" At the sound of his booming voice, it was like the sky opened up. The rain came down hard and fast, and before Emma knew it, Garrett had her hand in his and they were running toward the barn. The large doors were open so they could go directly inside, but they were both breathless. "Are you okay? I didn't mean to drag you like that."

Wiping the moisture from her face, she shook her head. "I'm fine. Really. I just don't know how we're going to find Axel." She stood as close to the opening as she could without getting wet and looked out. The sound of the rain meant it was doubtful the dog would hear her calling his name, and she felt utterly defeated.

Garrett stepped in close behind her and rested his

hands on her shoulders. "Has Ed moved any supplies in here yet?"

Glancing over her shoulder, she frowned. "Like what?"

"Umbrellas? Maybe some towels or blankets or tarps that we can use to protect us from the rain so we can keep looking?"

"Oh, um...I'm not sure." Together they turned and began walking around the barn and looked in every nook and corner for anything they could use. A lot more stuff had been moved into the space than she realized, but most of it wasn't of any use to them right now–lots of straw, dog food, harnesses and leashes, but nothing to use for cover. "I am going to go make sure to tell them to move that stuff over next," she murmured.

"Em?" Garrett called out from the other end of the barn.

"Yeah?" she replied even though she was determined to find something to use.

"Can you come here for a minute?"

It was on the tip of her tongue to ask him to simply tell her what he saw rather than making her stop what she was doing, but Emma was far too polite to do it. With a sigh, she walked over and found Garrett crouching in the corner. "What's going on?"

He moved and motioned for her to come closer.

And that's when she saw him.

Axel. Sleeping in a small pile of straw.

"That little stinker," she whispered as she knelt down beside him. And for the first time in several minutes, she felt like her heartbeat was returning to normal.

"He must have run in here before the rain because he's completely dry," Garrett said softly as he moved to sit on the concrete floor. "If you're up for running in the rain, we can get him back to the other barn and get you back to the house."

It was tempting, but the thought of being soaked to the skin and trying to peel out of wet denim wasn't the least bit appealing. "If you've got someplace to be, don't worry about us. I'm going to hang out here for a few minutes and hope the rain passes." Then she awkwardly maneuvered herself so she was sitting beside him.

"My plan was to hang out here this afternoon and visit some more with Ed since I didn't get to the other day."

"He's feeling much better," she told him. "Mom says that every once in a while the pain just comes out of nowhere and puts him out of commission. That's why they're finally doing the surgery. I still don't know how we're going to manage without him for six months."

"Six months? The recovery is that long?"

She nodded. "He'll be up and around before that, but he won't be able to lift or do anything too strenuous for a while. I have a feeling he's going to push the limits on that and make the doctors crazy."

"I know I would," Garrett said with a laugh. "I don't think I could just sit back and watch everyone else work while doing nothing. Everything just feels wrong if I'm not busy."

"Sounds like you," she teased, nudging his shoulder with hers. They sat in companionable silence for a few minutes before it started to get to her. "So...you head back to Norfolk tomorrow, right?"

"Yup. I'll probably leave by lunchtime. My mom's working, and I'm just going to grab breakfast with Austin and Mia. Jackson's already back on base today."

"How did everything go yesterday? Did the ground-breaking go okay?"

He nodded. "It was kind of fun. We each had a shovel and dug up a small spot before the big equipment moved in. Then we had a picnic lunch and hung out until it got too loud." He laughed again. "I don't think my mom and Mia really thought that part through. We ended up moving everything to Austin and Mia's rental place on the beach and spent the rest of the day together. All in all, it was a good day."

"That sounds nice. It was a good weekend." She smiled at him and he was looking at her and in an instant, something changed. Maybe it was the air or maybe she was imagining things, but...suddenly everything felt different. Garrett's expression went from smiling to a much more somber one and she felt her own smile fading. "Garrett...?"

"I swore I wasn't going to do this," he murmured even as he moved closer.

"Do...do what?"

"This," he whispered right before his lips touched hers.

For a moment, Emma was too stunned to react, but when one of his hands reached up and gently caressed her jaw, she was lost.

Her response was slow–shy–but it didn't take long for her to simply sink into it and melt into Garrett. His other hand reached up and cupped her face but he didn't attempt to take the kiss any deeper. It was like he was easing them both into it and it made her like him even more.

Sweet sips, soft caresses...it was everything and yet...it wasn't enough.

Before she knew what she was doing, Emma's hands reached out and gently gripped the front of his shirt to pull him closer. It was clearly the signal he was waiting for because one strong hand anchored up in her hair as he finally took the kiss deeper. His tongue teased at hers in a dreamy rhythm that still seemed to err on the side of caution. It had been so long since she'd been held or kissed that she was only willing to deal with being tentative for so long.

It was her turn to let her hand wander up into his hair as she moved even closer–her breasts pressed against his chest–and she heard the low rumble of need coming from him. It made her feel powerful and wanted, and it was the greatest moment of her life. For years, Emma had lived with the knowledge that she wasn't the kind of woman men went wild for and she had come to accept it.

Until now.

Now she knew that someone as attractive and sexy as Garrett Coleman could want her and it was a heady feeling.

And she wanted more of it.

It didn't matter that they were sitting on the floor of a barn, and it didn't matter that they were both wet from running in the rain. The way Garrett was kissing her said that none of that mattered. That he wanted to do this despite those things.

Wow...

Garrett's hands left her face, her hair, and smoothed down her back, and Emma felt herself being lowered until her back gently hit the floor. Her own arms wrapped around him as they awkwardly maneuvered to get comfortable, and all the while, neither broke the kiss. If it were up to her, she'd never stop kissing him. Everything about him–his lips, his hands, his scent...everything was perfect and had her on sensory overload. She hummed with appreciation as he settled over her.

And then the strangest thing happened...

Garrett was kissing her–his lips on hers–but suddenly, something or someone was licking her forehead.

Then she felt the cold little nose and realized Axel was trying to join in.

Reluctantly, they broke the kiss and both turned their heads to look at the puppy whose tail was wagging back and forth excitedly like he was waiting for them to play with him.

Dammit.

Garrett rested his forehead against hers as he closed his eyes and Emma did the same as she silently prayed he wasn't trying to come up with an excuse about why it was a mistake or how he maybe hadn't meant to do it or...

"Don't do that," he whispered.

Her eyes went wide. "Do what?"

"Frown," he replied softly, placing a kiss on the tip of her nose before rolling off of her and scooping up a delighted Axel.

Emma pushed herself to sit up. "I...I wasn't frowning."

The look he gave her told her he wasn't buying it. "Em, I was looking at you. Trust me. You were frowning."

"I was...thinking."

One dark brow arched as he continued to look at her. "About...?"

Ugh...I totally left myself wide open for that.

Huffing out a long breath, she answered honestly. "I was hoping you weren't going to try to say how you didn't mean to kiss me," she murmured, unable to look directly at him.

"I believe I gave you fair warning that I was going to kiss you, so...there's no way I'd try to say I didn't mean it."

Then she did look up at him and feared he'd see everything she felt in her expression. Swallowing hard, she asked, "But...why?"

"Why did I give you a fair warning?"

"No," she said with a shy smile. "Why did you kiss me?"

―――――

The simple answer to her question was that he wanted to.

The complicated response would mean telling her how he'd wanted to do that since middle school.

Probably best if I stick to the simple response for now...

The puppy in his arms was demanding attention–licking Garrett's face and biting his ear–but he did his best to focus on Emma. "I wanted to kiss you," he said and watched as she looked at him with disbelief.

"No, really," she chided. "Did someone dare you? Or were you just feeling sorry for me?"

Okay, now he'd had enough. He put the puppy down but kept one hand firmly on him so he couldn't run away. "Why would you even think such a thing?"

"Seriously? Um...look at me, Garrett. I'm hardly the kind of woman guys just can't help but kiss! I never have been and I never will be! Hell, even my husband left me because I wasn't enough for him! So excuse me if the thought of Mr. Hot Doc being so overcome with lust after getting stuck in a barn with me while I look like a drowned rat is a little hard to believe!" She jumped to her feet and walked back over to the opening to the outside. Axel squirmed to go after her, but Garrett scooped him up first so they could do it together.

"I take offense to that on several levels, Emmaline," he stated firmly when he was beside her. "For starters, I resent the Hot Doc comment. You know how much I hate that and how I'm not that guy. And I also resent the fact that you think I can't want you just because you're you!"

The eye roll she gave him spoke volumes, but he was prepared for this.

Sort of.

Okay, not really.

He honestly had no intentions of kissing her today, but once they were sitting there, he just couldn't help himself. And in the back of his mind, he knew if he went home tomorrow without doing...something, that he'd regret it.

Unfortunately, now that he *had* done something, the only thing he regretted was that he was going home tomorrow.

"Look, what is it you want me to say here?" he softly demanded. "You asked me a question and I answered it. You know I don't lie, Em. If I'm telling you I kissed you because I wanted to, then you should know it's the truth."

She didn't look the least bit convinced.

"It's fine, Garrett," she said wearily as she looked out at the rain. "I get it. You were curious and...I don't know... bored or whatever. It's not a big deal."

It took a lot to make him angry–to push his buttons–and it was like she had the complete list and was checking them all off. He moved to stand in front of her and had to seri- ously fight for control. "Curious? You think that I'm so shallow that I would do something like that? Just...just kiss you to pass the time?" He muttered a curse and paced a few feet away before standing in front of her again. "I thought you knew me better than that. Hell, I guess I figured you thought more of me! But you're no different from everyone else I've been telling you about. You look at me and you don't see me–the real me. You see some guy who doesn't exist except in your damn imagination!" And if it weren't raining, and he weren't holding the dog, he would have stormed off.

It was one thing for his brothers to tease him; they'd been doing that to each other their whole lives. And it was another thing for strangers to make blind judgments about him. But knowing that Emmaline thought them too?

That gutted him.

He mentally cursed himself for being impulsive and ruining a relationship he'd treasured for most of his life. But he also quietly cursed her for thinking so little of him.

Screw the rain, he thought, and handed Axel back to her. "I gotta go," he murmured once she had the dog securely in her arms. He stepped out into the rain and went all of ten steps before he heard her call his name, but he refused to stop. There was no way he could talk to her right now because he was mad at her for simply being herself, and even though Garrett knew he was being unreasonable, he couldn't seem to stop himself.

"Garrett, wait!" she called out again, and he heard her footsteps pounding through the mud and puddles.

His curse was vicious, but he did stop and turn around. "What?" he snapped.

She came to an abrupt halt two feet away, her eyes wide. "I don't understand why you're so upset! You tell me that I'm acting like I don't know you, and you're right! I don't know the Garrett Coleman who would kiss me!"

Her voice was shaking and he could tell she was frustrated and part of him hated how they were both getting soaked to the skin, but he was too damn stubborn to move.

Emma took a tentative step toward him. "We've been friends for far too long and you...you can't just throw something like this at me and expect me to just roll with it! It's not who I am!" He saw her swallow hard. "And you know what? It's mean, Garrett. It was just plain mean to do that. You resent me for saying what I said? Well, I resent you for doing what you did. So...there." Her shoulders sagged as she turned and walked back to the barn.

He stood there for a solid minute before following after her.

Once in the barn, he found her sitting in the corner where they had found Axel and he took another minute to collect his thoughts. A few minutes ago, the simple response seemed like the best response. But now? Now he knew he would have to lay it all on the line or risk losing her friendship forever.

It was crazy how they'd gone for years without talking to each other, but after this one weekend, he wasn't willing to let that happen again. She didn't have to want him the way he wanted her–hell, they never had to kiss ever again. But if she told him they could never be friends again, he wasn't sure what he'd do.

Letting out a long breath, he walked over. She was sitting on the floor and the dog was back in his little pile of hay, but Garrett remained standing.

"Do you remember our eighth-grade dance at school?" he asked quietly.

She looked up at him like he was crazy. "What?"

Nodding, he went on. "Eighth grade. At the end of the year, there was a dance. Do you remember it?"

It was her turn to nod, but she didn't say anything.

"You wore a pink dress and your mom did your hair in some sort of elaborate style that had a ton of curls that you held up with a sparkly clip. We danced together to *Chasing Cars.*" He paused and let out a small laugh. "It was your favorite song and I remember asking the DJ to play it. Do you remember that?"

"What does this have to do with...?"

"I wanted to kiss you that night," he blurted out. "Even before we danced to that song, but in my head, I thought we'd dance a slow dance and then I'd kiss you, but...I chickened out."

"Garrett..."

"Then when we went on the field trip to the battleship, you had a panic attack because you got claustrophobic. Mrs. Greene let us go sit up on deck by ourselves until they were done touring the lower part of the ship, and we sat outside, just the two of us. I wanted to kiss you then, too."

Slowly, Emma stood up.

"Sophomore year, I was failing Spanish, and I was freaking out because I didn't want to have to go to summer school, and I didn't want to mess up my chance to go to a good college. You worked with me every day after school for a month." He saw her expression soften a little. "When I got my final grade and it was a C, you were waiting out in the hallway for me and I picked you up and hugged you. But what I really wanted to do was kiss you right there in the middle of the crowd of people changing classes."

"Garrett, I..."

But he had one last thing he had to say.

"You went to the junior prom with Steven. I had planned on asking you, but he got there first," he said gruffly, forcing himself to hold her gaze. "I remember asking you to dance that night, but he told me to get lost." He shook his head. "And I always regretted not pushing back harder. Not that I think that would have changed anything, but sometimes..."

He never got to finish.

Emma launched herself at him and kissed him. Her arms were around him, she was up on her tiptoes, and they were both soaking wet, but it was perfect. It took him less than a second to wrap his arms around her, to press her even closer. Her hand raked back up into his hair and he couldn't believe there was a man alive stupid enough to let her go.

Their loss...

This kiss was nothing like the one they'd shared only a little while ago. This was incredibly hot and needy and Garrett wished there were someplace soft that he could lay her down and do this right.

There was nothing wrong with what they were doing, but...he wanted it to be better–special.

She was all wet curves and she smelled so damn good that he felt his control slipping. He wanted to touch more of her but didn't want to spook her in any way. Slowly, one hand smoothed up and cradled the back of her head. Her hair was clipped up in a ponytail and he gently released it and let the clip fall to the floor. At the same time, his other hand smoothed down and rested on her bottom and gave a tiny squeeze.

She was perfect.

From head to toe, she was perfection and he wanted her more than he had ever wanted a woman before in his life.

Maybe it was the fact that he had wanted this for so long that his senses were on overdrive, but he was reasonably sure it was more because Emmaline was...well...she was everything he admired and wanted. To him, she was flawless.

Slowly, the kiss became less urgent before it was nothing more than the two of them tenderly sipping at each other's lips. When Garrett lifted his head and looked down at her, her cheeks were flushed, her lips were red and wet, and her eyes were closed.

She was the epitome of beautiful.

When he rested his forehead against hers, he let out a shaky breath before whispering, "You okay?"

Wordlessly, she nodded.

"Should I apologize for that?" And he silently prayed that he didn't.

Emma's eyes were slightly dazed as she opened them, giving him an impish grin. "I believe I was the one who kissed you that time. Does that mean I should apologize?"

"Never," he stated. His hands gripped her hips and held her close.

When she pulled back and met his gaze, her smile faltered. "Where did that come from?"

"I told you..."

"No," she quickly interrupted. "I know what you told me, but...why now? Why didn't you ever say anything to me about how you felt?"

Good question.

"You were such an important person in my life and you never showed any interest in me beyond friendship. I didn't want to do anything to lose you." He shook his head but didn't release her. "Everyone thought I was a confident person–and in a lot of ways, I am–but where you're concerned, I didn't want to take the risk. And you have to know that I've regretted it for years."

She nodded and let out a soft sigh. "I wish I had known."

All he could do was nod solemnly. "I wish I had been brave enough to tell you. I should have told you. Maybe if I had, you wouldn't have..."

One slim finger pressed against his lips. "Don't," she

whispered. "Just...don't think like that. I don't want to go down that road of what-ifs, Garrett. I can't."

Her forehead rested against his chest and his hands released her hips so he could wrap his arms around her. Garrett rested his chin on top of her head and wondered where they went from here.

For right now, it was nice to just hold her. Over the years, they'd hugged–like buddies–but this was so much better. His hands rubbed up and down her back and it made him feel good that she wasn't pulling away.

Unfortunately, they really did need to talk because now that he'd kissed her and had a taste of the woman she'd become, he didn't want to go back into the friend zone. He'd do it if that's what she truly wanted, but...

"Where do we go now?" she asked quietly, as if reading his mind.

Looking around, he wanted to find a comfortable place for them to sit and talk. The rain was still coming down hard and it looked like they were going to be here for a while.

"What's up there?" he asked, looking up at the loft space. "Do you think Ed's put anything up there?"

Emma turned in his arms and looked for herself. "No idea. In the other barn, it's where he keeps extra hay. So maybe it's the same here?"

As much as Garrett hated letting go of her for even a second, he knew it would be worth it if they found some-place to relax and wait out the storm. He walked over and scooped Axel up in one hand and held the other out to Emma. There was a narrow set of stairs in the barn's front corner that led up to the loft. Normally it would just be a ladder, but he was glad Ed had upgraded. They climbed up in silence and his smile grew when he saw all the possibilities for them up here. Straw covered the floor, but there were also several bales that would make excellent seats. He placed Axel down and led her over to sit on one of them.

But when she looked up at him, words escaped him. All he could do was cup her face and lean in to kiss her again simply because he could.

So good...

Emma melted against him and Garrett realized another benefit to all these bundles of straw.

They were big enough to recline on.

At first he feared he was going too fast, but her hands came up and gripped his shirt and pulled him down with her when he hesitated.

They laughed and smiled against each other's lips before sinking back into another kiss. On and on it went—slow and tender one minute, wet and needy the next. He stretched out beside her before Emma shifted and wrapped one leg over his hip. Every kind of erotic image he could imagine involving her came to mind, and he was about to reach for the button on her jeans when he stopped himself.

Breaking the kiss with every reluctance, he let out a long breath as he sighed her name. His gaze scanned her face, and he loved how breathless she was. "This wasn't why I brought us up here," he said, forcing himself to sit up.

Once she did the same, he took her hand in his and marveled at how small it was and how soft her skin was.

Focus on your words...

"Em, I..." And for the life of him, Garrett had no idea what to say. He stared down at their hands as he tried to find his voice.

"How about I start?" she said, nudging his shoulder playfully. When he nodded, she said, "I think it's safe to say that neither of us planned this, right?"

He nodded again.

"You're leaving tomorrow to go back to Norfolk, and then you'll be traveling to work at a couple of different clinics to try to figure out where you're going to settle and which job you're going to take."

Another nod.

"So it's safe to say that...you're not going to be coming back to Magnolia any time soon." This time, her words were soft and she didn't even try to hide her disappointment.

That's when Garrett knew he needed to speak up.

"I can come back on the weekends. I'm not on anyone's formal schedule at any of the clinics. I'm going to observe and meet with the staff and see where I fit in best. I know it's not much, but I can be here on Friday nights and head back late Sunday afternoon. It's not ideal, but..."

Then he held his breath because he had a feeling this was the point where she was going to tell him it was too much work and not enough time and that the time just wasn't right for them.

He knew it was all true and the thought of all that driving back and forth exhausted him already, but she was worth it. He'd do it every weekend he possibly could—and maybe she'd be willing to come to see him too. It would practically take the planets aligning for this to work out, but that was a risk he hadn't thought about before kissing her.

One minute turned to two, and the suspense was killing him.

"Em?"

She looked up at him, her expression grim. "I hate to think of you driving so much after working all week," she began, and Garrett's heart sank. He'd waited too long and now he was going to lose her before they even had a chance to start.

"Like I said, I know it's not ideal..."

Her smile started small and then grew a little. "But I'd really like for us to try," she said, effectively blowing him away.

They celebrated by reclining on the straw again and kissing until the sun went down and the rain stopped.

6

"WHAT ARE YOU DOING TONIGHT?"

Emma got comfortable on her bed and cradled the phone in her hand to her ear with a smile. "Hmm...not a whole lot. I was just planning on getting comfortable and talking with you."

It was Thursday night, and she and Garrett had gotten into the habit of talking every night after dinner until one of them was just about asleep. It was crazy how they never ran out of things to say and how much she realized she missed having someone to talk to. It wasn't like she didn't have friends–she did–but...she just hadn't spent much time with any of them because she felt like they had nothing in common anymore.

But with Garrett, she found they still had everything in common.

And it made her miss him even more.

"What about you?" she asked. "It sounds like you're in your car. Did you work late?"

"I did. The clinic was a bit overscheduled and understaffed today. I was happy to help out, but I don't think it's where I'm going to stay permanently."

"Oh, Garrett, I'm sorry."

"Don't be. That was the point of this little exercise. I needed to work at the different clinics to see how I felt about them."

"I know, but...it's only been a few days and that's the second one you've crossed off your list. At this rate, you'll have no more options."

"Not really. These two weren't my first choice. The clinic up in Delaware is where I'm heavily leaning, but I needed to rule these others out before I made my final decision."

"So does that mean you're going to head up to Delaware sooner then?" Her heart was racing because she knew if he took that job sooner rather than later that there weren't going to be any weekend trips.

There probably wouldn't be any monthly trips either.

Disappointment washed over her, but she didn't want to bring him down. It was likely that she was just getting ahead of herself.

"There's a lot I need to take care of before I go back up there. They aren't expecting me right away, and I have to start looking for a place to live and then hire movers and work out all the logistics where that's concerned." He paused. "Hey, can you hold on a minute? I'm at the drive-thru getting some dinner and it's my turn."

"Of course. Go ahead." She pulled the phone away and sighed. It was crazy how much she had been looking forward to seeing him this weekend, and now it sounded like everything they had talked about and planned was never going to happen.

Then she wanted to kick herself because it wasn't

anything new. This sort of thing always happened to her–well, maybe not this exact scenario–but her low self-esteem made her believe that she wasn't enough to keep a man.

Any man.

It didn't usually bother her because she was thriving in many ways and was stronger than she ever imagined she would be. Steven had left her in a horrible financial and mental mess, but she was taking care of it all. The debts were getting paid and she was starting to believe in herself more.

Except where men were concerned, obviously.

Her job was wonderful, she was in great demand, and she knew if she ever put herself back out there socially in any capacity, she'd find a better version of herself.

And then something like this had to happen and bring some old insecurities back to the surface.

Dammit.

"I'm back," she heard him say and put the phone back to her ear. "Hey, remember those crazy burgers we used to get from The Sand Bar? Bacon, pepper jack cheese, onion straws, pickles, ketchup, and then ranch on the side for the homemade chips?"

Emma couldn't help but laugh. "Oh, my goodness! I haven't had one of those in a long time! I think sixteen-year-old me had an iron stomach!" She laughed again. "What made you think about those?"

"There's a place here by me that makes something similar. It's still a drive-thru, so it's not nearly as good as having it made fresh like we used to get, but every time I get one, I think of you."

It was both the sweetest and most ridiculous thing she'd ever heard.

"I only had a salad for dinner so that burger sounds even

more amazing," she told him. Her doorbell rang and she frowned. "That's weird."

"What? What's the matter?"

"Someone's at the door. Hang on."

She heard him crunching on his chips as he said, "No problem."

Opening the door, she froze,

There was Garrett–with a goofy smile as he ate a handful of chips–holding out a bag of food to her. She had no idea what to do first–grab the bag or the man.

She opted for the man.

"Oh, my goodness! What are you doing here?" she hugged him tight as he lifted her off her feet and carried her inside, kicking the door closed behind him.

He carefully put her down and grinned at her. "Surprise!"

Laughing, she hung up the phone and took the bag from him as they walked to the kitchen. "I don't understand. What are you doing here so soon? Why didn't you tell me you were coming?"

He shrugged. "I thought it would be fun to surprise you." Then he paused. "But if you're not cool with me being here..."

Emma never let him finish. She silenced him with a kiss and she wanted to cry because it felt so good to be in his arms, knowing he'd done this for her.

That she had been enough.

He pulled away much sooner than she wanted, but the lopsided grin he was giving her made her smile.

"I don't want to be rude, but...I just picked these up from The Sand Bar, and you know these burgers are best when they're hot."

Her eyes went wide. "These? How many did you get?"

"Two. One for me, one for you." He shrugged and began pulling food from the bag and setting it up on the table. "But if you're not hungry, I don't think I'd have a problem eating them both."

"Try it and die, Coleman," she said, taking one of the burgers and sitting down. "I told you I only had a salad for dinner."

Placing a kiss on the top of her head, he said, "And aren't you glad you did? Think about how disappointed you'd be if you were all full and had to sit here and watch me eat both of them?" He took the seat opposite her and winked.

"I don't know. Maybe," she said, unwrapping the burger. "We'll have to see if they're as good as I remember." And after one bite, she could confirm that they were–in fact–even better. "Oh my God, that's good." She moaned happily and caught Garrett staring at her and suddenly felt very self-conscious.

Was I seriously just making sex noises over a burger?!

Clearing her throat, she asked, "So, what are your plans for the weekend? Are you going to stay with your mom or Austin?"

"Actually," he began carefully. "They don't know I'm here or that I even planned on coming to Magnolia." He paused and carefully wiped his hands and mouth. "I was... um...I was thinking of seeing how you felt about me staying here. With you."

Oh.

Oh...

"I'm not saying anything has to happen, Em," he quickly added. "I'd be fine sleeping on the couch. I just really wanted to see you and spend some time with you. You mentioned that you have tomorrow off, and we had already made some plans for the weekend, so...please don't think I'm being presumptuous here. If we're only going to have a few days to see each other, I don't want to take time away by spending time with my family."

"Garrett..."

"No, no...I know. That sounds terrible. Last weekend I kind of ruined my mom and Dominic's date night, and Austin's mentioned more than once that having me around ruins his plans with Mia, so if you could just take pity on me..."

"Garrett..."

"I could just go to Magnolia On the Beach or even go and stay at my aunt's B&B, but..."

Reaching across the table, she put her hand on his. "Oh, my goodness! Stop already!" With a laugh, she squeezed his hand. "Of course you can stay here. I don't have a problem with that at all. If anything...I kind of like that you want to stay here instead of going someplace else." Emma couldn't believe she'd just said that out loud, but it was too late to take it back.

Plus, her burger was getting cold and she figured it would be safer to keep her mouth occupied with chewing rather than blurting out anything else to embarrass her.

The rest of the meal was spent commenting on the food and Garrett telling her about some of his favorite places to eat back in Norfolk. He seemed to enjoy living away from Magnolia Sound, but Emma could never imagine living anyplace else but here. Maybe that wasn't the healthiest way to live her life, but...this was home. She loved knowing her mom and Ed were less than ten minutes away and that she could drive by Henderson's Bakery and pick up a box of donuts to take with her when she visited them. There wasn't a small business in this town that she didn't know either the owners or someone who worked there. This was a close-knit community, and the thought of living somewhere without that kind of support was just too overwhelming for her.

Together they cleaned up the kitchen, and then Garrett went out to his car to get his suitcase while Emma sat on the sofa to find something for them to watch.

And immediately tossed the remote aside.

She had Garrett all to herself. Did she really want to spend that time watching TV?

Then she looked down at herself and groaned. This certainly wasn't the look of a seductress, she thought. The leggings and Happy Tails t-shirt were perfectly fine for sitting on her bed while talking on the phone, but it wasn't something anyone should wear when they were hoping to entice someone.

Ugh...I'm pathetic.

Walking over to the window, she saw Garrett standing next to his car with his phone to his ear. With any luck, he'd be on the call for a few minutes and it would give her enough time to freshen up.

Or at least make sure she brushed her teeth and made sure all the pertinent areas looked okay.

Racing into her room, she immediately went to work.

———

"I appreciate the call, Dr. Collins," Garrett said amicably, even though he was seething.

"We really hope you'll reconsider, Garrett. This is a tremendous opportunity for both of us. Let me send you a copy of the contract. You'll see there's a bonus incentive in there for you."

"For posing for a calendar?" he asked dryly.

"Well, that and posters and appearances at our adoption events," Dr. Collins explained. "I truly believe you'd be very happy with our clinic and should reconsider."

Even though the man couldn't see him, Garrett plastered a smile on his face. "Again, I appreciate the call, but I'm going to pass. Thank you for your time, and I hope you have a good night." He hung up and fought the urge to smash the damn phone to the ground as he growled with frustration.

Every offer he'd gotten was the same: Go work for the clinic, but be our poster boy.

He hated it—every last bit of it.

It wasn't fair, and it wasn't something he was ever going to cave on. For years he'd studied hard and buckled down to do this on his own. He had good grades and graduated near the top of his class. That should have been enough for him to get a decent job at any veterinary clinic anywhere.

But had it?

No.

All because he thought he was doing something good by doing those damn videos on social media. Now he was nothing but a joke.

He'd had a similar call yesterday with a clinic near Baltimore, and when Garrett told them that he was offended, their response was that there were worse things he could be known for.

Seriously?

All his life, he'd struggled with not feeling like he was good enough. It had started with his struggles with learning to read and had continued all through school. If it hadn't been for Emma, Garrett sincerely doubted he would have graduated.

His family was infamous because his father had left them, and then he and his brothers developed a reputation around town for being wild hooligans.

That description still made him laugh, but it added to the entire explanation of why he felt the way he did.

Hell, it was one of the main reasons–the only reason, actually–that he never made a move on Emma all these years. In his mind, he wasn't good enough for her. And now that he had finally made his move, what happens? He can't get a job.

Okay, he *could* get a job–several jobs if he wanted to–but none of them were based on anything that mattered.

They all wanted the Hot Doc.

It was beyond discouraging to him that he'd worked so hard to make something of himself and this one good deed was going to haunt him forever.

Looking back toward Emma's door, he sighed. This so wasn't the way he wanted their night to go.

"Why did I answer the damn phone?" he murmured before grabbing his suitcase and slamming the car door shut. All he knew was that he needed to clear his head before going back inside. It had been a huge risk to simply show up on her doorstep like this, and he wasn't going to ruin the night by whining about how all his "great" job offers were nothing but bogus.

He walked back up to her front door with a heavy sigh and then mentally counted to ten before stepping back inside. At first glance, he didn't see her. The condo wasn't particularly large–mainly an open floor plan where the kitchen and living room were one big space and then there was a bedroom off of it.

"Em?" he called out tentatively as he placed his suitcase down. The door to the bedroom was partially closed and he figured maybe she was in there. With a shrug, he walked over to the sofa and sat down. The remote was right beside him, but when he went to pick it up, he heard Emma clear her throat. When he turned to look at her, he almost forgot how to breathe.

Her long blonde hair was loose and wavy. Her lips were a little glossy and gone was the casual outfit she had on only minutes ago. Slowly, he stood and admired the soft-looking shorts trimmed with lace that showed off her long, tanned legs and the snug matching t-shirt.

His eyes lingered on the shirt because Emma never wore clingy clothes and this was the sexiest thing he'd ever seen on her.

And she wasn't wearing a bra.

Swallowing hard, he finally made himself meet her gaze and saw her very satisfied smile.

You little vixen...

"Everything okay?" she asked, and her voice was a little huskier than he ever remembered hearing.

"Um...yeah." He nodded and fought the urge to walk over to her. As sexy as she looked and sounded, he also saw the uncertainty on her face and wasn't sure if he would steal her thunder by going to her.

But he wasn't sure how much longer he could stay where he was.

"You were just out there for a little longer than I thought you'd be." She finally took one small step toward him and then another. Garrett admired not only the soft sway of her hips but also the way her breasts moved. Once she was standing in front of him, she placed her hand on his chest before letting her gaze slowly travel up to his face and her whiskey-colored eyes seemed to be asking him a million different things.

He gently caressed her cheek with the back of his hand. "Do you have any idea how beautiful you are?" he asked gruffly. "How sexy?"

She shook her head.

"I didn't come here for this," he clarified, because he had to. "You can set the pace, Em, but...I just thought it was important for you to know that." Her skin was so soft and he just wanted to touch her everywhere.

Somewhere in the back of his mind, he wanted to argue that this was too soon, that he should just risk ruining either his mother's night or his brother's because it was too soon for him to be here with her like this.

Then he remembered–eighteen years. They'd known each other for more than half their lives.

Emma took another step closer, which effectively had her pressed up against him and Garrett nearly moaned with pleasure. "When you stepped outside, I came over here to the couch to turn on the TV. I figured we'd watch something and just hang out." Pausing, she licked her lips in a very slow and deliberate way that left Garrett feeling more than a little turned on. "But then I figured that...you were brave enough to show up here and ask to stay over. We've watched TV together countless times. I wanted us to try something new." With each word, her voice got softer and a little less confident, and that's when he knew he had to speak up.

"Whatever it is you want to do, beautiful girl, we'll do it." Leaning in, he kissed her cheek and lingered. "We can sit down here on the couch and kiss like we did in the barn." Shifting, he kissed her other cheek before gently nipping at her earlobe. "Or maybe we can go inside and stretch out on the bed and talk."

It was Emma's turn to moan and he heard the slight catch in her breath when he nipped at her again.

"There's a third option," he went on huskily. "And it's one that I think could be mutually satisfying for us both."

"O...oh?"

Slowly, he kissed his way down the slender column of her throat before kissing along her collarbone. "We can go inside, stretch out on the bed, and...not talk."

Her hands moved up his chest, over his shoulders, and then up into his hair as she went up on her tiptoes. "I'm all for option number three."

"Thank God," he murmured before lifting her up and carrying her into the bedroom. Her legs wrapped around his waist as she locked her ankles behind his back, and it was crazy how sexy it was. He was careful not to bang into anything, and it wasn't until they were beside the bed that he finally gave in and kissed her lips.

And it was like coming home.

It felt crazy since it had only been four days–four of the longest days of his life–and he was this desperate for the taste of her. Maybe it had something to do with more than ten years of longing and hoping and dreaming about being able to kiss and touch her like this, but Garrett had a feeling it was always going to be like this simply because she was who she was.

He lowered them both to the bed, and as he stretched out on top of her, he couldn't help but smile. Reluctantly, he broke the kiss because he wanted to indulge himself by looking at her like this.

Garrett swore he'd never grow tired of seeing her like this–sprawled out on the bed, her long hair fanned out against the pale pink comforter. The room was totally feminine–totally Emmaline–and she was finally going to be his.

"Garrett?" she whispered.

"Yes?"

Reaching up, Emma stroked the line of his jaw, her expression serious. His heart sank because he had a feeling this was going to be the moment she told him she'd changed her mind.

"I need you to promise me something," she went on.

"Anything." And he would. He'd promise her the sun, the moon, and the stars if that's what she asked for.

"Promise me that nothing's going to change. That if we do this, we'll still always be friends." She paused. "Even if it's not good."

For a moment, Garrett could only stare. His mouth went dry as he tried to search for the correct response. He pushed up so he was still straddling her and looked at her with disbelief. When he saw her own expression go from shy to wary, he knew he was taking too long.

"Em," he began, "nothing's ever going to change the way I feel about you. We've been friends for too long and it's going to stay that way." Now it was his turn to pause as he took one of her hands in his. "As for nothing changing, I'm afraid I can't promise that, beautiful girl."

"But..."

"It's only going to get better," he promised. Leaning down, he kissed her softly, thoroughly, before lifting his head again. "And there is no way it's not going to be good. It's not possible." He placed another kiss on the corner of her lips. "You're far too soft..." Another kiss. "And far too sexy..." And still another. "I want you far too much for it to be anything but." This time he rested his forehead against hers. "If we do anything you don't like, you just tell me and we'll stop."

It would kill him, but he'd do it.

"It's just...it's us," she explained quietly. "This is a big change and sometimes...sometimes sex can ruin a relationship."

So many thoughts raced through his head, but the one that stuck was how her ex made her feel this way. Emmaline had always been a shy and quiet girl, but she was sweet and funny and full of life when she felt comfortable around someone. To see how Steven had somehow sucked all that life out of her and left her feeling insecure made him want to punch something.

Specifically, Steven.

But that wasn't going to happen–not now and possibly never.

The urge, however, was still strong.

"Only if it's with the wrong person," he reassured her. "If you want or need more time, Em, then we'll wait." Glancing around the room, he spotted a smaller television. "We can stay right here and watch some TV. I can just hold you if you'd like and nothing else has to happen."

She looked at him like she didn't believe him.

"I'm serious." He slowly rolled off of her and sat up, resting his back against the mountain of pillows she had on the bed. The remote was on the bedside table and he grabbed it and aimed it at the TV. "What are you thinking? Comedy? Drama? Any particular series you're binging on right now?" Garrett did his best to put her at ease because... well...that's just what he did–what he'd always done. Back when they were still in school, Emma would tutor him, and in return, he'd talk to her about things that bothered her–her insecurities about being a bit of an outcast because she wasn't part of the popular clique. By the time they'd hit high school, he had definitely become popular because he played football and baseball, and because she was his friend, she got invited to more things.

And she'd been nervous every time they went anywhere.

So what they were doing right now? It was the norm for them.

Sort of.

Back then, he wasn't trying to make her believe in herself so he could make love to her.

It's different, but the same...

With a grin, he started scrolling through the channels. "Do you get Netflix on this or is it just cable?"

"Garrett," she whined as she rolled over and sat up. Taking the remote from his hands, she turned off the TV and tossed it aside. "Talk to me."

"I thought that's what we were doing."

With a loud sigh, she maneuvered around until she was straddling his lap and all he could do was stare in disbelief.

And that's when it hit him.

She didn't take his offer of waiting as him being patient or honorable. She saw it as rejection.

Dammit.

Rather than say anything, his hands gently grasped her hips and pulled her closer and he saw a spark of surprise in her eyes.

Like that, do you?

Soft hands smoothed their way up over his chest and rested on his shoulders as she pressed even closer. "If I'd wanted to wait or simply sit and watch the television, I would have waited for you out on the couch." She played with his hair a little before continuing. "But this is new to me–to us–and I'm just a little...you know...scared."

"You never have to be scared with me, Emmaline. Never."

She was squirming in his lap and he was getting almost uncomfortably hard. Denim was definitely not his friend in this particular scenario.

"I'm not scared of *you*. I just...I know sex changes everything. And not always for the better. I don't think I could handle it if it happened like that for us. I realize we haven't seen each other or talked in so long, but once I saw you last weekend, it's like no time had passed." She ducked her head. "My marriage was...well...it was awful. And..." Pausing, she let out a long breath. "Steven is the only man I've ever...you know."

The urge to hunt the man down and kill him was back, but he couldn't let it show. Instead, Garrett gently cupped her face. "Forget about him and forget about everything he ever did or taught you about sex because I can guarantee you that he was wrong."

"Garrett, you can't know that."

Nodding, he said, "I disagree. I *can* know that. And you know how?"

Wordlessly, she shook her head.

"Because I've kissed you and touched you, and you are a very passionate woman. If the sex was bad before, that was on him. Not you."

Emma went to pull away, but he wouldn't let her.

"I know you, Em," he went on. "I've known you for more than half of my life, and I can say this with great certainty: There are close to six billion people in this world. Why are you letting one of them ruin your life?" Gently, he kissed the tip of her nose. "Forget him. Forget anything he ever said to you or made you believe about sex." Another kiss. "Let me show you how good it can be."

She looked at him with a mixture of sadness and uncertainty. "I don't want to disappoint you."

"That's never gonna happen," he murmured as he leaned in closer. There was little more than a breath between them. "It's just the two of us in this room, Emmaline. You and me." And then he was done talking. He kissed her–softly at first–but then he dove in.

And it wasn't strictly for her benefit. He was holding on by a thread, and he had a feeling they could talk about this all night and it wouldn't change a thing.

He wanted her–needed her.

And she wanted and needed him.

Now.

Garrett thought about letting her set the pace moving forward for a brief moment, but he reconsidered. What Emma needed was to know she was sexy and desirable and how he was desperate to have her.

She could doubt herself, but he never wanted her to question how he felt about her. This moment was years in the making and he wanted it to be perfect for her.

He kissed her as if his life depended on it while his hands slowly snaked their way under her shirt before pulling back so he could whip it over her head. Emma's eyes went wide, but before she could say a word or question herself, Garrett cupped her face and began kissing her again. From there, it was hard to tell who was seducing who.

They rolled until Garrett was on top and he broke the kiss again to strip off his t-shirt. Emma's hand came up and wrapped around him to pull him back down for another kiss. The skin-to-skin contact was electric, and as much as he wanted to sit back up and simply look his fill, he knew there'd be time for that later.

Her hands scratched down his back.

He cupped her breasts.

And in no time at all, he was pretty confident neither of them were second-guessing anything.

"Garrett," she panted as he moved down her body, her hands loosely fisted in his hair. "Please."

"Anything," he replied breathlessly between kissing all the smooth skin he'd been fantasizing about for far too long.

"I need you..."

"You have me. You have me, Em." And then he pulled those lace-trimmed shorts down her legs and looked up at her. She was flushed and panting, and his smile grew a little wicked.

She was finally his.

7

"It's been a long time since I've done this."

"Me too."

"Yeah, but for you it's a matter of logistics. For me, it's just laziness." Garrett's arms went around her, warming her as they watched the sunrise on the beach. "It's just so beautiful."

"Yes, you are."

She couldn't help but smile. "Not me. The sun and the sky."

"Sure, I guess it's a nice sight. But you are the most beautiful thing on this beach." His lips trailed along her throat and Emma couldn't imagine a more incredible way to start the day.

And after all the wickedly amazing things Garrett did to her last night, that was saying something.

Good Lord...when he told her to forget everything she knew about sex, he wasn't kidding. Emma knew her experience was extremely limited to one incredibly selfish man, but nothing could have prepared her for the way Garrett made her feel–repeatedly–all night long. It was amazing that she was even awake because she had only gotten maybe an hour or two of sleep the entire night.

And she wasn't complaining one bit.

Hell, she'd be willing to give up sleep all together for another night like that.

"What are you thinking?" he asked softly. His chin was resting on her shoulder as he held her close from behind.

"That I'm ready to go back to bed."

His laugh was so deep, rich, and masculine that she felt it all the way to her core. "Yeah, I could probably use a couple of hours of sleep too."

Twisting slightly, she grinned. "Who said anything about sleeping?"

It took him a moment to catch on, but once he did, he smiled with her. "I think I've created a monster."

"Complaining? Already?"

He jumped to his feet and held out a hand to her. "Never. I'm just mad that it's going to take so long to get back to your place."

In truth, it was less than ten minutes, but she knew exactly how he felt.

"I'll race you back to the car," she called out as she started running. Garrett still had to pick up their blanket so she had the advantage. However, it didn't take him long to catch up, and he somehow managed to swing her up into his arms without breaking stride. "Garrett!" They both laughed the rest of the way to the car, and it wasn't until she was on her feet that she was able to catch her breath.

He paused and glanced around, inhaling deeply. "Do you smell that?"

Emma sniffed and her stomach growled. "Unfortunately, I do."

With the boyish grin she adored so much, he took her by

the hand. "We have to go into Henderson's. We *have* to! That is the smell of freshly-baked cinnamon rolls! We can't pass them up!"

The bakery was across the street from where they were parked and Garrett was already tugging her along behind him. "And coffee! I definitely need coffee!"

Looking over his shoulder at her, he winked. "Sweetheart, I'll get you whatever you want if it will get us home faster with goodies."

First burgers and now baked goods for breakfast. She hadn't felt this decadent in a long time and it was a good feeling.

They ran across the street, and when they stepped inside the bakery, Mrs. Henderson herself was there to greet them. "Well, look at this!" she said, clearly delighted. "I feel like we must have gone back in time! The last time the two of you were in here together had to be around ten years ago!" Smiling, she added, "It's good to see you again, Garrett! And Emma, we don't see you nearly enough!"

Garrett must have sensed her unease because he sauntered up to the counter without her. "Do I smell fresh-out-of-the-oven cinnamon rolls?"

If there was one thing everyone knew about Mrs. Henderson, it was how she loved to flirt. "You sure do. Lots of icing on them too."

"Can you box up a couple of them for us and add two large coffees to the order, please?"

"You got it, Garrett."

While the two of them talked, Emma had been scanning the display cases and focused on the giant black and white cookies. It had been ages since she'd had one. Her grandmother used to get them for her all the time. It was sort of their thing. But she couldn't remember the last time she came in to get one for herself.

A hand reached into the case with a fistful of tissue paper and grabbed two of them. When she looked up, Mrs. Henderson smiled. "Your grandmother was a sweet lady and I remember her coming in here every Sunday to get these for the two of you. When I saw you eyeing them, I figured you might like some. On the house."

"Oh, no, Mrs. Henderson," Emma said as she walked over to the register. "I definitely want the cookies, but I insist on paying for them."

"Too late," the older woman said, handing the big pink box to her. "The whole order is on me. It's good seeing the two of you again, so don't be strangers, okay?"

Garrett accepted the box before handing one of the coffees to Emma. He grabbed the second one from Mrs. Henderson. "We promise we'll be back," he told her. "And thank you."

"You kids have a good day!"

"You too, Mrs. H!" Garrett called out as he held the door open for Emma. Together they walked back to his car, and once they were seated, he took the box from her hands.

"What are you doing?"

"There is no way I'm going to make it back to your place without tasting one of these," he said with a laugh, cursing the string Henderson's used to close their boxes.

Smacking his hand, she snagged the box back with a laugh of her own. "Just drive and I'll work on this."

"So bossy," he teased. "I like it."

Those words empowered her, and within minutes, they were halfway home and she was breaking off a piece of cinnamon roll and feeding it to him. He licked her fingers and playfully bit at them, and it was such a breath of fresh air to find that it could be fun to be sexy and teasing. Her mind wandered to how she could do more with the icing and licking when they were back at her place and in bed, but she had a feeling there wasn't going to be anything left for him by the time they got there.

When she broke off a piece of the black and white cookie for herself, he pouted. "Hey, I thought we were feeding me?"

Emma couldn't help but laugh. "You're not the only one who's hungry. I figured I could sneak in a few bites for myself while you chewed!"

"Hmm...I guess that's fair." He glanced at her. "So? Are they as good as you remembered?"

"Oh, my goodness, yes." She moaned happily.

"So your grandmother used to get them for you?"

She nodded. "Every Sunday, just like Mrs. Henderson said. She used to take me out on Sunday afternoons, just the two of us. We'd either go for a picnic in the park or sometimes when I slept over on a Saturday night, she'd go and get them for us for breakfast on Sunday. She was the best."

"That's a great memory, Em." He squeezed her hand. "Let's save the rest for when we get home so we can eat them properly."

"You don't like me feeding you?"

"Would you like to reach over here and feel for yourself how much I like it?" And with a lecherous grin, he winked. "I'm about ten seconds away from pulling the car over so I can kiss you properly."

"Garrett," she whined playfully. "We're only three minutes from the house. Surely you can wait that long."

"Oh, I can wait, but you better be prepared when I turn the car off."

It was exhilarating just imagining what he had in mind,

and Emma almost fanned herself in anticipation. This was all so...new and yet not. This was still Garrett–one of her best friends–and in all the times that she envisioned what it would be like to be with him, she never imagined it would be this good–this easy.

It almost made her worry that something was going to go wrong.

Don't think like that, you ninny. Stop looking for trouble!

The problem was that Emma had learned the hard way that most things weren't easy and when she got too comfortable, inevitably, something went wrong.

She'd thought her relationship with Steven was good and solid–until they got married. It was like a switch was flipped the morning after their wedding and every day after that was a nightmare. Now, she was thankful that it ended sooner rather than it dragging on for years and years, but until the last of those debts were paid off, she couldn't put it all behind her.

Garrett took her hand in his and licked her finger, which essentially pulled her out of her own depressing thoughts. She gave him a sexy smile and realized they were parked in front of her place.

"We're home," she said softly.

He nodded and took the box from her hands and his coffee. "Yes, we are." His grin was downright sinful, and she found herself scrambling from the car in her haste to get the front door open.

Garrett walked in first and she followed him. But when she went to stop in the kitchen, he kept walking straight through to the bedroom.

O-kay...

By the time she caught up with him, he was shirtless and kicking off his sneakers and her entire body began to tingle. The man truly was perfection and she could totally understand why those videos were so popular.

She'd never admit it to him, but she pretty much watched them daily since discovering them.

And now I get to watch him live...

The pink box sat on the corner of the bed and she wasn't sure what was going to happen first.

"Um..."

Emma watched as he stripped down to his boxers and climbed onto the bed. Reclined against the pillows, his hands stacked behind his head, Garrett looked very pleased with himself. "Breakfast in bed."

Emma knew she shouldn't feel shy—not after everything they'd done through the night—but stripping down in front of him was a little out of her comfort zone. So instead, she kicked off her shoes and unzipped her hoodie and tossed it to the floor. The yoga pants and cami stayed on. Picking up the pink box, she climbed onto the bed and straddled his lap.

"Hmm...this isn't quite the way I envisioned breakfast in bed," she murmured as she placed the box beside them and opened it.

"Really? What's wrong with it?" His tone was light and playful, and she had to hide her smile as her hair fell forward.

"Well, in my mind, I'd be asleep, and someone would come in with a tray full of food. You know, things like pancakes or bacon and eggs. Maybe some fruit." She shrugged. "And definitely coffee." Glancing over her shoulder, she realized she'd left her cup in the kitchen.

Drat...

No sooner had she turned back to face him than Garrett managed to twist them around so she was lying beneath him. "Tomorrow we'll do breakfast in bed your way," he all but growled as his hand began to roam up and down her body. "But for today, we'll do this my way."

Her heart raced and she had to wonder how much of his way involved them getting naked and how much involved them eating the rest of their bakery treats.

As if reading her mind, he leaned down and gently kissed the corner of her mouth. "I have plans for the icing on that second cinnamon roll. And it involves some very specific parts of your body and a whole lot of licking."

She met his heated gaze. "I think I'm going to like your version of breakfast in bed."

"Emmaline, I can guarantee you'll love it." Then he was kissing her and she could barely think at all.

Later, much later, she finally turned to him with a sleepy smile. "I'll never doubt you again." Then she curled up against him and fell asleep.

Sunday afternoon, Garrett pulled up in front of the Mystic Magnolia and let out a small laugh.

"What? What's so funny?" Emma asked.

"This place used to be such a dive. It's hard to believe my cousins did so much work to turn it into...well...this! It's crazy!"

"Oh, stop. Although I have to agree that it certainly wasn't the kind of place most people wanted to come to, it didn't start out that way. My grandmother used to tell me how it started out as one of the nicer pubs in town. It was only after the owner's wife passed away that it started to go downhill."

He nodded. "My great-grandfather invested in it over

the years and then left it to my cousin Mason. We all laughed when the Will was read and we heard about it. Who knew he'd end up taking after Pops and trying to turn the place around?"

"I'd say he didn't just try; he succeeded," she corrected.

"Well, he had Peyton's help too. It's not like he did it alone."

She turned and glanced at him. "Do I sense a little of hostility?"

He shrugged. "Growing up, Mason was the golden child. He could do no wrong. His mother used to love rubbing it in our faces just how perfect her children were. Especially Mason." Another shrug. "We're all grown up now, but sometimes I can't help but get a little annoyed at how everything works out for him."

"Well, you shouldn't think like that. I mean, look at you! Look at how great things are going! You've got veterinary clinics practically up and down the East Coast trying to woo you!" Reaching over, she squeezed his hand. "You should be proud of yourself. Don't waste your time comparing yourself to your cousin."

"Maybe..."

"No maybes about it." She moved away and opened the car door. "Now, let's go inside. I'm starving."

So was he.

And she was right. It was pointless to even try to compare himself to Mason.

His cousin would win every time.

Garrett just opted to keep that part to himself.

They walked inside and were seated right away, and he had to admit, the place looked fantastic. When he glanced at the menu, he was pleasantly surprised. "Okay, now I can see why you wanted to come here. The menu's pretty impressive."

"Rumor has it that your cousin Peyton is responsible for that. I know she has a little café in the heart of town, and I've gone in there quite a few times, but I prefer this menu."

He nodded. "How are the burgers here?"

"Good, but not as good as the ones we had the other night. No one does a burger like The Sand Bar."

"That's the truth."

They took several minutes and ultimately decided on splitting an order of tot nachos for an appetizer. Emma chose the lobster club and Garrett went for the fish and chips for their meals. Once their order was placed, he reached across the table and took both her hands in his and knew he was grinning like an idiot.

"What's that smile for?" she asked.

"I can't seem to stop," he replied honestly. "This has been an amazing weekend. Every minute of it has been...perfect."

She blushed. "It really has. I hate that you have to go home later."

Go home?

Oh, right. He hadn't told her that he'd had a change in plans since there were no jobs for him to rush home to.

"Listen, Em...about that..."

She smiled at him, and she was just so damn pretty and looked so happy and hopeful that it suddenly filled him with shame to have lied to her all weekend.

A lie of omission, he reasoned to himself, but a lie still the same.

"So I'm thinking of staying for a few more days," he said carefully. "I know you have to work, but I'm thinking of going over to Happy Tails and seeing where I can help out before Ed has his surgery. Maybe there's nothing I can do, but I feel like it's important to go and offer."

Her smile grew. "You are the sweetest man; you know that, right?"

"Em…"

"I think that is amazing and I know Mom and Ed are going to be so grateful for you. But…what about the clinics you were supposed to work with this week?"

"It's not a problem," he replied, looking down at their hands.

"Are you sure? I thought the point of all of this was for you to check and double-check that you were making the right decision." She paused and then gasped. "Oh, my goodness! Have you gotten some better offers? Is that why you were able to blow this week's stuff off?"

It was on the tip of his tongue to talk to her about what he felt because if anyone would understand, it was her.

But…he couldn't.

His pride wouldn't allow it.

Saying it out loud to her–or to anyone–would be admitting that he wasn't good enough on his own merits to get hired anywhere. And right now, when Emma looked at him, he liked what he saw there. She genuinely liked him and cared about him just because he was Garrett. But would that change when she found out he was a failure who couldn't get a damn job?

There was still the offer for the position in Delaware, so realistically, he knew all was not lost. But he did have a call scheduled with them for the end of the week. He'd feel better once that was done and he confirmed why he was taking the position and why they were hiring him.

Even though moving that much farther away from Emma was beyond unappealing.

Ugh...could my life be any more of a mess?

The waitress came back with their drinks and appetizer, and Garrett was thankful for the distraction. "So tell me about your week," he prompted. "Tell me what your schedule is going to be like."

"Well, my day starts at the school at eight. The school changes daily–and sometimes I go to more than one school a day–but I always make sure I'm there when the actual school day starts for the teachers. I take the time before the students arrive to talk to their teachers and go over their files. Most of the time, I work with a small group, but sometimes I get to do it one-on-one. That's my preference, but it doesn't always work out that way. That's why I've taken up tutoring in the afternoons because a lot of parents prefer for their child to have that personalized attention and lesson plan."

"I think what you do is amazing, Em, but it sounds like a very long day for you."

She nodded as she helped herself to some tots. "Some days are, but...I don't know...it's not like I have anything else going on. I do have a couple of shorter days where I'm done by lunch and I take that time to do my shopping and laundry, or I go over to Happy Tails and help out." She shrugged. "I like staying busy."

"I get that. I'm the same way, but I hate to think that you're just spending your life working and not living," he said and genuinely meant it. "Do you ever go out with friends?"

"Not in a long time," she murmured, focusing on her food.

"Maybe we should try to get together with some people this week. What do you think?"

With a sigh, she looked up at him. "Garrett, most of my

friends are married with kids or they've moved away. I haven't spent time with them because it felt weird after my divorce. I foolishly married young and was getting divorced when most of them were just getting married. I'm a little self-conscious about it, and after a while, they all stopped reaching out, so..."

Damn. That did suck.

Most of his friends had moved away from Magnolia and the few that were still here he hadn't talked to in ages either.

"Maybe we can hang out with Austin and Mia one night?" he suggested. "We could go over to their place for dinner or something."

Laughing, she took another tot from the platter. "Don't you think we should wait for an invitation rather than inviting ourselves?"

"Trust me. If I called my brother right now and told him I was with you, he'd invite us over tonight. Possibly even right now," he added as he pulled out his phone.

"Oh stop," she said, shaking her head even though she was still clearly amused. "You know I'd be a tongue-tied mess if you took me to their house."

"Because of Austin?"

Now she rolled her eyes. "No, because of Mia! I'm a huge fan. I told you that!"

"Once you hang out with her, you'll see that she's just like you and me. There's nothing to be intimidated by. She's very sweet and friendly and I'll bet the two of you will become instant friends."

She huffed with disbelief and turned her attention back to the tots. "These are seriously addictive. Who would have thought of using short ribs and tots to make something like this? I'm telling you, your cousin is a culinary genius."

Garrett nodded and scrolled through his contacts to get

to his brother's number and hit send. "So if they do happen to invite us tonight, would you like to go?"

"I have a feeling I won't be able to eat anything. Between this lunch and my nerves, I'll be a mess."

He sighed, shaking his head. "Any day this week better for you?"

"Um...Tuesday's a short day. I'll be done by two."

"Okay, then." He popped a tot in his mouth as Austin's phone rang. Garrett looked around the restaurant, recognized several familiar faces, smiled, and waved to a few of them. He continued to scan the room and wondered why his brother's phone waited so long to go to voicemail when he noticed someone walking in. It was an older man who looked vaguely familiar.

"Hey, it's Austin..." The message began and Garrett knew it to be lengthy because this was also his business number. So while it played out all about different ways to reach him, Garrett continued to stare at the guy by the door and tried to figure out where he knew him from.

A former teacher?

A former coach?

The man turned and looked his way and Garrett's heart kicked hard in his chest.

"Leave me a message and I'll get back to you," the message was saying.

As soon as he heard the beep, he murmured, "Austin, it's me. Call me back immediately. Something...something's happened and you need to get down to The Mystic Magnolia ASAP." He hung up and felt like he was going to be sick.

The only small consolation he felt was that the face looking back at him seemed to be equally shocked and uncomfortable.

"Garrett? Garrett, are you okay?" Emma was saying. "You've gone pale. What's wrong?" Her voice was laced with worry and he had no doubt that if he looked at her, her expression would say the same.

Should he get up and walk over? Call out something? Everything inside him screamed that he should, but he couldn't seem to move. And as for speaking, he knew his mouth was moving, but his throat had gone dry and he couldn't seem to force himself to utter a single word.

"Garrett," she said with more force. "You're worrying me! What is it?" Turning in her seat, she looked around and followed his line of vision. "Who is that? Do you know him?" When she looked back at him–even in his peripheral vision–he knew she was looking back and forth between the two men as if trying to figure it out for herself.

It took less than a minute for her to gasp.

"Oh my God!" she hissed quietly. "Is...is that...?"

Finally, he swallowed hard but never looked at her. With a nod, he said the words he never thought he'd say. "My father's here."

8

THINGS SEEMED like they were happening in slow motion, and for the life of her, Emma had no idea what she could possibly do or say. So she sat back helplessly as Cash Coleman–the man who had abandoned his wife and sons more than twenty years ago–walked over to his middle son.

"Garrett?"

She eyed the older man before looking across the table at Garrett. Everything in her screamed to get up and hug him–shield him–from the father who had caused him a lifetime of grief and insecurity, but she wasn't sure it would help. If he would only look at her, she'd know what to do.

Look at me, Garrett...

But his eyes never left his father's, and the silence was beyond awkward.

"Cash," Garrett finally gritted out, his jaw clenched.

His father scrubbed his hand along the back of his neck. "So, um...fancy running into you here."

"If you say so."

Cash looked from Emma and then back to Garrett before asking, "May I join you?"

Honestly, Emma was fairly certain her jaw was on the floor and she waited for Garrett to tell him to get lost.

But he didn't.

Instead, he motioned to one of the chairs and watched as Cash accepted and sat.

Emma glanced around the restaurant and wondered if anyone could tell what was going on or how uncomfortable she was. She looked toward the door and almost willed Austin to walk through it, but...no luck there either.

"Hi," Cash said when Emma's gaze happened to meet his. "I'm Cash Coleman. Garrett's father. And you are...?"

"Emma Ryan," she said stiffly and with a hint of disgust. How dare he sit down and introduce himself like this was perfectly normal.

"Ryan..." he repeated and then recognition hit. "You're Christine's daughter, right? She owns the animal rescue."

"Yes."

"I was planning on reaching out to them this week. I'm thinking about getting a dog and I know it's important to reach out to the shelters and rescues rather than going to the pet store, right?"

"What are you doing here, Cash?" Garrett interrupted with annoyance.

"What's with all this Cash nonsense? I'm your father..."

But Garrett never let him finish. "And why would you even consider getting a dog? That's a big commitment. Not as big as say...three children, but a commitment just the same."

Cash let out a low laugh as he eyed his son. "I would think you'd be happy to hear I'm adopting a dog. You're a veterinarian now. Surely you know the importance of finding homes for animals."

Emma saw a flash of surprise on Garrett's face and

knew exactly what he was thinking–his father knew what he did for a living. How much more did he know about his sons? But most importantly, why was he here? It was hard to sit back and not ask any questions, but that's what she forced herself to do.

Garrett's only response was a low growl as he pinched the bridge of his nose.

"Anyway," Cash went on, his focus on Emma, "I went to the website and saw several dogs that I'd really like to go and meet and see if I click with any of them. I need to make an appointment, right?"

He was looking at her expectantly, and as much as this man didn't deserve any kindness or consideration, she was raised with manners, so she figured she'd take one for the team and engage in conversation with him while Garrett calmed down.

"Yes. You can make one through the website, but some- times it's glitchy. Your best bet would be to call the office in the morning. Betsy Hamilton is our receptionist and she can tell you the best time to go in for an adoption consult." She paused and tried to think of anything else she should tell him. "There's an application you can do online, as well. If you have that done, it will speed things up when you go in."

"Why are you even telling him this?" Garrett asked wearily. "They can't approve him to adopt a dog. With his track record, he'll adopt it and then leave it on the side of the road somewhere!"

"Garrett," she began, but Cash interrupted.

"No, no. It's okay," he said calmly, easily, as he leaned back in his seat. His big arms crossed over his chest as he looked at his son. "I can understand why you believe I'm unfit to adopt a dog–and be a father–but the fact is that you don't know much about me or who I am now. You remember who I was when you were a kid and you're smart enough to know that people can learn from their mistakes and change."

Mimicking his father's pose, Garrett volleyed right back. "Oh, I believe some people are completely capable of change. You're not one of them."

In her heart, Emma felt for both of them. She knew the hurt Garrett had experienced as a boy and how his father's absence affected so many aspects of his young life. But then also learned that people could change. Her own father had divorced her mother when Emma was a baby and didn't play a part in her life until she was a teenager. They had a better relationship now that she was an adult and maybe it was something she would share with Garrett later when they were alone.

"It's not like you to be so judgmental," Cash countered. "You were always the one who thought things through when you were a kid." Then he smirked. "I guess you changed."

Garrett's hand slammed down hard on the table. "Now just a minute..."

"Holy shit! *Dad?*" They all turned to see Austin standing next to them with wide eyes.

Honestly, Emma had no idea who to focus on because everything became very chaotic all at once. All three men were talking–and not particularly quiet about it–until Mia suggested they take it outside.

Garrett stood and looked down at her. "I'm sorry, Em," he said gruffly. "I'll be back in a few minutes." Then he turned to Mia and introduced them. "Would you mind very much...?"

Mia waved him off. "Just go and make sure Austin isn't beating your father to the ground."

With a word of thanks, Garrett gave Emma a distracted kiss before storming out of the restaurant. Once he was gone, she smiled at Mia. "So...um...it's nice to meet you."

Mia Kingsley was beautiful in an almost exotic way. She was all dark hair and dark eyes and lightly tanned skin, where Emma was all...well...not that. Most women she had encountered who were this attractive tended to be more than a little conceited, so she was prepared for this to be strained and awkward.

Mia waved their waitress over. "Can I please get a glass of sweet tea, an order of crab cakes, and an extra plate? Oh, and some more sour cream, please." Once the girl was gone, Mia grinned at Emma. "Garrett is going to have to deal with me sharing the rest of these tot nachos with you. They're my favorite!"

And at that moment, Emma was relieved to be wrong.

"So, how long were you sitting here with Cash before we got here?" Mia asked, picking off a tot and popping it into her mouth.

"Thankfully, not long. You must have been driving right by to have gotten here so quickly."

She nodded. "We were going food shopping and about to walk into the store when the phone rang. Austin is terrible about answering it on the weekends, but I encouraged him to listen to the message. Now I'm glad I did!"

"Me, too." She shook her head. "I felt so bad for Garrett. He went white as a ghost when his father walked in."

"Why would he even come back after all this time?" Mia wondered. "It just seems mean at this point. What could he possibly want?"

"I've known Garrett a long time, and I know his father would sporadically reach out–just a call or a card every now and then–but as far as I know, this is the first time he's come back to Magnolia Sound." She shook her head again. "And he's talking about adopting a dog which makes me feel like he intends to stay awhile."

"Oh God. That won't be good."

"I know. Just hearing him say that nearly sent Garrett over the edge. This is going to be a nightmare."

"Wait," Mia said, looking mildly confused. "When did Garrett get into town? He didn't mention to us that he was going to be here."

Emma blushed and apparently it was enough of an explanation.

"Ah, a little privacy," Mia said as she helped herself to more tots. "I totally get that." She chewed thoughtfully for a moment. "Is he heading back home tonight?"

"Actually, he's planning on staying for the week."

"Really? That's odd. I thought he had all kinds of clinics lined up that he was going to work with to narrow down his job options."

"He was, but I guess he narrowed down the choice even more and he wanted to stay and volunteer at Happy Tails. I know my mom is going to appreciate it, but I hate to think of him taking time away from making a vital decision."

Mia's smile grew as she continued to eat.

"Of course, I'm thrilled that he's going to be here for a little longer. If he takes the job in Delaware, I'm not sure when we'd get to see each other, so I'm just soaking up all the time we have together while I can."

"And then Cash comes strolling back in and ruins it. The rat bastard." She paused. "He's the kind of guy I like to put in a book and kill off." As if she just realized what she said and how it sounded, her hand flew to her mouth as her eyes went wide. "I'm sorry! That was...well, that was a little rude and dramatic. Please don't think I'm a horrible person!"

Unable to help herself, Emma laughed. "Are you kidding? That's the greatest thing I've heard all day! And let me just say that I love your books! I promise not to get all weird on you or ask for any behind-the-scenes stuff on the book you're working on, but I just wanted you to know."

"I always love meeting a fan. And for the record, I don't usually talk about whatever book I'm writing to anyone. Not even Austin. It makes him crazy!"

"I can imagine! But really, don't worry. I'm not going to fangirl all over you. I'm just relieved that I'm not having to sit here by myself while they're outside doing...whatever it is they're doing."

Their food arrived and they both thanked the waitress. "Can you please box the fish and chips to go?" Emma asked. "I'm not sure he'll be back before it gets cold."

With a nod, the waitress took the plate and walked away.

"Smart move. If I had to bet money, I'd say we're going to have to either go outside to break things up or go to the police station to bail them out," Mia said, shaking her head. "But I'm finishing my lunch first."

"I really hope it doesn't come to that."

Mia looked up at her and laughed softly. "Emma, you've known the Coleman brothers much longer than I have. Can you honestly see things going peacefully out there?"

"Um..."

"Enjoy your lobster club and let's finish these tots. We're going to need all the strength we can get."

Yeah, Emma thought, she just might have found a new best friend in Mia.

"You have no right being here!" Austin was shouting when Garrett stepped outside. "Just get in your car and go! That's what you're good at!"

Cash held up his hands in surrender, but that wasn't what he was implying. "Look, I know seeing me is a shock, but I thought we could sit and talk like adults. Maybe we should go back inside…"

"Hell, no," Garrett said as he got closer. "We're not going back in there and making a scene. You may not care about reputations, but we do. Thanks to you, we were the talk of the town for years!"

"I've been coming in here for weeks without incident," Cash explained. "Everyone who works here thinks I'm a damn delight. Now I know your mother raised you both with better manners than this."

Garrett saw red. He had his father's shirt fisted in his hands as he slammed him against the nearest car. "You don't get to say a *thing* about Mom! You don't get to even *think* anything about her, do you understand?"

"Garrett," Austin said, pulling him off their father. "Don't. Don't do this. He's not worth it."

With a huff, he shoved Cash away. "You're right." He let out a long breath as he stepped away. With another glance at his father, he sneered. "You're not wanted or welcome here. I don't know what you thought you'd accomplish by coming back, but you're wrong. Whatever it is, you're wrong and it won't work. We've been fine without you all these years, and we'll keep being fine, so just…just do the right thing for once, and leave."

His heart was racing, adrenaline pumping, and the urge

to hit something was strong. Unfortunately, his brother was right–Cash Coleman wasn't worth it.

"You okay?" Austin asked quietly.

"Yeah. I will be. He just...he shouldn't be here."

Austin nodded before turning around and confronting their father. "Garrett's right. We're not interested in talking with you or hearing anything that you want to say. You lost that right to waltz back into our lives a long time ago."

For a minute, Garrett was confident they had convinced the man to leave, but in typical Cash fashion, he did what he wanted no matter what.

"I'm not asking for anything more than a bit of your time," Cash said gruffly. "The last thing I wanted was to come here and end up in a brawl with my sons in a parking lot. I truly just wanted to come and talk to you both. I know Jackson's deployed right now, and..."

"How do you know all this?" Garrett interrupted. "You know about me being a vet, Jack being deployed...I mean...how?"

"You may not believe this, but I always knew what was going on in your lives. I might not have been able to be here, but..." he shrugged.

"Um, yeah. That's not an explanation," Austin snapped. "Who's been telling you what's been going on? We know it's not Mom because she hasn't spoken to you in years. So who's your spy, huh?"

Cash sighed loudly. "Do we really want to do this in the middle of a parking lot? I realize we're on the edge of town, but people really are coming and going. Is an audience worth it to you?"

"I don't think the restaurant is any better," Austin reasoned.

"Yeah, I don't think Emma or Mia would appreciate

having to sit through this," Garrett murmured. "Whatever *this* is."

With a huff, Austin pulled out his phone and made a call. "Hey, babe. What?" He paused. "No, we're fine. But I think we need to go someplace else and do this." Another pause. "Yeah, I think that would work. Can you put Emma on and I'll give the phone to Garrett?" One last pause. "I love you too." He handed the phone to Garrett.

"Hello?"

"Garrett? What's going on?"

"Honestly, I have no idea, but I think we're going to go someplace to talk that's a little more private."

"Oh. Okay. Um...hang on."

He heard her saying something–presumably to Mia–but it was all muffled.

"Okay," she said when she came back on the line. "Mia and I are going to finish our lunch and she'll take me home. Call me later when you can."

"I hate this, Em. You shouldn't have to do that."

"It's okay. Really. Mia and I are getting to know each other, so it's fine. Go and do what you need to do and we'll talk later."

"I'm sorry."

"Don't be. I'm fine. You're the one I'm worried about."

"Yeah. Me too," he said grimly as he realized his father and brother were waiting on him. "I'll call you later and please thank Mia for me."

"I will."

After they said goodbye, he handed the phone back to Austin. "So, um...where are we going?"

"My place," Austin said. "I'll ride with you and he can follow." Then he looked at Cash. "Do I even have to tell you the address or have your spies already told you where I live?"

"I'll just follow you," Cash said.

Two minutes later, they were pulling out onto the main road and there were dozens of thoughts racing through Garrett's head. "Should we call Mom?"

"No. Not until we know what he wants. With any luck, he's just here to settle some twisted curiosity and when he sees we're not interested in having a relationship with him, he'll be on his way."

Garrett opted not to bring up the dog situation.

"What could he possibly want after all this time? No one's been able to even find him for years. I don't even know if Mom was able to divorce him because of it."

"She hasn't," Austin commented.

"You sure?"

"Positive. I've asked."

"You'd think she'd have found a way to do it by now. Even if she had no interest in getting married again, I would think she would have wanted to be rid of him in all ways."

"You would think. She's had so much on her plate for so long, maybe she was just too tired to deal with it."

"Maybe."

The rest of the drive was made in silence because anything they had to say would simply be speculation. Plus, Austin's place was less than five minutes away, so...

Once there, they followed Austin inside and sat down on the living room sofas facing one another–father versus sons.

"I won't waste your time with pleasantries and small talk," Cash began solemnly. "I briefly came back to Magnolia about a year ago. My plan was to get in contact with your mother and...see about getting together with all of you." He looked at Austin. "I actually saw the two of you having dinner at the Mystic Magnolia and almost walked over, but...I chickened out."

Austin muttered a curse under his breath.

"I didn't stay in town long and I never did make that call. The time just wasn't right."

"And now it is?" Garrett demanded, hating how angry he was.

Cash nodded. "It is." He shifted in his seat as he let out a long breath. "I found out a year ago that I have cancer. Liver cancer. It was caught relatively early but if I had a transplant, the survival rate wasn't going to be great. If it spread, my prognosis goes from five years down to less than a year."

"Obviously, you're still here," Austin murmured. "Were you hoping one of us is a match? Is that why you came?"

"No," his father replied with a small laugh. "Unfortunately, that ship has sailed. The cancer did spread, and I've opted to forgo any treatment. Basically, I've come to...make things right. Get my affairs in order."

And just like that, all the fight went out of Garrett, and beside him, he saw his brother sort of deflate as well.

It would be easy to hurl insults and hash out all the ways this man had done them wrong, but what would be the point? He might not deserve understanding–and he certainly didn't deserve forgiveness–but Garrett knew he didn't have it in him to be mean just for the sake of being mean.

They sat in awkward silence for several minutes before Austin spoke.

"O-kay...I'm not sure what we're all supposed to say here."

Cash looked at his sons and Garrett saw the sadness and

regret in his eyes. In all the ways he envisioned seeing his father again–if it were to ever happen–never in a million years did he imagine it would be like this. And suddenly he felt awful about how aggressive he'd been in the parking lot.

"Are you in pain?" he asked quietly. "Did I hurt you back there...?"

"I'm fine, Garrett. I deserved what you did back there and more. But overall, I have good days and bad."

"Why not get treatment?" Austin asked.

"What's the point?" Cash asked. "Even with treatment, the survival rate isn't good. I'd rather live out my days on my terms rather than hooked up to machines in a hospital bed." He let out another mirthless laugh. "Besides, I think we can all agree the world would be a better place without me in it."

Garrett and Austin exchanged glances and he knew they were both feeling mildly guilty because they'd said those exact words many times over the years.

"So what happens now?" Garrett forced himself to ask, doing his best to remain detached. If he let himself feel too much, he wasn't sure he'd be able to handle this.

"Now, I finally talk to your mother about a divorce. I'm not sure why she hasn't done that already."

"Hard to pin down a moving target," Austin said flatly.

"Yeah," Cash agreed. "I know." He paused. "That's first, anyway. Then my grandfather's attorney has been hounding me to come in and see him, so I'm guessing the old guy left me something. Lord only knows why."

No one disagreed.

"But more than anything, I wanted a chance just to see you boys face to face, to tell you that I'm sorry." He sighed. "I was a lousy husband and an even worse father. You deserved so much better than me. At the time, I honestly believed I was doing the right thing by leaving. I still do. Unfortunately, I didn't do enough to make sure you were all okay financially. I know that, and I regret it. If I could go back and do it all over again..." His words trailed off.

"Would you still leave?" Garrett asked, his voice quiet and unsure.

"I don't know, Garrett." He leaned back wearily on the sofa. "I can't regret marrying Grace and having you three boys because you're the only thing I did right in this world. No one's going to remember me when I'm gone, but the three of you are good men. Smart, caring, and successful men. You overcame the mess that I caused and came out of it as successes." He looked at Austin. "You're an extremely talented architect. I've seen pictures of some of the buildings you've designed and I see you're already putting your stamp here in Magnolia."

Beside him, he saw his brother blush.

"And you, Garrett," Cash went on. "A veterinarian. You overcame all your problems with reading and look at you now! Veterinary clinics are all trying to woo you to come work for them! You have your pick of almost any job you want and you're a social media sensation!"

Austin snickered and Garrett elbowed him in the ribs.

"I wish I had the opportunity to sit here with Jackson, too. I can't believe I have a son who's a soldier. A Marine!" He shook his head. "I know he was just deployed and won't be back for at least seven or eight months, but..."

He might not live that long.

"And what about the dog?" Garrett asked.

"What dog?" Austin looked between the two of them, confused.

"I thought a dog would make a nice companion. Especially an older dog," Cash explained with a shrug.

Now wasn't the time to discuss all the reasons why that wasn't the greatest idea in the world, Garrett thought.

"Where are you staying?" Austin asked after a moment.

"I'm renting a place down in Wilmington. A little bungalow on a month-to-month basis. I would prefer to be back here in town, but I wasn't sure if that was the smartest idea. I do have family here besides you boys and your mom, but I'm not sure I'd be welcome with any of them either." He smiled. "Although I am wildly curious to see what Susannah did with the old house. I saw some pictures online, but I'm sure it looks much better in person."

"Yeah, she did a great job with it," Garrett replied. "It's been very successful, too. It's the perfect setup for a B&B."

"Your great-grandfather knew what he was doing when he left it to her. He actually seemed to know what he was doing with everything he left for everyone. I'm almost a little afraid of what he left for me."

Neither of his sons commented.

"When are you planning on reaching out to Mom?" Garrett asked.

"The sooner the better. If I hadn't run into you at The Mystic Magnolia, I probably would have tried to see her today. I know she's still living in the same house and I planned on just showing up and knocking on the door."

"Yeah, um...maybe don't do that."

"Why not?"

Austin chose to answer. "She's got a life. A good one. Plus, she's dating someone. He's a great guy and I think you just barging in on them would do more harm than good."

"Oh," Cash replied quietly. "I guess I didn't think of that." He sighed. "So what do you suggest?"

Garrett and Austin exchanged glances.

"Let us talk to her first and then we can all meet

together. I think she'd appreciate having some time to deal with the shock of seeing you again and not having to do that in front of Dom," Austin suggested and both Garrett and Cash agreed.

Cash stood and nodded. "Okay, then. Why don't I give you my number and you can call or text me when you want me to come back and I'll let you both get back to your girls." He recited his number while both of them entered it into their phones. "Thank you for agreeing to see me and I'll wait to hear from you."

The brothers stood and there was an awkward moment where they were unsure whether they should shake hands with Cash, hug him, or simply say goodbye. Austin held out his hand and Garrett saw the flash of disappointment on his father's face. Maybe in time they'd feel differently toward him—more forgiving, more affectionate—but not yet.

Garrett shook his hand. "We'll talk soon," he said and hoped they weren't being set up for another big letdown—that Cash wasn't going to take off because things didn't go his way today.

Have a little faith...

Cash showed himself out, and once the front door closed, Garrett collapsed back on the sofa.

"Holy shit," Austin muttered. "I don't even know what to think right now."

"Yeah. Me either."

"I mean...I'd like to think he was telling the truth..."

"You mean you want him to have cancer?" he asked incredulously.

"That's not what I meant. I just hope he didn't make that up to gain sympathy, that's all. Honestly, I wouldn't put anything past him. That's why I want us to talk to Mom before he does." He glanced at his watch. "Do you think we should call her now?"

"I hate to have to call her at all. It doesn't seem fair that she's finally dating again and then he has to come and ruin it."

"Don't be dramatic," Austin chastised. "He's not going to ruin anything. Mom isn't an idiot. If anything, this is going to be great for her. She'll finally get her divorce and then she and Dom can do whatever they want. I don't think it's a big deal."

"Then why do we have to be the ones to break the news to her?"

His brother growled before sitting in the spot their father recently vacated. "Why are you like this?"

"Like what?" he demanded. "You're the one who's not making sense!"

"Okay, fine, I *do* think Mom's going to be a little shocked and upset to see him. That's why I wanted to talk to her first. Once she gets over that initial jolt, I think she's going to be fine." He paused. "And not only that, I don't like the idea of him coming around calling the shots. We all had to live by his rules for years–before and after he left–so he doesn't get to show up and have the upper hand in any way."

"How did we live by his rules after he left?"

Austin glared hard at him. "Why are you so literal?"

"Again, why don't you make sense?"

"Dad left us and we had to pay the price, Garrett! We had to struggle because he didn't want to stick around and have any responsibilities! So maybe *rules* wasn't the right word, but you do get what I'm saying, right?"

He shrugged. "Yeah, I guess." With a weary sigh, he leaned back against the cushions.

"You okay?"

"No. I think I'm still in shock. When I saw him walk through the door at the restaurant, it didn't register at first. Then he looked over at me, and...I froze. I completely froze. Emma was about to call 9 1 1 on me, I swear."

Smiling, Austin leaned forward. "So...you and Emma. How about that?"

Garrett seriously felt himself blush. "Yeah. Me and Emma."

"And I didn't even have to do anything drastic! I love it!"

"You still owe a donation to the animal rescue, don't forget about that."

Austin waved him off. "That's nothing and I'm happy to do it. I'm just glad that I didn't have to get involved and embarrass you or anything to get your butt in gear." He laughed softly. "So, how long are you here for? Are you driving back to Norfolk tonight?"

"Nah. I'm staying the week to help out at Happy Tails."

"Really? But...what about your plan—the whole working at different clinics thing? How are you going to make an informed decision if you don't work everywhere first?"

He knew his brother was mocking him, but he didn't care. In the grand scheme of things, his problem with the job offers had to take a back seat to what just went down with their father. So he shrugged and said, "I've got it all under control."

"Good for you then. Are you staying with Mom?"

Shaking his head, he said, "I'm at Emma's."

"Wow! Look at you moving fast!"

"I wouldn't say this is fast, Austin. We've known each other for eighteen years."

"I don't know," he teased. "I figured you'd be all slow

and methodical with this too. Testing the waters, not moving too fast...you know...overthinking all of it."

Garrett stood and did his best not to take the bait. "I guess you were wrong." Walking over to the kitchen, he helped himself to a bottle of water. "You got anything to snack on? Thanks to Cash, I missed lunch."

Austin joined him and grabbed a drink for himself. "I think it's funny that you won't call him dad."

"He doesn't deserve to be called dad," he replied simply. "He lost that right."

Neither spoke for several minutes while Austin pulled out some cheese, crackers, and grapes. "I've got the makings for peanut butter and jelly, but I figured this would do. Mia and I were about to walk into the grocery store when I got your call, so..."

"This is fine." They ate in silence before Garrett asked, "So you want to call Mom or should we just go over?"

"Why don't you go back to Emma's and I'll go over and talk to her in person?"

"You sure? I don't want you to have to do this alone."

"It's fine. If we both go over, she'll feel like it's a big deal and be worried more about us than she needs to be. Besides, your date got interrupted. Don't let Dad ruin that for you too."

It was hard to argue that logic.

Popping another grape in his mouth, Garrett pulled his keys from his pocket. "In that case, I'm gonna get going. Call me if you need me."

"I will. Tell Emma I said hello and I'm sorry I didn't think to do that at the restaurant."

"Are you going to call Mia or should I just tell her what you're doing?"

"I'm going to call her now."

"Alright." He turned to leave and felt oddly guilty. Glancing over his shoulder, he asked, "You sure you don't want me to go with you?"

Austin smiled. "I'm positive. But...thanks, G."

Returning the smile, he said, "Anytime."

Outside, he jogged over to his car, anxious to get over to Emma's. Maybe she could help him make some sense out of everything because even though he felt confident minutes ago, the truth was he wasn't okay.

With any of it.

Not his father, not his job options, and not his future.

9

EMMA WAVED goodbye to Mia and watched her drive away, but she stayed where she was because she knew Garrett would be back in a matter of minutes and she couldn't wait to talk to him.

"Maybe I should warm up his lunch..." Glancing over her shoulder toward the kitchen, she considered her options and ultimately walked over to preheat the oven. If he wanted to eat, she could heat it up for him right away. If he didn't, then she could just turn it off. No big deal.

Five minutes later, she found herself pacing and almost sagged with relief when he knocked on the door before letting himself in. She held herself back and tried to judge his mood, but he advanced on her and wrapped himself around her hard. She could feel the tension and it broke her heart.

"Hey," she said softly. "Are you okay?"

She could feel him shake his head and decided to let him set the pace. When he was ready to talk, he would.

So she held him and marveled at how lean and muscular he was. It was something she'd always admired about him, but being able to touch him like this was still new. They had spent every minute together since he arrived Thursday night up until he left her with Mia earlier. She hadn't had a proper moment to herself to think about the change in their relationship and how it didn't feel as strange as she thought it would. They had been friends for so long that she thought things would be awkward–especially the getting naked with each other part–but Garrett had put her at ease and made her feel confident.

Beautiful.

And Emma couldn't remember anyone ever making her feel that way. Her ex-husband had tried in his own pathetic way, but it always felt...dirty...like he complimented her simply to get his way. There was no sincerity in his words or actions. And with Garrett, it was in his eyes and the way he touched her. Closing her eyes, she could still see the look on his face Thursday night when he was completely naked beneath her. He'd looked at her with awe and it was the most significant moment of her life.

And so much more special because it was with him.

"Sorry about that," he whispered before placing a soft kiss on her neck. Pulling back, he smiled down at her. "And I'm sorry I left you at lunch the way I did. I hope it wasn't too awkward for you with Mia."

"Are you kidding? That was pretty much a major fangirl moment for me," she teased as she led him over to the couch and gently pushed him to sit. "I've got the oven heating up. Are you hungry? I can reheat your lunch for you."

"That would be great, Em. Thanks."

She went to the kitchen to put his food in the oven. "So? Do you want to talk about it?"

He hesitated, and Emma busied herself to give him time. "He's dying."

"What?" she cried, walking back over to him.

Nodding, he explained his father's illness, plans, and how Austin was going over to talk to their mother right now.

Taking one of his hands in hers, she gently squeezed it. "I don't even know what to say. That is a lot of information."

"I know." He paused, kissing the back of her hand. "And I feel guilty because I don't trust him."

"He hasn't given you a reason to. You have a lifetime of distrust to get past."

"Yeah, but…I was a kid then and didn't know any better. Now I do. If he pulls one of his stunts now and disappears, I don't know what I'll do."

"Garrett…"

"No, that's not true. I think I'd go and hunt him down and beat the crap out of him and I'm pretty sure Austin would go with me."

"Good thing Jackson's not home," she murmured.

He turned and looked at her. "I wanted to believe him," he admitted quietly. "I wanted to believe what he was saying and hug him and tell him everything was going to be alright, but I held myself back like a coward."

If her heart wasn't already breaking for him, those last few words sealed the deal. She hugged him tightly. "You are not a coward. There's nothing wrong with protecting yourself, Garrett. This man has a history of letting you down and breaking promises. The only coward in this situation is him." Pulling back, she gave him a weak smile. "You're a good person and it's in your nature to look for the best in people."

"This is different, Em."

She sat back and got comfortable. "You know my situation with my father," she began carefully. "He left when I was a baby and I'd see him maybe once a year. He was a stranger to me for most of my life. Then he started coming around more when I was older, and I honestly had zero interest in having anything to do with him." She let out a small laugh. "But he just kept coming around. He didn't push or make any big promises, but he was there."

"Emmaline, it's not..."

"The night before my wedding, my father came to see me and asked me if I was sure about what I was doing. At the time I was a little offended, but he said he was just looking out for me and if I ever needed a place to go, he would be there." She paused because she hated talking about this but knew it could possibly help Garrett. "Three years later...well... when Steven left me, I was mortified. My mom wanted to coddle me and I knew I could let her, but... in that particular instance, I needed my dad."

When she looked at him, his expression was grim.

"For some reason, I knew he would let me talk without trying to either defend me or bash Steven. He knew the importance of just letting me talk." She smiled at the memory. "I spent a week with him and he never once said 'I told you so' or mentioned how I should have listened to him. That week was a turning point for us. I realized I could be mad about all the years he wasn't there for me, or I could focus on all the years we still had ahead of us." She shrugged. "I'm not saying that's the attitude everyone should take, but I know it worked for me. He hasn't made me regret that decision, but I didn't know that then. I had to have faith."

Garrett nodded. "I want to be angry. I want to punch something and just feel better."

"Then maybe you *should* punch something. Keeping all that anger inside isn't good for you. Go to the gym or go for a run or maybe just talk to Austin or me or anyone about how you feel. I'll always be here for you, Garrett, and unlike most people, I *do* know how you feel."

His expression softened as he reached out and caressed her cheek. "I don't know how I survived so long without you and I don't know how I got so lucky to find you again."

"I was always right here. I wish you hadn't stayed away for so long."

"Yeah, well...you were married, Em. There was no way I could come around when you were still with him. It wouldn't have been right."

"We were friends, Garrett."

The look he gave her was almost comical. "Now you and I both know Steven didn't like that fact at all. As far back as junior year of high school he didn't like it. The last thing I wanted to do was cause any problems. I thought it was better for me to keep my distance. I didn't like it, but I thought I was doing the right thing."

That was a major confession, she realized. All these years, she had wondered what she did wrong to make Garrett stop talking to her.

Now she knew and she felt terrible about it.

But something else also occurred to her–this was a pattern for him. He didn't want to make waves. He didn't say how he really felt because he didn't want to upset or offend anyone. In some cases it was noble, but it seemed like he was a man just inches away from exploding from all this pent-up emotion.

And it just made her feel even worse for him.

It was her turn to reach out and caress his jaw–his beard a little scratchy against the back of her fingers. "I think you need to stop putting everyone else first," she said carefully. "You worry so much about everyone else's feelings that you're neglecting your own, Garrett. That's not healthy."

She paused and chose her next words carefully. "I understand the situation with Steven–I really do–but you have no idea how hurt I was because I thought I did something wrong."

"It was never you," he said gruffly, taking her hand and kissing her palm. "This is just how I am. Always." He shook his head. "Austin was the hellraiser, and even though Jackson and I followed right along, there were things I tried to keep to myself to cause a little less worry for my mom."

"Like what?"

"How much I struggled in school." He hung his head. "She knew I struggled with reading, but after that–all the stuff you tutored me on?–she never knew. I think she was thrilled that I wasn't failing anything, but she had no idea how much work I put in just to get a C in most of my classes."

"Oh, Garrett..."

"This is who I am, Em," he repeated as he looked back up at her. "I don't know any other way."

"There's nothing wrong with you," she said fiercely. "I just hate seeing you so unhappy, and to think this is something you keep doing...it just breaks my heart."

He was quiet for several minutes and during that time, the oven beeped, letting her know his food was ready. She kissed his cheek before she went to go and make his plate. Two minutes later, they were sitting at her kitchen table but he made no attempt to touch his lunch.

"Garrett?"

Once again, he hung his head. "For years, I thought I was the reason he left."

There wasn't anything she could say to that. All the years they'd known each other and all the things they'd shared with each other–including how much not having a father around bothered them–and this was the first time he made this admission.

"I thought he was ashamed of me for being stupid," he went on quietly. "As I got older, I realized there was a possibility that I was wrong, but I never quite believed it. And over the years, whenever his name came up, I lashed out so I would sound just as angry as everyone else. Then as more time went on, I just felt nothing." He shrugged. "And up until the moment he walked over to us at lunch, I would have sworn that was the way I still felt. But I was lying to myself."

"It was a shock," she reasoned. "Anyone would have felt that way in your situation."

But he was shaking his head and looked up again. "I didn't say what I really felt because..." He swallowed hard. "Because I didn't want Austin to think less of me, and worse, I didn't want to risk being rejected by my father right to my face."

Emma was out of her chair and crawling into his lap so she could hug him. She had no idea if it was what he wanted or needed, but she knew she should do it. Fortunately, his arms banded around her as he buried his face against her neck. Her hands smoothed down his back as she struggled to find the right words. And then something happened...

He was shaking...trembling in her arms.

She felt the dampness against her skin and knew he was crying.

Oh, my sweet, sweet Garrett...

There weren't any words she could speak to make things right. The only thing she had to offer was herself to comfort him in whatever way he needed.

And apparently, this was it.

So she held him.

Long after his lunch had cooled, and long after the sun started to go down.

And she vowed she'd do it again and again if it gave him some peace.

Late Monday afternoon, Garrett was driving over to his mother's and wished he could just crawl into bed and sleep.

Yesterday was emotionally exhausting, and after breaking down in Emma's arms, he wanted to just go someplace and hide.

But she wouldn't let him.

Instead, they had ordered takeout for dinner and she fussed over him most of the night. Sadly, he had let her because he felt completely drained.

Until they went to bed.

Then it was like he had all the energy in the world and spent the remainder of the night and into the wee hours of the morning loving her and showing her how much she meant to him.

When Emma's alarm went off this morning, they had both groaned unhappily. She had told him to stay in bed and sleep, but he couldn't do that. It wasn't fair. So they got up, and when she left for work, he drove over to Happy Tails to volunteer his services for the week. Both Ed and Christine were thrilled to have the help, and it was nice to be working someplace that just wanted him there to work with no ulterior motives.

There was a time earlier in the day when it was just him and Ed, and Garrett considered talking to him about everything that was going on, but Ed had been the one who needed to talk. He was nervous about the back surgery and worried about how things were going to go without him. So Garrett did what he could to reassure him that it was all going to be alright, and it seemed like they had a long list of volunteers to help out.

Garrett was great at encouraging people and whatever he said seemed to help because Ed was a little more relaxed by the end of the day.

Emma had shown up an hour ago, and as much as he wanted to take her home and pamper her for all the ways she took care of him yesterday, it just wasn't going to happen. She had a tutoring session, and he needed to go over to his mother's. The plan was to meet Austin over there and have dinner with her before Cash showed up. They had considered inviting him to dinner, but it seemed a little too soon to be trying to sit down for a family meal.

According to Austin, their mother took the news surprisingly well. She was a bit shocked, but overall, she didn't seem nearly as bothered by Cash's appearance as they were.

"So weird," he murmured. "Maybe this is all a dream and I just can't wake up."

That would make more sense than the reality he was currently living in. Never did he imagine that he'd be dating Emmaline Ryan–let alone sleeping with Emmaline Ryan–at the same time that his father came back into his life. It was as if every dream he had as a kid was coming true.

Then he remembered the not-so-dreamy part of his reality: no job.

Yeah, he was going to have to do something about that.

And soon.

He had a call scheduled with the Delaware clinic at the end of the week, and so far, they were the only ones who didn't add making videos and modeling for random crap a part of the negotiations.

And he prayed it stayed that way.

But if it didn't, he wasn't sure what to do.

Ed had mentioned that Doc MacEntyre was retiring, but he wanted to sell his clinic rather than take on someone to help run it. So that definitely left Garrett out. He might not have any student loans to pay off, but he certainly didn't have the money to buy a clinic–even a small-town one.

"Great, now I'm nervous *and* depressed," he said wearily. "This night's off to a great start."

When he parked in his mother's driveway a few minutes later, he was relieved to see that Austin's truck was already there. With any luck, he could sort of get lost in the background for the bulk of the night. This whole thing couldn't have happened at a worse time and he wasn't sure just how much more emotional stuff he could take.

As he walked up to the door, it occurred to him that maybe he should have stopped and picked up a bottle of wine or perhaps something for dessert. There was still time for him to drive into town to get some, but...

"You going to stand out there all night or are you coming in?" Austin asked as he pulled the front door open.

"What? Oh, um...yeah. I was just thinking that I should have stopped to pick up wine or dessert or something."

"It's already taken care of." He stepped aside so Garrett could walk in. "You look like shit. What's going on?"

Raking a hand through his hair, he glared at his brother. "You mean other than our father showing up after almost twenty years while I'm trying to figure out where I'm going to work because I'm essentially unemployed while finally dating the girl I've been in love with for half my damn life?"

Austin's eyes went wide and Garrett realized just how much he'd revealed.

Dammit.

"G, look...I get that the timing of all of this must really suck, but..."

"But you don't have to be here if you don't want to," his mother said as she walked into the room. She had changed out of the scrubs she wore for her work in the pediatrician's office and was dressed casually in a pair of black leggings and a long gray sweater. She looked completely relaxed–like this was just an everyday occurrence that the husband who abandoned her and their kids coming by was normal.

"I'm not leaving," he told her. "It's just...it's a lot to take in, that's all."

"Dude, it's a lot for all of us to take in, but you've clearly got a lot on your plate and I think Mom's right; you shouldn't be here if you don't want to."

It was so damn tempting to turn around and leave, but... he wouldn't. There was a part of him that needed to be here and see how it all unfolded.

When his mother walked over and hugged him, he felt himself start to relax. When he pulled back, he had to ask, "What about you, Mom? How are *you* doing with all of this?"

Sighing, she turned to sit down on the living room sofa. "I have to admit I was a bit shocked when Austin came by and told me the news yesterday, but...this is typical of your father. He just shows up when he wants to. I'm used to it." She shrugged. "As for the rest of the news, well...I don't think I've really processed it all yet."

He sat beside her. "Yeah, me either. I hate that it took him getting sick to come here to see us."

"Are we sure he's really sick?" Austin asked.

"That's a terrible thing to say!" Grace scolded. "Now I'll admit that your father has done some awful things, but I can't imagine he'd fake cancer just for sympathy."

"Again, are we sure?" Austin repeated.

Rather than respond, Grace stood. "Come on. Dinner's ready." She walked toward the kitchen. "Thank God for the crockpot so we could eat sooner rather than later. I just made some beef stew. I hope that's alright."

Alright? His mother was a fantastic cook and her beef stew was one of his favorite meals. "You didn't have to do that, Mom. We could have just ordered a pizza or something. We know you worked all day."

"Nonsense. That's the beauty of a crockpot meal. It practically made itself." The three of them worked together to make their plates before sitting down at the table. "So," Grace said after a moment. "How was everyone's day?"

Austin talked about the progress on the house he and Mia were building and a new shopping center he was submitting designs on. His mother mentioned how the pediatric practice she worked for was looking to move to a bigger location and how they should maybe consider building from scratch. When they both turned to Garrett, he considered how much to share with them.

"I had a good day with Ed over at Happy Tails. I was able to examine the dogs and make notes for Doc MacEntyre so when he comes in next week, things will be a little more organized." He took another bite of his dinner. "Ed's having back surgery in two weeks so they're going to be short-handed. I wanted to help out where I could."

"That's very sweet of you, Garrett. It's a shame Doc MacEntyre is retiring. I know a lot of people are scrambling to find new vets," Grace commented. "Any chance you can get financing to buy the practice?"

He almost choked on his dinner, and while he was coughing, Austin spoke up.

"Mom, Garrett's got a plan already. He's practically got the position at a clinic up in Delaware. Why would he want to get into a heap of debt for a small-town practice?"

She shrugged. "I don't know...I just thought it would be nice if he moved closer to home."

"Doc's practice isn't closer, Mom; it *is* home," Austin countered. "Besides, Garrett's famous now. He's the Hot Doc, the social media sensation!" With a laugh, he grinned at Garrett. "All he has to do is take off his shirt and snuggle a puppy and he can have his pick of any practice he wants. Why here?"

Garrett felt like his face was on fire as he focused on his meal. Clearly his mother must have noticed because she quickly changed the subject to whether they would tell Jackson about what was going on.

So he ate the rest of his dinner in peace, but it was only a matter of time before she would want to talk to him about his reaction to Austin's teasing.

But at least it wouldn't be tonight.

Ultimately, Grace decided that she'd be the one to tell Jackson when she heard from him. With his deployment, their communications were sporadic, but she didn't feel like this was something urgent that they needed to worry him with. And once dinner was over and everything was cleaned up, they had nothing to do but wait for Cash to show up.

And he did.

Right on time.

It was the first time the man was ever where he was supposed to be when he was supposed to be there, and it felt weird.

And felt even weirder when his father walked into the home they had all shared at one time and Garrett was hit with just how much had changed. Not only were he and Austin older, but...so was Cash. His dark brown hair was all gray, and the giant of a man he always remembered suddenly didn't seem quite so larger than life. Now he was just a man–not overly large or powerful...just an ordinary man who was a stranger.

They all sat, and he noticed how his parents seemed to only have eyes for each other.

Oh, God...

Garrett and Austin exchanged nervous glances, and luckily his brother knew how to get things started.

"So, Dad," he began loudly, effectively snapping everyone to attention. "You wanted to talk to all of us."

Cash seemed to reluctantly tear his gaze away from his wife and cleared his throat. "Um, yes. Thank you for agreeing to see me again." Then he did look directly at Grace. "I appreciate you opening your home to me."

Before she could reply, Austin spoke up again.

"Yeah, okay. You're welcome. Did you happen to go and speak to Pops' attorney like you said you were going to?"

"Actually, I did." Shaking his head, he let out a low chuckle. "My grandfather left my inheritance in a trust until I came to Magnolia to claim it in person." He paused. "Richard McClellan informed me of everything Pops left to everyone." Glancing at his sons, his smile was sad. "I'm glad he gave you boys the opportunity to go to college." And then to Grace, "And that he took some of the burden off of you with the house."

They all nodded silently and waited for him to go on.

"Anyway, I was more than a little shocked at what he left me. I thought for sure he would have left me out of things, but Richard had gotten in touch with me and mentioned an inheritance when he died. Then I thought it was going to be something small–like a token gesture." Raking a hand through his hair, he let out a long breath. "Boy, was I wrong."

"Cash," Grace said, reaching out a hand to him. "Are you alright?"

He nodded, and once again, Garrett and his brother exchanged glances.

"There's some...uh...property at the northern tip of town," Cash explained. "About ten acres worth that he left to me. Richard's been handling the taxes on it all these years, but it's all undeveloped. I went and looked at it and it butts up to where all the revitalization seems to be happening in that part of town. The land is worth...well...a lot." He looked up at the three of them. "Like 1.5 million."

You could have heard a pin drop in the room and Garrett had to wonder just what his great-grandfather had been thinking in leaving something that valuable to someone who was never around. At times, Pops had been openly hostile where Cash was concerned, so this simply didn't make sense.

"I think at the time the Will was written," Cash explained, "the property wasn't worth nearly that much. All the work happening up there really pushed the value up." He shrugged. "I was still in total shock, but then there was a letter from the old guy, and...it's been a hell of a day."

Maybe no one was saying it, but they all had to be thinking the same thing–now Cash had the money to do all the things he wanted to do his whole life, all the things that were more important than his wife and kids. And the irony was that he might not live long enough to enjoy any of it.

If that wasn't karma, Garrett wasn't sure what was.

"O-kay...," Austin said. "So...now what?"

"Now I have to talk to a realtor and see about getting the property sold and hope I can get more than what it's worth." He looked at all of them before adding, "It makes sense for me to do that. I hope to get two million for it, so that would be half a million to each of you. Including Jackson."

"What?!" Grace cried. "Cash, you can't be serious! Think of what you could do with that money! You can get better treatment, talk to some specialists about the cancer! You...you can..."

But he held up a hand to stop her. "Grace, I'm not looking for any more opinions on my disease. It is what it is, and believe it or not, I've already had multiple doctors weigh in on it. I'm at peace with my decision." Pausing, he sighed again. "All this time, I was trying to think of some way that I could do something good for all of you. There's no way I can make up for the things I did and I'm certainly not trying to buy your forgiveness, but by doing this, it feels like a way for me to know that you're all going to be okay."

So many thoughts raced through Garrett's mind, but as usual, his brother spoke up with his thoughts first.

"Dad, take some time to think about this before you do anything you might regret."

"Don't you get it, Austin? I've had a lifetime full of regret. For the first time, I'm going to do something selfless." His voice cracked, and he took a moment to compose himself. "I like knowing that this money can help you pay off that new house you're building." Then he looked at Garrett. "And maybe you can start up your own veterinary clinic." He paused. "I have no idea what Jackson plans on doing after he comes home from deployment, but I'm sure he wouldn't mind having a little financial freedom to do whatever it is that he wants." Then he looked at Grace.

"And you deserve not to have to work so hard. I made your life hell, and you worked hard to be both mother and father to our boys. Let me do this for you."

"Cash," Grace said softly. "Believe it or not, I'm okay. Your grandfather helped me out over the years and taught me how to invest my money, so financially, I'm good. If you're really going to do this, then do it for the boys. I don't want to be part of the equation."

"You're always part of the equation," he replied gruffly. "Always, Grace."

There was an awkward silence and Garrett finally spoke up. "I think this is a lot for all of us to take in. Why don't you take a few days to think it all through?" he suggested.

"There's nothing to think through, Garrett. This is what I'm doing, and Richard is going to make some calls for me and get back to me tomorrow with the name of an agent who deals in property deals like this." He gave a grim smile. "With any luck, we can have a deal by the end of the month."

"Let's just...see how it goes," Grace said. "I picked up an apple pie from Henderson's and some brownies. Why don't we have dessert?" She rose and walked to the kitchen with Cash following.

Once they were out of earshot, Garrett looked over at his brother. "Is it just me or are you not getting your hopes up on this either?"

"It's not just you. I think this all sounds too good to be true, and I can't believe Pops would have left him something that valuable."

"That was my thought, too. So now what do we do? I mean...if he wants to stay local and play at being a dad, are you interested in that?"

"Yeah, Mia asked me about that last night. Like where did I see our relationship as father and son at this point."

"And what did you say?"

"Yesterday, I wasn't so sure I wanted a relationship with him and I felt guilty about it. Now I feel guilty if I do suddenly want one because then I have to ask myself if I'm doing it only because of the money." He paused. "What about you?"

"Pretty much the same and I'm not proud of it." Sighing, he leaned back on the sofa. "The bottom line is that he's dying. How petty would it be for us to turn him away?"

"It's no more than he deserves, G."

"Maybe."

They were both quiet for a moment.

"I just think maybe...maybe we give him a chance," Garrett said quietly. "I'm not saying we become his best friend, but..."

"That's exactly what Mia said," Austin replied wearily. "I'm just not going into this with any expectations."

"Me either."

"Although...this could be great for you. With that kind of money, you really could start up your own practice instead of going to work for someone else." Then he laughed. "And you'll be able to keep your shirt on!"

"That would be a perk," he murmured with a little more heat than he intended.

Austin stood and stared down at you. "Are you okay? Is there something going on?"

"It's nothing," he said, standing. "Just...this is all a lot to take in."

His brother continued to stare at him until he started to squirm.

Then the sound of feminine laughter–almost a giggle–had them both turning toward the kitchen.

"Oh, God," Austin groaned. "I never thought we'd have to worry about how the two of them still felt for each other."

Garrett shuddered. "Do we even want to go in there?"

Grace laughed again, followed by, "Oh, Cash, you always could make me blush."

Now they both groaned. "I think it's important that we go in there and put a stop to whatever that is," Austin grumbled as he turned and walked away.

And all Garrett could do was follow.

10

Axel was his usual excitable self when Emma walked into the barn a few days later. He danced around her legs, and by the time she sat herself down on the ground, he was already in her lap and giving her happy puppy kisses. She loved this time with him and wished more than ever that she lived someplace that was pet-friendly so she could just take him home with her.

Someday...

Her phone rang, and she laughed hysterically as she tried to maneuver the two of them so she could pull it out of her pocket. "Axel," she chided playfully, "let me get this!" It took a little work, but she finally had the phone in her hands and frowned at the name on the screen. "Hello?"

"Hi, Ms. Ryan. It's Jason Harber. How are you?"

"I'm fine, Mr. Harber, thank you. What can I do for you?" The only time she heard from her attorney was if he needed money from her or he had something new to report in his efforts to locate Steven.

So far he'd only been successful in needing money from her.

"I'm calling to let you know that we tracked your ex-husband to Nevada and served him papers."

Gasping, she asked, "Really? You found him?"

"Well...we did. Temporarily."

"Oh, no..."

"The papers were served and when a colleague of mine went to reach out the next day to follow-up, he was gone. The landlord said he moved out the night before."

She knew better than to get her hopes up–even temporarily. "So what happens now?"

"Since he was officially served, it means when he doesn't show up for his court hearing, a warrant will go out for his arrest. Unfortunately, he's been able to stay ahead of us every step of the way, so there's no telling when we'll catch up with him."

"Oh."

"I know it's not particularly helpful news, but I did want to keep you informed."

"Can't we put out a warrant for him now?" she asked.

"I'm working on it. The courts are backed up, and the alimony owed to you isn't something a judge is willing to issue a warrant for just yet."

It was so unfair.

All of it.

With a weary sigh, she asked, "Okay, so then what happens next?"

"I'm going to keep trying to track him down, but his court date wasn't set for another thirty days. At that point we could probably get a judge to hear us on the warrant for missing the date and the alimony. I know you've been patient, Ms. Ryan, but please continue to be for a bit longer."

It was the story of her life.

Be patient...take all the crap life throws at you...don't fight back...

Yeah, she was done with that.

"Mr. Harber, you have thirty days to make something happen," she said firmly. "This has gone on for three years, and if you aren't capable of handling this, then I'll find a law firm that can. Do I make myself clear?"

"Um...yes. But you have to understand..."

"No," she interrupted. "*You* have to understand. I'm done living in limbo and I'm tired of paying for you to do nothing but waste my time. Thirty days and that's final."

"Yes. Yes, of course. I'll be in touch," he said meekly before wishing her a good day.

Emma slid the phone back into her pocket and hugged Axel close. "If it weren't for that guy, I'd be able to move someplace with you," she said, kissing his nose.

In a perfect world, she'd not only be able to take Axel home, but she'd be going home to Garrett as well.

Okay, technically, she *was* going home to Garrett for the last several days. He was here for the week and he was staying with her and it was wonderful.

She just knew that it wasn't going to last because he had to go back to Norfolk and deal with his job search.

Off in the distance, she saw Doc MacEntyre walking around with Garrett and wished there were something he could do to help him out. Even if he wasn't looking to keep his practice, maybe he knew of someone who was looking for help. Or perhaps just take Garrett on until he could possibly get some financing to buy the clinic.

Of course, these were all just musings in her own mind. Garrett hadn't mentioned even wanting to purchase Doc's clinic. If anything, he seemed pretty set on settling up north a little more, much to her dismay. And while Emma knew it was pretty much too soon to be thinking about their future together, she couldn't help *but* think about it.

Could she leave Magnolia Sound and her family to be with him? Would she be able to find work with a school district somewhere else?

But the biggest question was...did Garrett even want her to go with him?

Again, it was too soon for either of them to broach that subject, but if things progressed the way she hoped, they would have to talk about it.

Hopefully sooner rather than later.

"Maybe I should be looking at jobs up in Delaware," she whispered and considered pulling her phone out again, but Axel was squirming and she knew he'd rather go out and run around with her and a ball or frisbee than sit here in a corner while she scrolled on her phone.

Besides, she could always look for jobs later.

"Come on, sweet boy. Let's go play," she said as she stood and put him on his feet. He immediately began barking and dancing around her again, and he was just the cutest thing in the world.

And as she grabbed a frisbee on her way out of the barn, she allowed herself to imagine they were out playing in their own yard while waiting for Garrett to come home.

"You're a hard man to get together with."

Garrett wasn't sure if that was an insult or a compliment, but as he took his seat across from his father, he forced himself to smile. "I've got a lot going on."

"So it seems," Cash said easily. "Thank you for finding some time to meet with me."

They were back at The Mystic Magnolia for lunch. After dessert Monday night, his father asked if Garrett would join him the following day, but Garrett declined.

Then he texted.

And called.

It was pointless to keep putting it off, so he finally agreed and figured he'd just get it out of the way. Now that he was here, however, he wasn't feeling nearly as confident as he'd hoped.

They sat in awkward silence for several minutes until Garrett decided that he needed to be the one to break the ice. "How are you feeling?"

Cash seemed to relax a bit. "Today's a good day. I'll admit that it's taking a little longer for me to get up and do things, but for the most part, I can't complain. How about you? How are things going?"

They had talked the other night about his job search, and no matter how much his father tried to tell him he had no reason to keep looking for employment, Garrett wasn't ready to believe it yet.

"Good," he replied. "I was over at Happy Tails again today lending a hand. They're pretty much full to capacity so I'm helping them with the dogs who are going into foster care and making sure they're clean and healthy and their charts are up to date."

"So you're just volunteering your time?"

"Yup. They're good friends of mine, and Ed really encouraged me when I was growing up and first became interested in becoming a vet." He shrugged. "Now Ed's getting ready to have back surgery so I'm glad I can be of help."

"You're a good man, Garrett. Everyone says so," Cash said quietly. "I know it probably doesn't mean much to you, but I'm proud of everything you've done. You worked hard and went through so many years of school, and your mother said you graduated at the top of your class. That's quite an accomplishment."

As much as he didn't want to admit it, the praise felt really good.

"Thanks. I struggled a lot in school when I was younger...hell, probably through most of high school too. Once I hit college, I knew I had to work even harder, but it was all worth it."

"Good for you. You deserve a practice of your own for all your hard work and I'm glad I'll be able to help you with that."

"Yeah, um...about that..."

Cash held up a hand to stop him. "Don't. Just...don't." Sighing, he continued. "Look, I get it. You don't trust me, and if you had your way, we wouldn't even be here talking right now. I get it. But I'm trying to do the right thing for you and your brothers. You ask anyone around here and they'd tell you I've been selfish my entire life, but when you know that life is coming to an end, you want to at least try to make amends." He paused, and Garrett saw a sheen of tears in the old guy's eyes. "Let me do this for you. You don't have to thank me." He let out a mirthless laugh. "Hell, you don't even have to like me. I just need to know that I've done something for you after everything I cost you growing up."

Well...damn. There was no snarky comeback for that.

"Listen, Cash..."

Hanging his head, Cash shook it. "It's really weird hearing you call me that." He looked up. "Any chance you might try calling me Dad?"

Raking a hand through his hair, Garrett glanced around and seriously wished a waitress would come by and interrupt them. When he realized no one was coming, he looked across the table. "You have to understand…I spent most of my life not calling anyone that. You're basically a stranger to me. Maybe in time, I'll be more comfortable with it, but…"

He let out another mirthless laugh. "I don't have a lot of time, Garrett. I wish I did. I wish we were looking at years of getting reacquainted, but that's just not going to happen."

And now he felt like crap for being honest.

"This has all been a lot to take in. You have to realize that."

"Hey! Welcome to The Mystic Magnolia! I'm Jasmine. Can I take your orders?" She was young and perky and Garrett noticed his father straighten in his seat as he talked to her about today's specials.

Apparently, the man flirts with everyone…

Jasmine giggled and wrote something down before looking at Garrett. "And for you?"

"I'll get the fish and chips, please. And a Coke."

"You got it!" She winked at Cash before she walked away and Garrett fought the urge to roll his eyes.

"Anyway…"

"I do understand what you're saying," Cash said, his expression going serious again. "Your mother said I should just give you time, but like I said, I don't have a lot of it. I was hoping we'd talk a bit and you'd relax and give me a chance."

"The fact that I'm here should tell you that I'm giving you a chance, but I can't force myself to feel something that just isn't there yet. I'm not a liar and I would think you'd appreciate that."

With a curt nod, Cash replied, "You're right. I do appreciate that. You're an honest man and that's admirable."

Pausing, he shifted in his chair. "So tell me about this girl you're seeing. Is it serious?"

Emma's name came up several times Monday night over dessert, so it wasn't like the man had been secretly spying on him or anything.

"Emma and I have been friends since the third grade, but I always had a crush on her. I was just too insecure to do anything about it." He shrugged and smiled when Jasmine put their drinks down. "Anyway, we ran into each other recently after not seeing or talking for years and things just sort of fell into place."

"Why didn't you talk for years?"

Ugh...

"Well, she started dating someone our junior year of high school who didn't particularly like the fact that Emma and I were close. We started drifting apart and then I left for college the next year and so did she, but the boyfriend went with her. Then they got married."

"Damn. That had to be rough for you."

He nodded. "It was. And honestly, I thought I was over her. I mean...I missed her and thought about her a lot, but I certainly didn't live like a monk either."

Cash chuckled. "Good for you."

"Then I found out she was divorced, and so when Austin called and asked me to come home for the weekend when they were breaking ground on the house, he sort of dared me to go and see her." He shrugged again. "Turns out we ended up running into each other at the Publix and we've been together ever since."

"Sometimes the best things in life are worth the wait," Cash said grimly. "And sometimes you miss your chance." He looked over at Garrett. "I'm glad you didn't miss yours."

"Me too." He smiled. "She makes me happy, happier

than I can ever remember being. Things are still complicated because all my job offers aren't around here,
but..."

"All the more reason you should be happy that I'm here
to help."

Unable to help himself, Garrett chuckled.

And it felt good.

Resting his arms on the table, he tried to keep his tone
light. "You'll have to forgive me if I'm a bit in the I'll-
believe-it-when-I-see-it mentality."

Cash didn't seem to take offense. "I respect your
honesty, but I want you to promise me something."

It seemed ironic that he'd be asking, but Garrett figured
he'd humor him. "Yeah, sure."

"When I give you that check and you get your clinic, I
don't want you to thank me; I want you to make it a
success."

"Seriously?" Because it seemed like an overly selfless
request and it didn't line up at all with who Cash Coleman
was.

"That's all I want, Garrett. And I seriously hope that
I'm here to see it happen. Your mother and I believe in you,
and I think..."

He held up a hand to stop him. "Okay, I think there's
something I have to say."

"You *think* there's something?"

Nodding, he amended, "No, I *know* there's something I
have to say."

"O-kay..."

"I think it's very...admirable that you're here and trying
to reconnect with us. And by us, I mean me and Austin, and
Jackson if he were here. However...you need to stay away
from Mom."

"Excuse me?" Cash's expression went from mildly amused to indignant in the blink of an eye.

"You have no idea how much she's struggled–the things people said to her or the way she was treated by members of your family all these years. She's done some amazing things with her life and she's finally in a good place and deserves to be happy. Don't come here and get all flirty with her or chummy with her or whatever it is that you're clearly doing. Give her the divorce she deserves and leave her be. Dominic's a good man and he makes Mom happy." His heart was racing and he still couldn't believe he'd just said all that, but...it had to be discussed.

They stared at each other, both leaning back in their seats with their arms crossed as if it were a showdown. There was probably a lot more that Garrett could say, but he opted to wait and see how the old guy responded.

"I appreciate you looking out for your mother," Cash began gruffly. "However, there are things that don't concern you. She's my wife."

"But they do," he countered. "You see, her being your wife is really just a technicality. My brothers and I were here–you weren't. For far too many years, she had to be both mother and father to us. When we were all old enough, we did what we could to help ease some of the burdens she had to carry because her husband wasn't around. We all worked and helped with the bills, we learned how to do home repairs, and had far more responsibility from a young age than we would have if we had a father around. Mom's happiness is most definitely my concern and you don't get to swoop back into town and play the part of the loving husband."

"Garrett..."

"And if my saying this means you're not going to give

me the money for the clinic, I don't care. It needs to be said and you need to hear it. So...if there are conditions on your gift, then you can keep it. My mother comes first."

They were back to staring each other down and that was when Jasmine decided to come back with their lunches. Luckily, she didn't linger and simply placed their food down and walked away.

A solid minute passed before Cash leaned forward and looked at his burger and seemed to relax. "You want to know the best part about dying?" he asked with a grin.

"I wouldn't think there'd be a best part."

"I eat whatever I want. My doctor doesn't harp on me about my cholesterol or how I should be scheduling colonoscopies. It's very freeing." Taking a bite of his burger, he moaned with pleasure. "Everything tastes better with extra bacon." Nodding toward Garrett's plate, he asked, "Well? Aren't you going to try it?"

"Um...yeah."

"When you were little, you would only eat fish if it were breaded like that. And you'd pour an almost obscene amount of ketchup on it," he explained with a laugh. "Promise me you outgrew that."

Unable to help himself, he laughed. "That is something I can definitely promise. I can't even remember the last time I put ketchup on fish."

"Thank God."

It was the most bizarre meal he'd ever had. One minute they were strangers, then they were friendly, and then they were adversaries. Now it seemed they were veering toward being father and son.

Garrett knew it was a long time coming and knew the path was going to be bumpy, but for the first time in a long time, he wasn't quite so hostile about it.

11

Life was good.

Seriously, Emma couldn't remember the last time she had spent so much time just being happy.

And she owed it all to Garrett.

She woke up next to him every morning, they left for work at the same time, she would meet up with him at Happy Tails before coming home to have dinner together, and then they'd spend their nights talking and laughing and making love. It was just...perfect.

Years ago, this was what she envisioned married life would be like. Unfortunately, her life with her ex didn't even come close. For the longest time, Emma had simply convinced herself that she over-romanticized what her life was supposed to be and that the relationship she dreamed of didn't exist.

But it did.

And she'd never been happier about being wrong.

It was a little after two on Friday afternoon and she was done for the day. Rather than going over to Happy Tails, she decided she was going to go food shopping. Most nights they'd had takeout or gone out to eat, but tonight she wanted to cook a meal for the two of them. Part of it was because she loved the idea of doing it and partly because today Garrett had his final interview over the phone with the clinic up in Delaware that he was really hoping for. They postponed the call last week, and today they were supposed to make him an offer. As much as she hated the thought of him working so far away, he talked so much about it that she knew it was important to him.

That thought stopped her because she realized he talked less and less about it lately. And, now that she thought about it, he was being rather vague on when he was heading back to Norfolk. Any time she mentioned it, he would tell her that he didn't want to think about it and how they needed to just enjoy the time they had right now. For the most part, it seemed incredibly sweet–like he couldn't bear the thought of having to leave her–but now she was wondering if something was going on.

Actually, a lot was going on that wasn't about them.

Well...not directly.

After his dinner with Austin and their parents, Garrett had been a little tight-lipped on what exactly happened. Oh, he'd told her they had a good visit and how it was weird to see Grace and Cash together and how they were flirting a little with each other, but it didn't seem like it had been any kind of life-altering meeting. Then he'd had lunch with Cash and didn't talk much about it, either. She had asked when he planned to see his father again and he said he wasn't sure, and when she pushed him on it, he'd gotten frustrated and said he didn't want to talk about it.

That had put her in a bit of a bad mood, but he'd more than made it up to her since. It bothered her that he kept things from her–especially since they'd always told each other everything. Why he chose now when they were intimate to hold part of himself back was a mystery to her. But because everything else was going so great with them, she didn't want to ruin it by harping on the things that were obviously weighing on him.

So tonight, she wanted to prepare a nice dinner for them where they could sit and talk and hopefully figure out what happens next for them. If he were to get the position in Delaware–and really, why wouldn't he?–then they'd have to figure out what that would look like for them. She wasn't much of a traveler and wasn't completely comfortable flying, but if they were going to continue in this relationship and only have the weekends to see each other, it was something she was going to have to get used to. Why waste seven hours of driving one way when she could take a 90-minute flight?

Because, yeah...she'd already researched it a bit.

Either way, there were things they were going to have to discuss whether Garrett wanted to or not. It was one thing to live in this bubble for a few days, but eventually they were going to have to deal with the real world.

And Emma said a small prayer that the real world would be a continuation of the bubble.

She pulled up to the Publix shopping center and parked before pulling out her phone to make a list of what she wanted.

"Steaks," she said as she typed it into her notes app. She had a small gas grill on her back patio, and it had been a while since she'd grilled anything. "Stuff for a salad and maybe some sort of potato." It wasn't the most creative meal she'd ever thought of, but she knew it would be delicious. "And dessert. Definitely grab something for dessert."

Feeling good about her list, she grabbed her purse and headed into the store.

"Emma!"

Turning, she saw Mia waving at her and tried not to act like a giggly schoolgirl because a famous author was now her friend and walking her way.

Don't be a spaz...

"Hey, Mia," she said and mentally congratulated herself on sounding casual. "How are you?"

"Good! I'm so happy I ran into you. I was going to call you later."

Oh, my God...Mia Kingsley was going to call me...

Just breathe...

"Oh, really? What's up?"

"Well, I'm guessing that Garrett is finally heading back to Norfolk Sunday night, and Austin and I would love to have you guys over for dinner tomorrow. You know, if you don't already have plans." Before Mia could answer, she added, "We really meant to do it last week, but I'm on a deadline with this next book and was pretty much chained to my laptop all week!"

"That is so sweet of you! Thank you! We'd love that!" she gushed and then wanted to kick herself for not playing it cool.

They started browsing through the produce section together. "So tell me," Mia said after a moment. "What do you think about all this business with Cash giving the guys his inheritance?"

"Um..."

"He met with the realtor last week, and we saw the ad online, but we haven't heard if he's had any offers yet." She paused and picked up a bag of grapes. "Does Garrett believe it's going to really happen? Because Austin's on the fence, but leaning more toward believing it."

"Um…" Rather than let on that she had literally no idea what she was talking about, Emma shrugged. "I think Garrett's erring on the side of caution. You know, not wanting to get his hopes up over anything to do with his father."

That sounded logical, right?

"Still," Mia went on as she examined some bell peppers. "It's a lot of money. Potentially life-changing." She moved on to the cucumbers before looking over her shoulder at Emma. "It would be amazing if it happened. Austin's already talking about using it to pay off the house we're building, and he said Garrett would be able to buy his own practice! I think that would be amazing for you guys! Especially if he bought one here! The local vet is retiring, isn't he?"

Emma felt like someone had kicked her in the gut and she had no idea how she kept a smile on her face or kept from being sick. Fortunately, Mia was focused on her shopping as she talked, but it wouldn't be long before she noticed that Emma wasn't saying anything.

They were over near the bakery section when Mia's phone rang.

Saved by the bell…

Emma waved and murmured, "Text me what time for tomorrow," before walking away. Looking down at her empty cart, she realized she never grabbed anything for a salad or the potatoes. The thought of heading back to the produce section and walking past Mia wasn't appealing, so she just figured she'd loop back around in a few minutes. Meanwhile, she had to wrap her brain around why Garrett hadn't told her about this inheritance business.

And that had her thinking again about all the other things he wasn't telling her.

Which reminded her of how his refusal to tell her how he felt all those years ago led to her getting involved with–and marrying–the wrong man.

Suddenly, she didn't want to make dinner. She wanted answers.

Normally, Emma prided herself on her patience and her ability not to make waves or rock the boat, but right now, she definitely wanted to make all kinds of waves.

And throw something–or someone–off the boat.

Damn the man, she thought.

Damn him for making her feel so freaking good and happy and making her believe she deserved all of it.

And she cursed herself while she was at it because she'd been so dazzled by the attention he was giving her that she was willing to overlook all that he was keeping from her.

"When am I going to learn?" she whispered as she walked back down the next aisle and then right out the doors of the store, shoving her shopping cart aside as she did.

There were two options she could take. She could go to Happy Tails and demand that he talk to her right then and there. It would be the fastest option, and she'd get her answers sooner rather than later. But that meant there would potentially be an audience, and she wasn't sure that was what she wanted. Or...she could go home and bide her time until he got there. It would give her time to calm down and think things through so she didn't come off like some sort of crazy person. She could make a list of all the things she wanted to ask him, and then they could have a calm and rational conversation.

It was beyond tempting to go the crazy person route, but

once she was in her car and pulling out of the parking lot, she knew she'd go home and think.

"Heaven forbid I make a scene," she muttered. As she drove down Main Street, she kept reminding herself that she was making the right decision–the logical decision. However, about halfway home, she said, "Screw this," and turned the car around and headed to Happy Tails.

Maybe they'd have an audience, but it was her family and she could tell them to give them some privacy or simply tell them to get lost.

She let out a snort at that thought. She'd never told anyone–especially her family–anything as hateful as "get lost."

Still, it felt good just to think that she might do it.

Five minutes later, she was driving down the long dirt drive–a trail of dust blowing wildly behind her. She pulled up in front of the house and was out of the car almost instantly.

"Hey, Sweetheart!" her mother called as she walked out the front door, full of smiles. "You were driving like the hounds of hell were after you. Everything okay?"

"Is Garrett around?" she asked curtly.

Christine's smile faltered slightly. "He's back in the new barn with Ed and Doc MacEntyre. Why?"

"I need to talk with him. Now." Before she could walk away, her mother stopped her.

"It's been so busy this week and I've been going with Ed to doctor appointments that I haven't had a chance to talk to Garrett about doing a video for us. Have you?"

"Mom, it's really not a good idea."

"I don't see why not. He's done it for other clinics. If you're not comfortable asking him since you're seeing each other..."

And for some reason, that was her breaking point. Facing her mother, Emma straightened. "You will *not* ask Garrett to do one of those videos, okay? He hates doing them and they've been nothing but a nightmare for him! You'll just have to think of something else to help out with the crappy situation around here, but it's not going to be at Garrett's expense!"

"Emmaline!" Christine gasped. "What in the world?"

"I don't have time for this right now, Mom. And I'm serious. Do *not* ask him to do a video."

Her mother gave her a curt nod in response.

"Thanks." And with barely a wave, she took off across the property with a determined stride.

Emma Ryan was many things, but she was done being a pushover.

"And then next month, we'll host our annual adoption carnival. We've got you signed up for the kissing booth, and hopefully you'll consider doing a shift in the dunking booth," Dr. Mills was saying. "We're all team players here, Garrett, and I believe you're going to be a perfect fit!"

Garrett's heart sank. His top choice clinic was no different from all the others.

They'd simply waited until he was ready to sign the contract to throw all this at him.

Besides the carnival, there were promos with the local news station—where it was suggested he do the segment without his shirt—and a photoshoot so they could make a life-sized cardboard cutout of him to go in the lobby of the clinic.

Shirtless, of course.

Pinching the bridge of his nose, he listened as the man droned on about how excited he was to have Garrett starting at the clinic.

"Dr. Mills, I'm going to have to stop you right there," he finally said.

"Sorry," the man said jovially. "I know it's a lot to take in, but I'll send you the itinerary in an email along with the employment contract. I'm guessing you'll need at least a week to pack up and move, but we can help you with a place to stay. There's one of those executive suite hotels right across the street. I'd be more than willing to cover your stay for the first month while you look for a place of your own."

"That won't be necessary."

"Oh? Have you found a place already?"

"No, but I won't be needing one. I'm sorry, but I'm going to have to decline your offer," he said firmly.

"But...but...I thought we were on the same page!" Dr. Mills reasoned. "You said you loved our facility and that we were in a desirable location. I don't understand what the problem is."

"The problem is that I'm a veterinarian, not some sort of cover model," Garrett explained with annoyance. "I want to work at a clinic that is interested in how I treat the animals rather than how I attract female clients. So if it's all the same to you, I'm going to thank you for your time and wish you luck finding another vet."

And before Dr. Mills could comment, Garrett hung up and turned his phone off.

All while willing himself not to get sick.

Okay, it's not the end of the world. There's still the inheritance from Cash...

Yeah, he hadn't wanted to let himself even consider

getting that money because his father had never come through for him before. But maybe things were finally turning around. Maybe this was why none of the other job offers were working out. Maybe the universe was finally going to give him a break and he'd be able to show the world that he was good enough.

Maybe.

Letting out a weary breath, he raked a hand through his hair and walked back into the barn where Doc MacEntyre and Ed were treating a new litter of Labrador puppies with their second round of vaccinations. Once that was done, they were all getting general exams before moving on to an older group of pups who were ready for their third round of shots. It was a little chaotic, but the room Ed had built in the barn was geared for this sort of thing. He walked back in and gave them both a smile. "How's it going?"

Ed took one look at him and seemed to know that something was wrong. "I take it the call didn't go well?"

Garrett looked around and realized it was only the three of them—and the dogs—and maybe it would help to talk about it.

"I've had no less than two dozen job offers," he began. "All of them with well-known and successful clinics here on the East Coast. There were more from around the country, but I didn't even entertain them because this is basically where I want to stay to be close to my family."

Both Doc and Ed nodded as they worked with the puppies.

"Anyway, I knew the offers were coming in because of the videos I did at those shelters." He shook his head. "It seemed like a harmless thing to do and it truly helped find so many dogs their forever homes."

"It was rather impressive, Garrett," Doc commented. "I

can't remember ever hearing about so many dogs finding homes in such a short amount of time."

He sighed. "I know. And I wouldn't change that for anything."

"But...?" Ed prompted.

"But...every job offer I got came with a marketing plan that included me doing the shirtless doctor thing for all their clinic promos. No one wanted to hire me because I'm smart or talented or because I was at the top of my veterinary school class. As a matter of fact, no one even talked to me about my qualifications other than the fact that I took my shirt off on social media and looked good holding dogs! It's great for business, they all said. And while that might be true, that's not who I am!" He growled and began to pace, picking up a puppy as he did. "My whole life, I've felt like I'm not good enough. I struggled all through school. My family was the talk of the town thanks to my deadbeat father. Hell, I didn't feel worthy of anything! I couldn't even ask out the girl I wanted to because I didn't think I was good enough for her! And then..." He looked up and saw both Doc and Ed staring at him with wide eyes and realized he should probably reel it in a bit.

"Garrett," Ed began, placing a hand on his shoulder. "We all deal with insecurity. Even the people who seem the most confident are insecure about something."

"Yeah, but..."

"I can understand how you felt as a kid. Your father leaving messed with you in a lot of ways that most of us can't understand. But you overcame so much. For all those struggles in school? You ended up graduating from veterinary school at the top of your class! That's an amazing accomplishment."

"Not if no one wants to hire me unless I'm the shirtless Hot Doc," he murmured.

"Then those weren't the right places for you," Ed went on. "There are thousands of other practices you can work for."

"I don't have that kind of time, Ed. I thought I had everything planned out! I'm organized. I keep a schedule. I think everything through until every aspect of my life is planned out."

The older man stood back and considered him before saying, "And nothing's going as planned."

"Exactly. I need a job, Ed. A paying job that's going to help me not only pay my bills but help me start planning my life. I've been in school and doing internships for so damn long that I'm ready for my life to begin! And now... now I'm a damn joke in the veterinary community."

"Doc," Ed said as he turned to look at him. "What about your practice? What about not selling it and letting Garrett take it over?"

It was on the tip of Garrett's tongue to rebuke him because this wasn't how he wanted to get a job, but...beggars couldn't be choosers, right?

As soon as Doc MacEntyre's shoulders dropped, Garrett knew it wasn't going to happen.

"I really wish I could help you, son," he said sadly. "But I need to sell the practice so I can retire. The missus and I want to move to New Mexico to be near our son and grand-kids. We've got a house picked out and we're just waiting on me selling the practice to make it all happen. I'm sorry."

"Thanks, Doc," Garrett said quietly. "It was a longshot. I appreciate your honesty."

They were all quiet for several minutes except for the puppies. Ed spoke up first.

"There's got to be something," he said. "I find it hard to believe that every clinic is only interested in you for your social media status."

"Well, believe it. Everyone's looking for free publicity and I'm it, apparently." He paused and considered sharing his other news.

Or potential news.

Then opted against it.

If Cash pulled a typical–and expected–move and took the money from the property and ran, he didn't want to deal with everyone's pity.

Please don't let me down...

"Can I ask you something?"

Garrett turned toward Ed. "Sure."

"Why are you here?"

He looked at him oddly. "I thought you needed the help."

"No, not here at Happy Tails, but...okay, yeah...here at Happy Tails, if you're so worried about a job. Not that we don't appreciate everything you're doing, but maybe this isn't the best use of your time."

"If anything, it's given me time to think," Garrett told him.

"About what?"

"Yeah, Garrett, about what?" Emma said from the doorway, and she did not look the least bit happy.

"Hey," he said softly, walking over and kissing her on the cheek. "I was getting worried about you. I thought you were supposed to be here like an hour ago."

"I went shopping to make us a nice dinner."

Her words should have made him feel good, but her tone told him something was up. "Really? That's great! What are we having?"

"Nothing," she stated, crossing her arms over her chest. "I didn't get anything."

"Um..."

"Hey, Em!" Ed called out. "If you'd like some privacy, I set up the office across the hall."

With a curt nod, she turned and walked out, and Garrett had no choice but to follow her. Once they were inside, he quietly closed the door. "What's going on?"

"That's what I'd like to know," she said as she turned to face him.

He took a cautious step toward her. "Okay, I think I'm missing something here. Did I do something wrong?"

"I guess it depends on your definition of wrong."

"Emmaline..."

"Your father offered you his inheritance to buy a practice–which is huge, by the way–and you don't mention it to me?" she asked, her voice rising with each word.

"Okay, yeah, but..."

"Then I just hear you pouring out your heart about how all these job offers are bogus and people just using you, and you didn't think to share that with me either?"

"I told you about that in the beginning," he countered.

"But it's still happening and it's been all the offers! Why? Why wouldn't you talk to me about this? Why keep it to yourself?"

He began to pace because...well...he knew this was going to happen. Eventually she was going to find out, but he hadn't wanted it to be like this.

"Who told you about the inheritance?"

Her eyes went wide. "It should have been you."

Nodding, he told himself he was focusing on the wrong thing.

"What is going on, Garrett? It sounds like this could be

the perfect solution for you! You can start your own practice anywhere you want to and do it on your terms! No one asking you to take silly pictures or videos! You'd be doing it on your own merit!"

"It's not that easy!" he shouted, surprising them both. He never lost his temper and the thought of doing that with her didn't sit well.

And yet...

"I have no idea if Cash is going to make good on his offer! And even if he did, I have no idea how long it will take!" He growled with frustration and paced like he did over with Ed and Doc MacEntyre. "I don't have time to sit around and wait, Emma! Don't you get it? A few months ago, I felt like I had the world in the palms of my hands! I had more job offers than anyone in my graduating class! And call it ego, but it felt pretty freaking awesome to finally be the guy that everyone envied. Now, all those same people who envied me have jobs and I don't!"

"But you could..."

"No! That's not the way I want it. I don't want to be the spokesperson that no one takes seriously. Becoming a vet was everything to me because I love helping animals. All everyone seems to want me for now is posing for the camera. You know what kind of message that sends? That I'm not good enough to actually care for animals."

"You know that's not true, Garrett. Anyone who knows you..."

"That's just it, Em, no one *wants* to know me! Not the real me! They want the shirtless guy in the videos who cuddles puppies!"

She stared at him for a minute. "What is it you think is going to happen, Garrett? You may not like how it happened, but the truth is that you *did* help a lot of animals.

No one's saying you're not a good vet." She paused and seemed to consider her words. "You own a mirror. You have to realize that you're a good-looking man. Women will ogle you and want to have you smile and flirt with them no matter what. The fact that you also help puppies is like crack! Why not embrace this and make a difference?"

"Because I don't want to be a joke, Em," he admitted gruffly.

"You're *not* a joke," she argued lightly. "That's just how you're taking it."

"No, it's not. People are making fun."

"People make fun of everything!" she shouted with frustration. "It doesn't matter what other people think! You're the one who used to tell me that back when I had a stutter! You used to say, 'Who cares what they think?' and that I should ignore them!"

"But my brothers…"

"Brothers tease one another, Garrett! It goes with the territory! Are you saying you've never teased them for anything?"

He supposed that was true…

"I'm floundering here," he said after a moment. "I don't know where to go or what to do because none of this is working out the way I planned. None of it. I had it all worked out and now…my confidence is gone. Even if I go back and accept any of those offers, sure, the head vet or partners might think I'm great, but you don't think the rest of the staff is going to be offended that I got the job based on social media exposure?"

She took a step toward him. "There are always going to be co-workers who are petty and jealous. If you're looking for the perfect work environment, Garrett, you're going to be very disappointed. It doesn't exist. Every job, every company has issues. It's human nature. Instead of focusing on all that could go wrong, why not focus on everything that could go right? If you could open your own clinic..."

"Please," he said with disgust. "I can't possibly believe that's going to happen. And even if it did..."

Now they were practically toe to toe. "Even if it did, you're scared that it still wouldn't work because you don't believe in yourself." She sighed. "I know what that's like, and I wish I could say it's easy to overcome, but it's not. You're never going to believe that you can succeed because you keep focusing on things that don't matter." She let out another sigh. "And by doing that, you're missing out on some amazing things–jobs, relationships...all of it. You're not just hurting yourself in the process, you're potentially hurting others."

He hung his head. "I should have told you years ago how I felt." His throat felt raw as he spoke the words, and he couldn't even look at her. "If I had, you never would have married Steven and had to suffer through a bad marriage."

"Wow," she murmured and stepped away from him. For a moment, he was confused about whether that was a good wow or a bad one, but once he saw the look on her face, he knew.

Bad.

"You are not responsible for the decisions I've made," she snapped. "We were kids back then, Garrett. Kids! We were friends, and I never thought you felt anything romantic toward me, and I would have been too scared to risk our friendship! Was Steven a bad decision? Yes! Do I regret it? Yes! But that's not to say you and I would have become anything either!" With a huff, she added, "You're not responsible for my bad marriage. I am! I should have seen the warning signs and believed in myself enough to walk away."

He swallowed hard and stared at her.

"All these job offers...you saw the warning signs and you walked away. You should be proud of it. Own it. Only you can know what's right for you. But this opportunity from your father? You not only have to decide to have faith in him but to have faith in yourself too."

Dammit, she was right. But man, was that asking a lot of faith. If he had to choose one or the other, it would be one thing, but...it was terrifying.

"You know why I think it was so easy for you to walk away from those offers?" she asked.

"Why?"

"Because you don't have that faith in yourself and I honestly don't know why." She let out one last sigh. "But what I do know is that it's something you have to work through on your own."

He didn't like the sound of that.

"It hurt me, Garrett, that you've been struggling with all this and you never talked to me about it."

"I didn't want to bog you down with my bullshit, Em. You have enough on your plate without me adding to it."

"You know what? I *do* have a lot on my plate, but I would have gladly made room for you, too. That's what friends do! That's what people in a relationship do!"

He saw tears in her eyes and it was killing him. "Emma..."

"You liked protecting me when we were kids and I liked letting you. But you know what happened? There was a time when you weren't there to protect me and I had to learn to protect myself. I'm not perfect at it, but I'm not a failure either. I don't need you protecting me from things that you think I can't handle."

"Yeah, but..."

"You're still trying to protect me now and I can't have that. Not like this. It's not fair and it's not right. If we're in a relationship, then we're in it together–the good and the bad."

"Okay, I get that now. Just give me..."

But she was shaking her head. "No. Now I need a little time to myself because I have some thinking to do, and God knows you do as well. We went from being best friends to being strangers to being lovers. It went from one extreme to the other and it's all...it's just too fast."

"Emma, I don't want it to end like this," he begged. "I screwed up. I should have talked to you. I get it now. This is all new to me, too. I don't want to leave and never see you again."

She rolled her eyes. "Does everything have to be an extreme with you? I'm talking about maybe spending a couple of days where we're not in each other's pockets, and you're breaking us up!" With a look of disgust, she headed for the door. "I think you should either go home or go to your mom or Austin's tonight because...just because."

And then she was gone and Garrett didn't even know if he wanted to go after her because he was ashamed.

He'd just ruined the one relationship that meant the world to him, all because he thought he was protecting her from all the negative stuff going on in his.

"Idiot," he murmured. It was no different from the night they'd first made love. Emma needed to feel in charge–to feel sexy and wanted–and he'd almost taken that away from her because he was afraid he was rushing her. Now he'd gone and done the same thing by not letting her decide for herself if she could handle things.

Raking a hand through his hair, Garrett sat down in Ed's chair and wondered how a guy who was smart enough to graduate from veterinary school with honors was so damn clueless.

12

THE WEEKEND HAD BEEN MISERABLE.

She didn't go to Austin and Mia's for dinner, and she didn't see or talk to Garrett at all. He'd come over to get his things, but he had a key to her place and managed to do it while she wasn't home.

And she couldn't even be mad about it.

If anything, she was glad he did it that way.

Ed had his surgery on Monday and everything had gone well. Now here it was on Wednesday and he was home. The last few days were hectic for all of them, but Emma knew her mother would be able to relax a bit more now that he was out of the hospital.

It was amazing how he was up and walking around–slowly–but still up and moving. He couldn't do much, but just seeing him moving around the house seemed to do wonders for everyone's spirits.

"Em, I've got a call with Georgia Bishop that I need to take. Can you bring Ed his tea? I shouldn't be more than fifteen minutes."

"Sure, Mom. No problem." Walking into the kitchen,

she grabbed the steaming mug of tea and went into the living room where she found Ed sitting in his favorite chair and reading. "Somebody order some tea?"

He smiled up at her as he carefully put his book down and reached for the mug. "Thanks, Em." After taking a sip, he motioned for her to sit on the sofa. "So, how are you doing?"

"Me?" she asked with a small laugh. "You know me–same old, same old. How are you feeling?"

With a patient smile, he studied her until she started to squirm. "I think we all know how I am. I'm going to be like this for a while and we're all expecting it. I'm more concerned about you."

It was pointless to pretend she didn't know why he was asking. He had been relatively close by when she and Garrett fought on Friday, so...

With a sigh, she got comfortable on the sofa. "It sucks, Ed. Like...a lot. Garrett was always different, the one guy I could always count on and trust."

"I'll try not to take offense to that," he murmured before taking another sip of tea.

"You know what I mean." Her head leaned back against the cushions. "He keeps everything to himself and it's not right. It's like he doesn't trust me or he thinks I'm too weak or stupid to handle anything."

"I'm pretty sure that's not what he thinks..."

"But we don't know, do we?" she said flatly. When she straightened, she tucked her feet under her. "I don't only want to be there for the good times or the happy times. I believe when you're with someone you care about that you share each other's burdens. I'm a big girl. A grown woman. I've lived through a crappy marriage and an even crappier divorce. I'm not the same person I was the last time he truly knew me. A lot's changed since he's been gone."

"That's fair, Em, but he doesn't know that, and it's only been a few weeks."

"Yeah, I get that, but so many things were going on and it's like he shared just a small fraction of it with me. And you know what, it was brutal. Seeing his father again was devastating for him and we talked it through and I thought that was it. Then I find out there's so much more! I mean, why only share part of it? And the stuff he was keeping to himself was actually good news! If he gets the inheritance, then he can say 'screw you' to all those practices that just wanted him because he's hot!"

Ed snickered behind his mug.

"You know what I'm saying," she whined. "I've already been in a relationship with a man who thought I was an idiot. I'm not looking to go there again."

"But…"

"I know, I know! Garrett's different and it's not like he really thinks that of me, but…that's how it makes me feel."

They sat in silence for a few minutes while Ed drank more of his tea. When he finally put the mug down, he glanced at her. "May I make a suggestion?"

Emma shrugged.

"Instead of making this about you–which you totally are–why not think about all the ways Garrett is hurting and struggling?"

"I…"

"Look at this from his perspective–he's had a thing for you for years and he finally gets the chance to be with you. But all around him, his life is basically unraveling. He's struggling with insecurity and betrayal and the emotional roller coaster of having his father come back. And rather than being a safe haven for him, you pushed him away." He shifted awkwardly in his chair and grimaced in pain. "I understand why you were upset, but...I believe you could have handled things better."

She hated that he was right.

"Oh, God. I was a total bitch," she groaned, hiding her face in her hands.

"I didn't want to be the one to say it."

Peeking at him over her hand, she glared. Fortunately, Ed was probably the only person who could have said all this to her without her taking offense. He was good like that. As far as stepfathers went, he was the best. Ryleigh, Madison, and Wyatt were lucky to have him as a father. He was wise and caring, and he had a gift for knowing exactly what to say to get you to see the error of your ways.

After allowing herself a minute to be dramatic, she looked at him. "Okay, how do I fix this?"

"Call him. Invite him over to talk. Or you can just go over to Austin's and see him."

Frowning, she asked, "Wait, how do you know he's at Austin's?"

"Because I've talked to him every day. He's called, he came to the hospital...you know, because he's a good guy."

"Ed..."

He smiled sweetly at her. "Go. Go over there now. I know he'd really like to see you."

"I want to. I really do."

"But...?"

"But I promised Mom I'd help with dinner, and Ryleigh mentioned needing help with her biology homework."

Holding up one finger, he gingerly reached over to the table beside him and picked up his phone. She watched as he typed something and when he was done, he simply sat there looking thoroughly at peace.

The sound of a stampede coming toward them had her spinning in her seat.

"What's going on?"

"Are you okay?"

"Are you in pain? Do you need your meds?"

All the questions came out at once from all three of her siblings, and it was incredibly sweet how much they worried about their father.

"Here's the deal, kiddos," he began softly. "Mom's on the phone dealing with some important stuff for Happy Tails, and Emma has someplace that she really needs to be, so here's what's going to happen. Wyatt, you're going to go out and make sure the dogs are all fed. Ryleigh, you're going to bring your biology homework down here and we'll work through it together. Maddie, you're going to go and help Wyatt with the dogs and make sure they all get a good run around before it gets dark." He looked very pleased with himself. "And if all that gets done, I'll order pizza for dinner. How does that sound?"

No one answered because they all took off running.

She looked over at Ed. "Wow. That was impressive."

"They're highly motivated by pizza, so..." He shrugged. "Go and tell Garrett I said hello and I look forward to beating him at chess tomorrow."

"Chess?"

He nodded. "We used to play it when you were younger and he would come over to hang out. We started playing again last week. I'd forgotten how much I enjoy it."

Standing, she couldn't help but smile. "I'll be sure to let him know." She walked over and kissed him on the cheek and whispered, "Thank you for being awesome."

"I do what I can," he replied with a wink.

"Tell Mom I'll call her tomorrow and if she needs me..."

"She won't. We have more volunteers than we know what to do with. Just go, Em."

She walked into the kitchen with a small sigh and grabbed her purse and headed out the door. Once she was outside, she saw the dogs running around and Axel came sprinting toward her. She opened the gate and bent down to snuggle him a bit. "I know, baby boy. I haven't been around to play and I'm sorry." He licked her face as she hugged him close. "I promise we'll find some time this weekend. Maybe we'll go for a walk on the beach. How does that sound?" He gave her another round of puppy kisses as Wyatt called out that it was time to eat and Axel pretty much leaped out of her arms, making her laugh.

There was nothing else for her to do, so she walked over to her car and prayed Ed knew what he was talking about and that Garrett really did want to see her.

And that she hadn't ruined this relationship before it even had a chance to begin.

"Why are we doing this?"

"It's relaxing so shut up."

Garrett stared out at the water and sighed. "It's boring. I don't think I've ever been this bored in my entire life."

Beside him, Austin groaned. They were standing on the beach with their fishing poles, trying to catch...something. Fishing had never been his thing, but when Austin suggested it, it seemed like something to do to break up the monotony of the day.

But it hadn't.

This was the equivalent of watching paint dry.

"I heard from Dad today," Austin casually began. "The property sold."

For a moment, it felt like he couldn't breathe. Was it possible that this was really going to happen? Could he truly be in a position to have his own practice? Here in Magnolia? He'd be closer to Emma and…

Emma.

He missed her so damn much it hurt. He'd done his best to respect her wishes, but it was hard. Every day he had to fight the urge to call her or simply show up at her place or even arrange to be at Happy Tails when he knew she'd be there.

But he didn't.

And he hadn't just been moping around either. While she was at work, he went over to help out with the dogs. He'd applied for several positions with veterinary clinics in North Carolina, Virginia, and Tennessee, but he wasn't excited about any of them. Yesterday he took his mother to lunch before going to visit Ed in the hospital. He was keeping busy, but it wasn't helping. Sighing, he shook his pole and began reeling it in.

"For the love of it," Austin muttered. "Just go inside already. Forget that I tried to have a conversation with you."

Oh, right. The property sold.

"You're right. Sorry. I'm just distracted."

"Yeah, I know. We all know. I thought this would distract you from all the sighing and moaning you've been doing for days."

"Are you going to tell me what else Dad had to say or not?"

Glancing at him, Austin smirked. "Maybe."

"Austin…"

"Okay, fine. The property sold. They're going to go to closing in two weeks. It's all being expedited. The buyer's very motivated."

"Really? That's...wow."

His brother's smile grew. "Yeah. I knew Ryder would be the perfect buyer for it. He's been looking for property here. So once I called him and told him about it..."

"Wait, wait, wait...Ryder? As in the guy who owns this house you're renting?"

"That's the one."

"Holy shit! I can't believe you did that!"

Shrugging, Austin reeled in his own line. "Two birds, one stone. Everyone wins."

"That still remains to be seen," he murmured.

For several minutes, they collected their things and when they turned back toward the house, Garrett noticed Mia was out on the deck talking to someone.

Emma.

His heart kicked hard in his chest and he made sure he didn't appear too anxious. Once he and Austin were up on the deck, Mia turned and smiled at them.

"Seriously, can the two of you just put shirts on? I mean, how hard is it to wear clothes?" she said with exasperation.

Austin took her in his arms and kissed her soundly. When he raised his head, he teased, "You know you prefer me like this. And be honest, I look better shirtless than Garrett, right?"

"I am *not* getting in the middle of this," she said with a laugh, pushing against his chest. "Come on inside and give me a hand with dinner."

"Yes, dear," he said, following her into the house with a small wave to Emma.

Garrett put his gear down and simply took in the sight

of her. She looked tired and uncomfortable, and he wasn't sure what he could say to put her at ease. Once he heard the sliding doors close, he moved a little closer. "Hey."

"Hey," she replied softly. "Catch anything?" She motioned to the fishing poles.

"Nah. I haven't fished in years. Austin loves it, but it's too tedious for me." The silence stretched before he finally invited her to have a seat at the dining set on the deck. "Can I get you something to drink?"

"No, I'm good. Thanks."

He nodded.

How had they gotten here? Even after not seeing each other for years, they slid back into their comfortable relationship. And now, two weeks of sleeping together and one fight undid all of it.

Great.

"I'm sorry I..."

"No," Emma interrupted. "I'm the one who needs to apologize." Her gaze met his and he could see the regret there. "I made it all about me without taking into consideration how much pressure you were under. I should have been more patient, and instead, I acted like a bully."

He couldn't help but chuckle. "Emmaline Ryan, you are many things, but a bully isn't one of them."

"Oh, please. I could have encouraged you to talk to me instead of totally crashing your conversation with Ed and Doc MacEntyre and making a scene like that." She shook her head. "I'm so embarrassed."

"You shouldn't be. You were right to call me out on it. All of it." Pausing, he reached across the table and cautiously took one of her hands in his. "Here's the thing, Em; I couldn't believe that my life could be so awful and so wonderful at the same time. So much was falling apart around me and then...there you were. I didn't want any of my bullshit to taint what we were doing. Some of it did, and we talked it through and you made me feel better, but... God, it just kept coming, and...I know I didn't handle it well."

"To be fair, I don't think anyone could handle all you've been dealing with and do it with a smile on their face." She studied their hands. "So what happens now?"

He glanced toward the house. "I'd love to go back to your place and have dinner with you. I don't have to spend the night, but I'd just love the chance to be alone with you and talk. You know, without an audience."

She smiled so sweetly and it gave him hope for the first time in days. "I'd like that very much."

Together they stood and walked into the house. Mia and Austin were nowhere to be seen and Garrett saw that as a blessing. His shirt was folded up on the arm of the sofa, so he grabbed it and slipped it on. With his fingers over his lips, he pointed to the front door and whispered, "I'll text them later," and they tiptoed out the front door. "I'll meet you at your place, okay?"

Nodding, Emma went to her car while he climbed into his, and ten minutes later, they were parked outside her condo. Neither spoke as they walked up to the door, and once they were inside and Emma put her keys down, Garrett knew he had to confess.

"I lied," he said with a mixture of remorse and defiance. All she did was look at him. "I do want us to talk, but...I'd really like to stay the night. If that's okay with you."

She blinked but didn't say anything, and he didn't take it as a good sign.

"I'm not going to pressure you or try to change your

mind–the decision is yours and yours alone–but...I've missed you."

In a move he never saw coming, he had his arms full of Emma as she wrapped herself around him, kissing him.

Relief washed over him as his arms banded tightly around her as he kissed her back. It was wet and untamed, and as he backed her up to the wall, all he could think was...*mine*. This beautiful, brave woman was his, and he'd do whatever it took to keep it that way.

His lips left hers as he trailed hot kisses along her jaw and throat.

"I missed you so much," she panted, rubbing against him in the most erotic way. "We can talk later, right?"

All he could do was nod because he had her shirt pushed up and was busy kissing and nipping and sucking at all the soft skin he exposed.

She had no idea how sexy she was, how desirable. He'd always thought she was beautiful, but what made her even more so in his eyes was the way she had come into her own. Gone was the shy girl he knew, and in her place was a fierce and independent woman who wasn't afraid to take what she wanted.

And he was beyond relieved that she wanted him.

As sexy as up-against-the-wall sex sounded, what Garrett really wanted was to have Emma sprawled out on the bed under him. Reluctantly, he lifted his head and told her exactly what he wanted.

"Good," she said breathlessly. "Bed is good."

As soon as they were beside it, they tumbled onto it with a laugh. Emma had her shirt off before he could even touch her again and he gladly whipped his off. He reached for her, but she scooted away and took off her bra and shimmied out of her pants before lying back against the pillows. "Okay, now we're good," she said with a sexy grin.

This girl...

He quickly shucked his own jeans and settled himself between her thighs, and the skin-to-skin contact was the best thing he'd felt in a long time. One soft hand reached up and raked through his hair and he let out a very satisfied moan.

"I have a confession to make," she said softly.

That...wasn't what he was expecting...

Her other hand smoothed over his chest. "I know you might not want to hear this, but...I used to watch those videos of you and wish I could touch you like this." Her gaze slowly traveled up to meet his. "You may not like them, but they truly were everything to me—even though I had only recently discovered them."

Garrett swallowed hard. "I know they served a purpose and I'm proud of that, but knowing how much you enjoyed them makes it all the more worth it." Dipping his head, he kissed her because he was done talking. There'd be enough talking later and for now, he wanted to touch and kiss and lick every inch of her until neither could form a coherent thought.

So that's what he did.

"I know this is decadent, but you know what would be even better?"

"What?"

"If Henderson's delivered," Emma said before taking a bite of her burger. It was a little after eight and they were in bed, eating burgers they ordered from The Sand Bar.

"I knew I should have ordered dessert too."

She waved him off. "It wouldn't have been the same. The Sand Bar does decent brownies and apple crisp, but you need to eat that right there while it's still hot. If Mrs. Henderson hired a delivery service, I can guarantee the people of Magnolia would completely utilize it."

Garrett finished his burger and leaned back against the pillows. "I didn't realize how hungry I was. I basically inhaled that."

"You still have some fries left..." And she emphasized that by stealing one.

"Hey! You said you didn't want fries!"

She shrugged with a giggle. "I lied."

Wrapping an arm around her, he hugged her close, kissing the top of her head. "Brat."

Emma finished eating, and they put all their trash in the bag the food came in before relaxing again. Garrett had a feeling they should probably talk now, but he wasn't even sure where to begin.

Luckily, he didn't have to.

"So here's the thing," she began, her head resting on his shoulder. "I think we have something good here, Garrett. Something special. But mostly, something worth fighting for."

He nodded.

"However, I need you to be all in." Lifting her head, she met his gaze. "No secrets, no keeping things from me because you think I can't handle it or because you think I'm dealing with too much...whatever it is, I want to know, okay?"

He nodded again.

With a weary sigh, she put a little space between them. "When Steven left, he not only wiped out our bank account, but he ran up all our credit cards. I was able to work with a financial service to get fees waived and we've gone after him with no luck. So I rent this tiny condo and work more than I want because I have a lot of debt to pay off."

"Geez, Emma. How...how is that even fair? Why aren't the credit card companies going after him?"

"Because no one can find him."

There wasn't anything he could say to that because it sounded a lot like his father. "O-kay, so..."

"I'm telling you this because you need to know that I can handle more than you think I can. My life isn't glamorous or exciting, but you know what? It's mine and I'm in control of it."

"But still, you shouldn't have to pay..."

She held up a hand to stop him. "Oh, I know, and when we do find him, he *will* pay. I've got a lawyer working on things. He'll never be able to fully repay everything he should, but for now, my credit isn't ruined, and in another year or two, I should be able to breathe a little easier."

"Okay, now...hear me out," he cautioned. "I know I can find a job–we both know I've had offers–but I can't take them, Em. Maybe it's me being a coward or a diva or just a damn jackass, but I want a job where I'm respected." Falling back against the pillows, he let out a long breath. "If my father stays true to his word, this is all a non-issue. I can buy Doc MacEntyre's practice and be here with you and help out at Happy Tails and everything will be alright."

"I really wish you had told me about that."

"I know. I should have, but...there's a part of me that doesn't believe it. I'm waiting for the other shoe to drop. He's here and he's doing everything he said he was going to do, but...I'm afraid to trust it."

"That's only natural. He hasn't given you any reason to trust him. But maybe he's truly changed. Once the property sells..."

"It sold today," he told her. "Austin told me while we were out fishing. They're scheduled to go to closing in two weeks."

Emma sat up straight, wide-eyed. "Garrett! This is fantastic news! You should go and talk to Doc MacEntyre tomorrow and see if you can get things started there, too!" Hugging him, she continued to talk about all the ways that this was a good thing.

But he still didn't feel it.

Slowly, he maneuvered them so she was sitting up again. "I can't help having pride, Em. It feels wrong to be here with you and making plans when you're struggling financially and I'm unemployed."

"But I don't care about that. It's not a big deal..."

"It is to me," he countered sternly. "I grew up poor thanks to my father. Even before he left us, he wasn't keen on working. I don't want to be like that and I certainly don't want people looking at me around here and comparing me to Cash."

She gave him a patient look. "Garrett, you are nothing like your father and no one would ever make that comparison."

"I'm not sure I'm willing to take that risk. So many things are up in the air right now and...I'm not comfortable with it."

"I don't think anyone's life is ever totally settled. There's almost always something going on that isn't quite like we plan. I'm dealing with a wayward ex-husband and that has kept me from doing a lot of things. I've missed out on doing things with friends, mainly because I was embarrassed and couldn't afford to go out and do anything. Being poor truly sucks."

He studied her for a moment. "If you were done with all of that and got reimbursed for the money he essentially stole from you, what is the first thing you'd do?"

"Well, I don't think I'll ever get all the money back, but the first thing I'd love to do is move out of this place and into a house. One that I owned. And if I couldn't buy it, then at least a house that had a fenced-in yard and accepted pets." She smiled wistfully. "Then I'd bring Axel home with me."

"Really? No big vacation or spa day or new car?"

She shook her head. "This place is functional and it's fine for just me, but...I grew up with pets so not having one is very hard for me. Steven never wanted one so I've been without one for a long time. But the thought of finally having a dog again is what keeps me going."

"What if Axel gets adopted before then?" And yeah, it was a crappy thing to ask, but he knew she was practical and was more than likely prepared for that.

"I'd be incredibly disappointed, but as long as I knew he went to a good home, I'd learn to be happy for him. There are so many wonderful dogs at the farm that I don't think I'd have a problem picking one. Axel's just special to me because I seem to be the only one he depends on and trusts. It's a nice feeling."

"He's got excellent taste," he said softly, pulling her back in for a hug. "I hope that happens, Em. And I hope it happens for you soon. You deserve to be happy."

"Believe it or not, I am." She paused. "Of course, you have a lot to do with that. Before you came back to town, I was doing okay. But now that you're here? I'm genuinely happy." Then she playfully jabbed him in the ribs. "At least I am when you're not so darn secretive."

Laughing, he rolled them over until she was sprawled on top of him. "Yeah, I'm working on that. Trust me." He loved looking at her. Even tousled and a little sleepy, she was still the most beautiful girl in the world to him. Reaching up, he caressed her cheek. Her smile was soft and dreamy, and he knew he'd never get tired of looking at her.

"Mmm..." she hummed. "This is nice."

Garrett nodded. "I love you, Emmaline."

Her eyes went wide.

"No more secrets, no more keeping things to myself," he went on. "I love you. I've loved you for a long time and I know I'm always going to love you. Maybe it's too soon for you to hear it, but for me, I should have said it years ago."

"Garrett," she whispered, her eyes scanning his face. "I...I don't even know what to say."

It was wrong for him to be disappointed that she didn't say it back to him, but that was truly where he thought they were both going. He meant what he said and he'd give her time, but she was it for him.

"Don't say anything," he said quietly as he cupped her face in his hand. "I just wanted you to know how I felt." Pausing, he smiled. "This is me not being secretive."

She smiled as she leaned down to kiss him and Garrett felt it...she might not be able to say the words, but she said it in the way she kissed him. Touched him. And for now, it was enough.

13

Everything was better.

Emma knew the moment Garrett said he loved her that it would be.

Now, a week later, things seemed to be falling into place all around her.

Ed's recovery was going well and things were being handled perfectly at Happy Tails. A dozen dogs were adopted in the past week thanks to several fun videos Georgia's daughter-in-law Scarlett did for them.

And no one had to take their shirt off.

Garrett was in talks with Doc MacEntyre to buy his practice, and the two had been working together so Garrett could get a feel for the day-to-day operations. Every day when he came home, he was practically giddy from everything he was learning and all the plans he was making for improvement. Next weekend they were supposed to go up to Norfolk to pack up his apartment and get him moved back to Magnolia Sound. Most of his stuff was going to go into storage since he was moving in with her. Once things got settled for him with the clinic, they'd look into moving someplace bigger, but they could totally make do for now.

It was Friday night and they were pulling up to Austin and Mia's for dinner. It was actually going to be a family affair, with Grace and Cash Coleman joining them to celebrate the sale of the property. No one seemed to want to openly talk about it, but Emma knew she was dying to know what was going on with the two of them and what had happened to Dominic. She kept wanting to ask Garrett, but any time she tried, he got really upset.

And he wasn't afraid to show it.

When they were walking up the steps to the front door, Garrett stopped her.

"It's going to be weird in there," he warned her. "And I can't promise we'll all play nice."

"Garrett..."

"I'm serious, Em. I've been very straightforward with Cash and so has Austin. Neither of us is thrilled that he's still sniffing around our mother." He shook his head. "And I'm not too thrilled with her either because she refuses to talk about it, so...yeah. There is potential for this to be a disaster."

She held up the big pink bakery box. "Then it's a good thing I picked up lots of cookies and brownies. I think Mia and I can sit back and be spectators while indulging in sweets, so don't worry about me."

Pulling her into his arms, he kissed her soundly. "God, I love you."

She smiled sweetly. "Let's do this."

Yeah, she still hadn't been able to say the words back to him. She wanted to–deep down, she knew she was in love with him–but she was still being cautious for some reason.

"Hey, you guys!" Mia said when she opened the door. "Come on in!"

Garrett kissed her on the cheek as he walked in and Emma hugged her. "I brought cake," she said. "Well, technically brownies and cookies, but...you know..."

"Two of my favorite things," Mia assured her but held her back when Emma went to follow Garrett into the house. Her voice lowered as she moved in close. "Okay, I don't know about you, but I'm worried about tonight. Grace is here, Ryder's here, and Cash is due any minute. Austin's already argued with Grace about everything going on and demanded that she invite Dominic, but...it was awkward." She pulled back and offered a weak smile. "I just wanted you to be prepared."

"Thanks. Garrett warned me too, and I told him if all hell broke loose, you and I would sit back with this box of goodies and observe." She smiled. "I hope that's okay."

Mia grinned broadly. "I knew you and I were going to be good friends!" Hooking her arm through Emma's, she led her into the house. "Let's think of a code word just in case we need to pull away from the group." She paused. "Ooh...I know! Coconut. If you use the word coconut in a sentence, that will tell me you're overwhelmed and I'll do the same. Deal?"

Emma laughed. "Deal."

Austin introduced Emma to Ryder, and she was a little taken aback at how...everything he was–tall, built like a linebacker, and almost movie-star handsome. What in the world was he doing buying property in this little town?

"It's a pleasure to meet you, Emma," he said, shaking her hand. He had an easy smile and she almost let out a very feminine giggle because he was just that good-looking.

One glance at Garrett, however, and she knew exactly where her heart belonged.

"You too, Ryder," she said before moving closer to Garrett.

"I was just getting ready to pour some champagne," Austin said to them, "to kick off the celebration, but I supposed it would be rude if we didn't wait for Dad."

They all agreed and moved out to the deck to chat and relax while waiting for Cash.

"Ryder, how do you feel about fishing?" Garrett asked as the men moved over to the edge of the deck. Meanwhile, Emma, Mia, and Grace sat down on the cushioned benches around the fire pit.

They made small talk, and Emma did her best to bite her tongue and not ask what she desperately wanted to ask.

"I hope Cash gets here soon," Mia commented. "Austin picked up some fabulous steaks from the butcher and I managed to snag us fresh seafood. I made a crab dip and lobster bruschetta, and if I do say so myself, they're both delicious."

"Oh, that does sound yummy," Emma agreed. "I ate a very light lunch because Garrett warned me there'd probably be a lot of food tonight."

"I brought scalloped potatoes and a salad," Grace added as she discreetly looked at her watch. "Cash was supposed to bring the wine. Maybe that's what's taking him so long."

Emma and Mia exchanged glances.

"Grace," Mia began, beating Emma to the punch, "I know it's really none of my business, and I know you and Austin just talked about it earlier, but...what about Dominic?"

Her shoulders sagged as she looked at the two of them. "Things are a little...confusing right now," Grace quietly explained. "When the boys told me that Cash was back, I really didn't feel much of anything. It was like...okay. Then he showed up at the house and..." She sighed and shook her head. "It's crazy how some feelings just don't go away."

Mia gently patted Grace's hand, and Emma was pretty sure her eyes were about to bug right out of her head.

"The night he first came over, we stayed up all night talking," Grace went on. "He kissed me goodbye and asked if he could see me again." She looked at them helplessly. "And I said yes."

Emma quietly cleared her throat. "Well, there were a lot of unresolved emotions there."

Grace agreed. "I felt so guilty that I called in sick to work that Tuesday and went to see Dom at the shop. We sat in his office and talked, and...honestly, he's way too forgiving. If the roles had been reversed, I would have wanted to scratch someone's eyes out."

Both Emma and Mia nodded in understanding.

"Anyway, he suggested that I take some time to sort things out." She shook her head again. "He said if he had another opportunity with his wife, he'd take it." She paused. "It's not the same thing, of course. His wife died tragically young and they had a good marriage. Cash and I...everything was a struggle. But I took one look at him and was ready to fall all over again."

"It has to be very confusing," Mia said after a moment. "I can't even imagine how you're feeling."

"And knowing he's dying makes it so much worse. How can I possibly be mean and hateful or drag up the past when he's suffering like this? No one deserves that kind of treatment."

Emma definitely kept her mouth shut because she didn't agree at all. While it was unfortunate that the man was dying, it didn't give him a free pass or a blanket of forgiveness for all the hurt and hardship he'd caused his family.

But considering Grace was already struggling with enough, she didn't want to share her two cents.

"So what happens now?" Emma asked instead.

"Well...Dominic asked that I not reach out to him until I know what it is that I want. He didn't want to be part of the equation."

He already is, Emma thought.

"Cash and I have gone out together several times and...it's been nice. We've gone to dinner and the movies, to the aquarium, and for walks on the beach. All the things we did way back when we were dating." She paused and let out a weary sigh. "Nostalgia is a funny thing. The lines between past and present are getting blurred and I'm not really sure how I feel. Maybe part of me wants the man I thought I married, and he's finally trying to be that man."

"But...?" Mia prompted.

"But...I'm not that same girl I was all those years ago and I don't want to ever be her again. I'm afraid being with Cash will force me back into that person." Reaching out, she squeezed Mia's hand. "It's been a bit of an emotional roller coaster." After another pause, she added, "And it's nice having the two of you to talk to about this. The boys don't quite understand."

Before anyone could comment, Austin walked over wearing a fierce scowl.

"What's the matter?" Mia asked.

"He's thirty minutes late," he snapped. "I've had lunch with him several times and he's always early. He actually bragged about how important it is to him to be punctual."

SINCE YOU'VE BEEN GONE   223

"O-kay," Mia replied cautiously. "Maybe something's happened? Have you called him?"

"Three times and it goes directly to voicemail."

A soft gasp had them all turning toward Grace. "What if something's happened to him? What if...what if he's lying unconscious somewhere?" She jumped to her feet. "We should go to his place and check on him! And if something happened on the way–like an accident–surely we'd see it, right?"

Everyone seemed to nod in agreement, and when Garrett came to sit beside her, he asked the group, "Does anyone have his address?"

"Um..."

"Uh..."

"I never thought to..."

Ryder held up a hand. "It's on the contract," he stated firmly, looking more than a little put out at the entire situation. Pulling out his phone, he scrolled until he found it. He read the address and looked up. "I thought he wasn't living here in Magnolia?"

"That's my address," Grace said wearily before closing her eyes. "He lied about his address on a legal document."

"Give me a minute," Ryder said, walking away with his phone.

"This is bad," Grace said. "This is very, very bad."

"So...wait," Mia said, looking around in confusion. "No one knows where he's been staying?"

"He said he was renting a bungalow down in Wilmington," Austin said with frustration as he began to pace. "There was no reason to go there because he was always here! How the hell are we supposed to find him?"

Everyone started talking at once and Emma did her best to fade into the background because there wasn't a damn thing she could add. How do you go about finding someone who wasn't honest about...well...anything? Short of going door-to-door on the streets of Wilmington—if that was actually where he was staying—there wasn't a whole lot they could do.

Ryder rejoined them and announce, "He's staying at a place on Lansing Street in Wilmington."

"How do you know?" Austin asked.

He shrugged. "I always look into the people I do business with. And knowing your family history, I wanted to dig a little before agreeing so I wouldn't be blindsided by anything. The address thing got past me, so for that, I'm sorry." He looked around. "Okay, let's go find him."

Now they had to decide who was going.

"Alright, I'm not trying to be sexist or anything," Austin began, "but why don't I go with Garrett and Ryder?" He looked at Mia. "But promise to save me some of the dip and bruschetta."

"I make no promises," she teased before standing and kissing him.

Grace stood. "Maybe I should go with you. I could..."

This time it was Garrett who spoke up. "Mom, just stay and visit with Mia and Emma. I'm sure we won't be gone long."

She wasn't happy about it, but she didn't argue either, and in a matter of minutes, the men were gone and Emma heard the car drive away.

She and Mia looked at each other at the same time and said, "Coconut," before bursting out laughing.

"So, um..." Grace began, looking at them like they'd lost their minds.

"Wine," Mia said as she walked back toward the house. "And open the bakery box, Emma. I think brownies and wine will go great with crab and lobster, don't you?"

The GPS said it would take them forty minutes to get to Cash's place, but Ryder promised to get them there in thirty.

Garrett chose not to question it.

He'd been relegated to the back seat and it was fine with him because his mind was racing with every scenario that could possibly be played out once they hit their destination.

His brother had kept up a running commentary from the front passenger seat, and Ryder pretty much only commented when necessary. The only thing the three of them had in common at the moment was that none of them had any idea what to expect.

Part of Garrett resented that Ryder was even here with them. This wasn't any of his business. However, the alternative was leaving him behind with his mother, Mia, and Emma, and...yeah, it was probably better that he was here in the car.

"What do you think, G?" Austin turned and asked.

"Um...what?"

Austin groaned. "Can you please focus here? I think Dad just fell asleep and lost track of time. He turned off his phone and we're all freaking out over nothing."

"I'm not sure I agree with that."

"If anyone wants my opinion," Ryder interrupted. "I think he maybe stopped to get the wine and perhaps wanted to get something for your girls and lost track of time." He glanced at Austin. "What? You don't think that's possible?"

"Who knows if it's possible," Garrett murmured. "The man's never done anything for anyone else in his entire life. These last few weeks have bordered on the bizarre and the fact of the matter is we can sit here and speculate all we want because we don't know him."

"Shit," Austin hissed. "I think it's safe to say that we're all trying not to say the one thing we're all thinking."

"That he took the money and ran?" Ryder suggested. "Um, yeah. That was my first instinct, and I'm rarely wrong."

"He wouldn't do that," Austin argued. "Not after everything these last few weeks. He knows what we're all going to do with the money that he's promised. I mean, I can deal with it because it was all extra for us and for the house, but he knows Garrett's only able to buy Doc MacEntyre's practice because of the inheritance. He wouldn't do that."

Garrett slammed his head back against the seat cushion and cursed even as his heart sank. He didn't have a good feeling about any of this and no matter how many times he told himself not to panic and that everything was going to be alright, he was seriously beginning to lose hope.

"Okay," Ryder said simply. "Then let's hope it's one of the other scenarios we just mentioned or that he's too sick to answer his phone."

The rest of the drive was made in silence, and when they finally pulled up to the address, one thing was abundantly clear.

Cash's car wasn't there.

Ryder parked and climbed out, and Garrett and Austin followed.

"Wait, why are we getting out?" Garrett asked.

"Look in the windows," Ryder said as he walked up onto the front porch of the small house. He looked in the window on the right of the front door while Garrett looked in the one on the left. Austin walked around to the back, but it wasn't necessary. "Son of a bitch!"

"It's empty," Ryder confirmed and walked down the front steps and over to the house next door. All Garrett could do was remind himself to breathe. He was definitely going to be sick as everything around him began to spin. He was sliding to the floor when Austin ran up and grabbed him.

"G, come on," he said quietly. "It's gonna be okay."

No words came out, but he shook his head.

Nothing was going to be okay. He'd already started a contract with Doc MacEntyre to buy the practice. He had to be out of his place in Norfolk in a week. He had promised Emma that their lives were going to get better. He vowed he'd take care of her better than anyone ever had.

And now he couldn't.

His brother loosened his grip as they both sat on the porch floor.

"I can't believe he did this," Garrett whispered.

"I know this looks bad, but...maybe we got the wrong address or something."

"Why are you defending him?" he yelled, finally snapping. "Look around, Austin! This is where he was supposedly staying and no one lives here! Even if by some small chance he did use a bogus address, it still doesn't explain where he is or why he's not answering his phone!"

Ryder jogged back over to them. "Yeah, I talked to the neighbor lady and she said she saw Cash moving out this morning. She called the landlord, who's a friend of hers, because he was taking some stuff that wasn't his."

"Great. He's a thief, too. Awesome," Austin said with disgust.

"Look, I don't think we're going to get any answers tonight, but I can certainly get someone working on this. The same guy who did the background check could dig around into where Cash went." Ryder stared at the two of them. "I wish I could stop payment on the money, but it was a cashier's check and I'm sure he's already deposited it somewhere."

No one moved for several minutes. The sun was starting to go down and Ryder finally suggested they head back to Magnolia.

"Do you think we can talk to the landlord?" Garrett asked.

"To what end, G?"

He shrugged. "I don't know. Maybe he knows something, or maybe after finding out that Cash was essentially robbing the place, he called the cops on him. It can't hurt to talk to him."

With a small huff, Ryder decided to handle it. "I'll go talk to Judy...I mean, Mrs. Robinson and see if I can charm the phone number out of her."

"Judy? Really?"

Ryder nodded and grinned. "She told me I was cute." He winked. "I'll be right back."

"Why would he do this?" Austin wondered out loud. "I mean, why go through the whole charade of giving a damn and wanting to help us if he was simply going to take the money and run?" He muttered a curse. "And now I'm even wondering if he was really as sick as he said he was."

"Oh, he's sick," Garrett replied. "And twisted, and the sorriest excuse for a human being in the world." He shook his head. "I don't understand, and I'm mad at myself for believing him. I struggled with it all this time, but when he suggested I talk to Doc about buying the practice and how much he wanted that for me, I started to let my guard down. I'm so screwed, Austin." His head fell forward into his hands as he blew out a long breath. "This not only ruins my plans for buying the clinic, but it ruins everything with Emma."

"How do you figure that?"

Sadly, he looked up. "She's already dealing with getting financially screwed by her ex-husband and is paying off the mountains of debt he left her with. How can I possibly stay here with her when I have no job?"

"Garrett, it's not..."

"There are no jobs around here for me," he said firmly. "None. You don't think I've been looking? You know I always have a plan and a backup plan and even a backup for the backup. And you know what I have now? Nothing!" Raking a hand through his hair, he gently banged his head against the house. "I can't mooch off of her and now I'm going to have to take one of those crappy job offers that I turned down–if they'll still hire me."

"I'm sure you don't..."

"No, someone will hire me. They'll all use me for their stupid Hot Doc calendars and charity auctions and I'll be a fucking joke. And as if that's not bad enough, I won't have Emma. She won't leave Magnolia and her family, and I don't want to even ask that of her."

"Wow. That's a lot of brand-new information." He stared at Garrett for a long moment. "I didn't realize all the fuss about the videos bothered you that much. We joked about it and I thought it was cool with you."

"Yeah, well...not so much," he admitted. "Turns out all those job offers? They didn't want me because I was smart or good at my job. They wanted me for promotional purposes." Closing his eyes, he braced himself for more teasing.

But it never came.

"I'm sorry, G. Had I known...well..." Austin let out a small chuckle. "Well, I probably would have still teased you a bit, but I would have felt bad." He paused. "And all of them...?"

He nodded. "All of them. I had a total of twenty-two job offers in the last three months, and every one of them presented me with their marketing plan and how they were going to utilize my online celebrity. It was insulting and ridiculous."

"I don't even know what to say, man. I had no idea."

"Being able to buy Doc MacEntyre's practice was like an answer to a prayer. It killed me that Cash was the one making it happen, but once I got over that, I knew it was a blessing. Now I'm back to square one, and...I don't know how to come back from this, Austin. I worked so damn hard in school, and I learned to do it on my own after struggling so much, and where did it get me, huh? Nowhere. I don't even know how I'm going to explain this to Emma."

"Yeah, let's talk about that now. I had no idea the ex-husband left her with so much baggage. Why hasn't anyone forced him to pay this crap off and take the burden off of her?"

As much as Garrett hated sharing something so personal with his brother, it was too late to take any of it back. "No one can find him, apparently. The guy seems to stay one step ahead of the people looking for him. Plus, I think she's got a lazy attorney handling the case because it doesn't seem possible that this guy's been skating by for three years without being detected. I knew Steven back in high school. He wasn't that smart."

"Damn."

Ryder came walking back over, talking on the phone.

He gave them both a thumbs-up, but Garrett had no idea what exactly that could mean.

"If anyone can get information, it's Ryder," Austin quietly commented.

"It must be nice to have that kind of power. Maybe we should have talked to him before letting Cash back into our lives."

"Hindsight and all…"

They tried listening to the one-sided conversation, but Ryder was pacing and it was hard to follow along. It took a solid five minutes for him to finish up, and then he held up a finger to them again before making another call.

This one he walked farther away to talk.

"That's not a good sign, is it?" Garrett asked.

"Maybe it had nothing to do with us and it was business-related. You can't blame the guy for wanting privacy."

"Maybe."

"I'm going to call Mia and give her an update," he said, pulling out his phone.

"What are you going to tell her? We don't know anything."

"We know Dad's not here," he huffed with annoyance. "Why don't you call Emma? Maybe the sound of her voice will help you relax."

It was tempting, but he shook his head. "Mia can tell her what's going on. I think I'd just freak her out."

"Suit yourself." Austin rose and stepped down from the porch and walked around to the side of the house, leaving Garrett by himself.

He did his best to try to relax; otherwise, he'd throw himself into a full-throttle panic attack. He was about to start counting backward from one hundred when he saw

Ryder walking back toward him, sliding his phone into his pocket.

"Where'd Austin go?"

"He went to call Mia. Any news?"

Ryder looked toward where Austin was and shrugged. "The landlord managed to stop Cash before he left town. He said he literally pulled up beside him at a gas station and blocked him in."

"O-kay..."

"Cash played on the guy's sympathy. He claimed he was going to pawn the stuff because he needed money to get home." He shook his head with a snort of disbelief. "The guy just made over two million dollars and he's going to hock some silver candlesticks and a few paintings? Who the hell does that?"

While that definitely was bizarre, Garrett was only focused on one thing. "Did he call the cops? Is he possibly in jail someplace local? Is that why we can't get a hold of him?"

"Cash convinced him not to press charges and gave him the stuff back."

And the hits keep coming...

"But when he was giving the landlord the sob story, did he mention where he was going? Where home was that he needed money to get back to?"

"All he said was he was heading back home for a family emergency." With a shrug, Ryder added, "I honestly don't even know what to say to that, Garrett. I'm sorry."

Austin came walking around the side of the house and spotted them. "Well?"

"He's gone," Garrett said, coming to his feet. "Told the landlord he was going home for a family emergency. We know home isn't Magnolia, but who the hell knows where he was heading. All we can say is that the only emergency was that he wanted to leave as fast as possible before he had to part with any of the big money."

"Son of a bitch..."

"Guys, we can stand here all day calling him every name in the book. Let's get back in the car and head home. Obviously, we're not going to be celebrating, but maybe we can just have a nice dinner and try to move on from this."

"You don't understand, Ryder," Austin began as they walked to the car. And then, to Garrett's shame, his brother repeated everything he had told him only minutes ago. All of it. He was mortified that even more people knew what a shitshow his life was and how it was only going to get worse.

They were on the road when Ryder looked at him in the rearview mirror. "Damn. Sorry, Garrett. Is there any way this vet guy will work with you on the purchase of the clinic?"

He shook his head. "He needs the cash so he can move near his grandkids. Retirement is his only goal, and if he can't sell the practice, he'll sell the building and property and take the money from that. He just wants out."

Ryder nodded. "And the debt that Emma's dealing with? What's happening with that?"

Garrett groaned. "I really don't think Emma would appreciate us talking about this. It's kind of private."

Holding up a hand, Ryder assured him, "No worries. Just was curious, that's all."

"Yeah, well...Austin could have left that part out of the story."

His brother turned and glared at him. "It's an important part of the story and adding to the stress you've got going on right now."

They drove in silence for several minutes before Ryder

spoke again. "So what's going to happen when we get back to your place? I know I mentioned dinner, but it seems to me like maybe I should just go. This is a family situation, and just like Garrett mentioned how his stuff with Emma is private, I'm sure your mom would probably feel the same way."

"I don't know. Maybe," Austin replied. "Considering you know as much as the rest of us, it's not exactly private, but it will be awkward and probably boring for you to sit and listen to us hashing things out."

"What's to hash out?" Garrett asked wearily. "I'm screwed, my future with Emma is gone, Mom's going to feel like a fool for trusting Cash again, and you're in no different of a situation than you were before he arrived. Your share of the money was going to be a bit of a perk, but you didn't need it. Not like I did..."

He was busy staring out the side window that he didn't see Austin and Ryder exchange glances.

Once they were back at Austin's, Ryder said goodbye to them and seemed more than a little anxious to leave, and Garrett couldn't blame him.

Together, he and Austin stood in the driveway and stared up at the house. "I really don't want to go in there," his brother said. "I feel completely helpless and there isn't a damn thing I can do about it. You're devastated, Mom's going to be devastated, and knowing that you're going to go home and try to break things off with Emma...I can't. I can't freaking do it."

"We really don't have a choice," he mumbled, walking up the front steps. "There's no point putting it off. Might as well go and get it all out there and just...move on. Again."

The thing was, they'd gone through this before–Austin, Garrett, Jackson, and Grace. They'd been left behind before and they'd survived and Garrett knew he would too. But this time, it felt far more personal, and the loss was going to be that much greater.

And when he opened the front door, he braced himself. Maybe they'd have a family dinner and maybe they'd all do their best to encourage one another. But by the end of the night, Garrett knew the life he'd been dreaming of was going to be over.

14

Sunday morning, Emma watched with tears in her eyes as Garrett put the last of his stuff in his suitcase. She knew this moment was coming, yet a part of her felt like it was all a bad dream and she would wake up from it any minute.

She'd pinched herself until she was black and blue and she knew she was awake and this was her crappy reality.

"I think that's everything," he said quietly as he glanced around the bedroom.

After he and Austin got back on Friday night, they'd all sat and talked until well after midnight. Grace had cried and begged her sons' forgiveness and they all cried with her. By the time she and Garrett arrived back at her place, they were both mentally exhausted and decided they needed to sleep more than they needed to talk.

Now she wished they had stayed awake because sleep robbed them of time together–time they could have spent trying to come up with a way for things to work out. She hated how he was heading back to Norfolk alone and going through his list of previous job offers and accepting the first one that still wanted him. She hated how he was degrading himself because he felt like he didn't have a choice. He swore he was doing it for her–for them–and that did nothing to make her feel any better.

If anything, it made her feel guilty.

If her own life hadn't been such a mess, she'd be packing up with him and following him wherever it was that he landed. But she had her own debts to pay and couldn't afford to be out of a job either, and it made her want to curse Steven that much more. Like it wasn't bad enough that he'd already robbed so many years of her life - first on a crappy marriage and then a divorce. And as if that wasn't enough, the last three years of making her pay for it all financially, but he was robbing her of her future; she wanted to scream out at the universe and demand to know why.

Not that she'd get an answer.

She never did.

So now she had to sit and watch the man she loved leave her.

They talked about the long-distance relationship thing, but neither could afford to fly back and forth if he took a job anywhere north of Virginia. She had thought it would be plausible, but somehow the cost of flying a short distance almost cost more than flying cross-country.

Just another way the universe clearly hated her.

"Please tell your mom and Ed that I said goodbye," he said, zipping the suitcase closed. "I know I should have gone over to see them myself, but...there just isn't enough time."

She nodded. They'd discussed this as well, and she knew he was just struggling for something to say because neither of them wanted to say goodbye.

"Are you going to stop and see your mother on your way out of town?"

Shaking his head, Garrett walked out of the bedroom and put the bag by the front door. "I'll call her when I get home. Hopefully she's working on patching things up with Dominic."

Emma stood in the bedroom doorway and watched him wander around the tiny condo looking for...something. "Do you think she's going to?"

"I hope she does. He seems like a pretty understanding guy, and this was just an incredibly awkward situation."

Small talk was fine and well, but it wasn't what she wanted. They'd made love all through the night–each time more urgent than the one before–and yet she still wanted more. Walking over, she wrapped her arms around him and kissed him.

Deep and wet and full of promise.

He kissed her back with the same passion, but as she tried to maneuver them back toward the bedroom, he broke the kiss. With his forehead resting on hers, he took a moment to catch his breath. "I have to go."

Tears streamed freely down her face as she shook her head. "No. Don't go. We can find a way for this to work, Garrett. I know we can. We've had less than two days to really think it through. With a little more time..."

He placed a finger over her lips. "Em, the longer I'm not working, the worse things get. I need to go back home and sort through everything, and I'm going to start making calls in the morning. We'll talk every day, and hopefully, in time, things will work out. But for now, this is what I have to do."

"I love you," she said fiercely, holding his face in her hands. "I love you so much and I'm sorry I didn't say it sooner. I should have said it right back to you the night you said it to me, but...I don't even have a good reason." She met his gaze. "I love you, Garrett Coleman, and it doesn't matter if you have a job or not. I don't care if you have to do those silly videos or if you have to wear a disguise so no one recognizes you from them. I just love you. Don't go. Don't do this."

For a minute, she thought she had him.

Then he kissed her softly and took one step back and then another.

"I'll call you when I get home, beautiful girl," he whispered before turning and walking toward the door. Picking up his suitcase, he opened the door and looked at her one last time. "I love you."

And then he was gone.

Emma stood exactly where he'd left her for countless minutes and when she finally moved, it wasn't to throw herself down on the bed or couch to cry; it was to grab her purse and keys because she refused to accept this fate. She'd been a victim long enough and she was over it. On her way out the door, she took out her phone and called her mother first.

"Hey, Em! What's up, sweetie?"

"I need to hold a meeting at your place in an hour. Will you and Ed be able to be there with me?"

"A meeting? A meeting for what?"

Closing and locking the door behind her, she replied, "I can't get into it right now. I just need to know that you and Ed will be available."

"Of course. Is there anything I can do?"

"As a matter of fact, you can. Please invite Doc MacEntyre and Georgia Bishop. I know it's short notice but tell them it's urgent."

"Will do. See you soon."

When she climbed into her car, her next call was to Mia.

"Hey, Em," Mia said sympathetically. "Did Garrett leave?"

"He did," she said, feeling stronger by the minute. "What are you and Austin doing right now?"

"Um...nothing really. Why? Would you like to come over? Or I can come by you. I'll bring brownies..."

"Actually, I would love it if the two of you could meet me over at my parents' place in an hour. Happy Tails. I'm pretty sure Austin knows where it is."

"What's going on? Is everyone okay?"

"That's what I'm trying to make sure of."

"Okay, we'll be there. Can I bring something?"

Emma didn't even have to think about it. "You can bring two somethings."

"Name them."

"Definitely some brownies and...Ryder Ashford."

"Seriously? You want Ryder there?" Mia asked with disbelief. "Why?"

"I'll explain it all later. But if he's in town, I need him to be there. And if he's already on his way out of town...well...make him turn the car around and come back."

Mia laughed. "If I can't, I know Austin can. No problem. Anything else?"

Emma considered reaching out to Grace, but she figured she had enough going on right now working things out with Dominic.

"That should do it. I'll see you soon."

As Emma drove through town, there was no place she needed to go just yet. What she needed was a little time out on the beach to clear her head and organize her thoughts. She wasn't picky about where on the beach she went, so she pulled up to the first public access spot she could find and parked. Within minutes, she had her toes and butt on the sand and stared out at the ocean.

Just breathe...

And for several minutes, that was all she did, and once she felt calm, she reasoned out everything she was about to do. If Garrett had been willing to stay longer, she would have told him all of this and chances are he would have balked at her and refused to listen.

So maybe it's a good thing he's not here...

For all the years he protected her and helped her, it was her turn to do the same for him. She may have helped him with his schoolwork by tutoring him, but what he gave to her with his friendship and always looking out for her was so much more.

Now it's my turn.

She allowed herself a total of fifteen minutes before she stood and walked back to her car. She was sure that everyone was curious about what she wanted, and really, she was anxious to see if they could pull this off.

When she arrived at the farm, her first instinct was to go and find Axel and have a few minutes of puppy snuggles with him, but she decided to wait. Right now, she needed to focus. Her mother greeted her at the door, looking wildly concerned. Emma kissed her on the cheek as she walked in.

"Okay, Doc and Georgia are on their way and should be here any minute. I put on a pot of coffee and put together some cheese and crackers trays and baked some cookies. You were a little vague, so..."

Smiling, Emma continued to walk toward the kitchen. "That all sounds wonderful, Mom." She looked around. Will Ed be more comfortable in here or in the living room?"

"Well...I would think everyone would be more comfortable in the living room, but..."

"But I think the kitchen will be better. I like the idea of sitting at this large table and looking at everyone. We'll set up in here."

Together they worked to put out the food Christine prepared. Within minutes, Ed walked in with Doc MacEntyre. "I must admit that I'm intrigued," Doc said as he took a seat. "Does this have anything to do with Garrett or is it about Happy Tails?"

"Thanks for coming," Emma replied evasively. "If you'll wait for everyone else to arrive, I'd rather only go through it once."

Georgia Bishop arrived five minutes later along with her husband, her son Mason, and his wife, Scarlett. "When you said it was urgent," Georgia explained, "I thought it couldn't hurt to bring a little more power to the table." She smiled. "Plus, we were all having lunch, so..."

"That's fine," Emma said, smiling at everyone. "The more the merrier."

In the distance, the doorbell rang, and soon Austin, Mia, and Ryder were walking in. "I hope we're not late," Mia said, holding up a large pink box. "I think we bought out the entire brownie display at Henderson's, along with a few other goodies."

"Thanks, Mia." Emma took the box from her and motioned for them to take a seat at the table. Fortunately, everyone seemed to know each other–except for Ryder–but introductions were quickly made. With a steadying breath, she took her spot at the head of the table and said a silent prayer that she wasn't going to sound like a crazy person.

And she opted to stand as a show of being in charge.

"Thank you for coming on such short notice," she began calmly. "Most of you are aware of what transpired two days ago, but for those of you who don't, let me explain." Then she gave the abbreviated version of how Cash Coleman had once again destroyed his sons' lives and what exactly that had cost them. Georgia's eyes went wide, Beau shook his head, Mason and Scarlett both cursed, while her mom and Ed just looked sad.

She wanted to say so much more to bash the man, but that wasn't the reason for this little get-together.

"I think we can all agree that Doc MacEntyre has been a huge blessing to us here at Happy Tails and the entire Magnolia Sound community," she went on. "Losing him is going to be sad, but I think I speak for everyone when I say how much you deserve to retire after giving us and our pets so many years of tireless service. However, the town as a whole desperately needs a veterinarian, and I believe no one would do a better job than Garrett."

She knew enough about the Bishops that she expected some sort of pushback, but fortunately, they were quiet.

"Obviously, without the money his father promised him, Garrett cannot buy Doc's practice." She turned to the vet. "Do you have other offers on it?"

He shook his head. "I'm afraid I've been procrastinating a bit on that. My wife has been pushing me to get it done, but...it's hard to let go after all this time. She's the one who gave me the three-month time limit, but I didn't want to sell it to just anyone. My patients mean the world to me."

"And it shows," Emma said sympathetically. "No one knows more than we do how much you love all your patients." With a smile, she added, "And that's why the right person needs to take over for you."

Ryder raised his hand from the opposite end of the table and Emma had to fight not to giggle. "Um...yes, Ryder?"

"I'm not really sure why I'm here."

Her smile grew. "I've got a proposal for you," she said

bravely, her eyes never leaving his. "I want you to buy Doc's practice and put Garrett in charge of it. You can come up with the proper legal way to do it and make a deal where he can purchase it from you in five years. That timeframe would give him enough time to truly make the practice his own and put the money aside that he'd need and build the credit required to purchase it from you."

"Um, I'm not..."

"But know this," she interrupted, "I don't want you trying to make a profit off of it. This is something vital to this community, and here in Magnolia Sound, we take care of our own."

"Emma, I..."

"It seems to me you just purchased a large parcel of land from Cash Coleman and you've made it public knowledge that you are looking to invest more in the town. You've already bought a house locally, so clearly there's something here that you find desirable. All I'm asking is that you take an interest in something a little less selfish and give the locals a show of faith that you're not just looking to come here and dominate and change the town." Resting her hands on the table, she leaned forward slightly. "I can guarantee you that in doing so, you'll meet with a lot less resistance when you want to start building whatever it is you plan to build."

He arched a dark brow at her. "That sounds a little like a threat."

Her smile never faltered. "Consider it motivation." She paused. "Or a promise."

All he did was nod.

Straightening, she took a moment to calm her rapidly-beating heart. "Now, should Mr. Coleman be found and he actually holds true to his word, then all this is moot, but I don't believe we have the time to wait around for that."

Next, she looked over at the Bishops. "I understand that we had a busy adoption week last week and the adoption event was a success. I was curious if there was anything more we could do to benefit both Happy Tails and the clinic. In the past, Garrett has been very successful in drawing attention to shelters and animals that need homes, but moving forward, he is not to be used for that purpose." Then she grinned again. "But I'm sure there are other good-looking men in the community who might not mind volunteering their time for a good cause. Maybe the local firemen or police force...is there a way we can reach out?"

Scarlett raised her hand. "One of my brothers is a firefighter and I am sure I can reach out to them and get the word out in general. Social media marketing is what I do for a living and I would love to organize something like this," she said excitedly. "Do you have any idea how many posts or how many volunteers you'd like?"

"Oh, my goodness...I hadn't gotten that far," she admitted with a nervous laugh. "But if we can get maybe...a dozen? Is that too much?"

"Not at all," Scarlett assured her. "What's my timeframe?"

"I'd like to have things rolling in a week if we can swing it."

"Perfect!" Scarlett began typing on her phone and Emma felt like they were definitely making progress.

"Mrs. Bishop, is there anything you can think of that I'm missing on this particular project?"

Georgia cleared her throat and Emma thought she looked uncomfortable. "I...I need a little time to think about it, but I do have something to say."

"O-kay..."

Glancing at Austin, Georgia sighed. "This is all my fault."

His eyes went wide. "Um...what is?"

"Your father. I'm the reason he came to town and back into your lives!" she cried miserably. "I had no idea what our grandfather had left for him in the Will, but you have to know that I never would have reached out to him if I thought he was capable of this sort of thing!"

"You did *what?*" Austin shouted, coming out of his chair. Mia quickly tugged him back down.

"Maybe now isn't the time for this discussion," Mason interrupted. He looked at his mother. "Although I am dying to know what on earth possessed you to reach out to Cash, I believe Emma has an agenda that needs to be addressed first." Then he glanced at his cousin. "Austin, come home with us when we're done here and we'll get to the bottom of this."

Austin nodded, but it was obvious that he was furious.

After that, there was talk of another adoption event and then an event to welcome Garrett back to town to celebrate his taking over Doc MacEntyre's practice. Everyone had a job to do, and they agreed to meet back at Happy Tails the following Saturday.

As everyone was leaving, Emma felt a little guilty about what transpired between Austin and the Bishops, but she had a feeling she'd find out about the outcome soon enough. She hugged Mia and thanked her for her help and the brownies.

"I'm not sure it will do much, but I can certainly do some promotion on my social media accounts and maybe do some auctions of signed books or Zoom calls with me to raise money to use wherever it's needed."

"That would be amazing. Thank you." They hugged and Emma stood in the front doorway and watched them all drive away.

Doc had gone out to the barn with her mother and Ed just to check on all the dogs, and when Emma turned around, she realized she wasn't alone. Ryder was still there.

He strolled toward her, looking oddly somber.

"That was very impressive, Emma," he said, his voice low and deep. He was dressed impeccably, like he would for an important business meeting, and it just hit her how out of place he looked in her family kitchen.

"Thank you."

"Does Garrett know about this?"

She shook her head. "Garrett's too prideful and would never ask for help."

"And yet you went ahead and essentially took matters into your own hands. Don't you think he's going to resent that?"

"Maybe. But I already know he's miserable with the options he's going to pursue. He might be a little upset that I put things in motion, but I love him and want to see him happy. Once he gets over the fact that we all wanted to help, he'll be fine."

He studied her, his expression was unreadable. "I never agreed to your terms."

And just like that, her heart sank, but she refused to let it show. She stared back defiantly. "Are you going to?"

A slow smile spread across his face. "I have a few terms of my own that I'd like to discuss with you, but I think we can come to an agreement."

Now she wasn't sure if that was a good thing or a bad thing.

"No need to look scared," he told her, motioning to the

kitchen table. "Have a seat. I think you'll be quite pleased with what I'm proposing."

———————

All week Garrett had been miserable.

Worse than miserable.

And he had no one to blame but himself.

Well, okay, he certainly had his father to blame for a lot of things, but leaving Emma and Magnolia Sound had been the worst decision yet.

His landlord gave him an extension on his apartment–but only another month–so now he had to add finding a place to live to his list of things to do.

Awesome.

He reluctantly made almost a dozen calls this week and received almost a dozen rejections. His ego was beyond battered and his next option was to apply for work bagging groceries just so he could pay his bills.

"I've officially hit rock bottom," he murmured Saturday morning as he rolled out of bed. He'd talked to Emma every single day, and as much as she was the only bright spot, he hated being such a downer during their conversations. If something didn't give soon, he knew he'd have to start limiting their calls until he just stopped talking to her all together.

In the kitchen, he made himself a cup of coffee and reached for his phone. He had a few texts from Austin asking him to call him. He avoided doing that all week, but he guessed his time was up there too. So he made himself comfortable on the couch and called.

"It's about damn time," Austin said when he answered. "I've been waiting to hear from you all week."

"Yeah, well...the phone works both ways," he murmured before taking a sip of his coffee.

"Fair enough, but listen...you need to drive down here today."

"Um...no."

"Yes."

"No, Austin, I'm not doing it. I'm busy."

"Bullshit," his brother countered. "Are you working?"

"No, but..."

"Got an interview?"

"No, I'm..."

"You need to get your ass in the car as soon as possible, G. I'm not joking. Something's happened and you need to be here."

Okay, that sounded ominous. "What's going on? Is it Mom? Is she okay?"

"She's fine, but it's about Dad, and...you just need to be here."

"Austin, I just woke up..."

"It's just a little after eight and it's a three-hour drive. You can be here by noon." He paused. "Ryder's gotten some information, but...I don't want to hear it without you. Please."

It was so rare that his brother even used the word "please" that Garrett was inclined to say yes for that fact alone.

"Can't we just...you know...do a conference call or something?"

"Oh my God...why are you like this?" Austin demanded with a growl. "Just...get in the car and I'll see you at noon. Do *not* let me down!" And he hung up.

It was still possible to refuse to go, but...now his curiosity was piqued. Muttering a curse, he took his coffee and walked back into the bedroom where he packed an overnight bag before taking a shower. Thirty minutes later, he was in his car and heading back to Magnolia. He thought about calling Emma, but he didn't think he should. If he told her he would be in town, she'd want to see him, and considering he had no idea what he was going to find out from Ryder, he thought it best to just wait.

Even though he was dying to see her...hold her...sleep beside her and wake up to her saying she loved him.

Yeah, he wanted it all, and unfortunately, the odds were not stacked in his favor.

Again.

Rather than drive in silence and obsess about the things he couldn't have and how much he wanted to strangle his father, Garrett opted to turn on the radio and focus only on listening to the music and watching the road.

Surprisingly, it worked, and before he knew it, he was pulling into Austin's driveway. He recognized Ryder's car and wondered how weird it must be for the guy to come to this house that he owned and not be able to stay in it. He supposed Austin had invited him to at least stay with them, but as far as Garrett knew, Ryder stayed elsewhere.

"So weird," he whispered as he climbed from the car.

"Right on time!" Austin greeted him as he opened the door. "Glad you could make it." He gave him a brotherly hug and ushered him into the house.

Mia was in the kitchen and kissed him hello before offering him something to drink. He turned her down before walking over and shaking hands with Ryder.

"Thanks for coming, Garrett. I'm sure you're beat after a long drive," Ryder said. "You want to sit?"

"Actually, I'd rather stand after being in the car for so

long." And honestly, he just wanted to get to whatever news it was that Ryder had about Cash.

Austin walked into the room and kissed Mia before ushering them into the living room. "Okay, Ryder. The floor is yours."

Ryder opted to sit on one of the sofas with a nod and made himself comfortable before saying anything. "Cash left Magnolia last week and flew out to Seattle."

"Seattle?" Garrett asked. "What the hell is in Seattle?"

"We're not sure yet. According to my guy, there are no family connections there–as in Cash doesn't have any relatives or another secret family–living there or anywhere. I wasn't sure if the two of you know anyone who live in the Pacific Northwest."

Both Garrett and Austin shook their heads.

"Obviously no one knew where he was going when he left, so we were a day behind, which means no one knows where he went once he landed in Seattle. All we can say with any great certainty is that he didn't fly anywhere else."

That was it? That was what he just drove three hours to hear? For real?

"Um...I'm not trying to be a jerk or anything," Garrett began hesitantly, "because you didn't have to look into helping us with this situation..."

"But...?"

"But..." He glanced at his brother. "There wasn't a reason for me to drive here for this. You could have told me this over the phone!"

Austin shrugged. "I've missed you."

Rolling his eyes, Garrett walked over and sat down on the other end of the couch Ryder was on. "Seriously, dude?"

"What? A guy can't miss his brother?" He shook his

head. "I let myself be vulnerable and open up to you and...and..."

Mia pat him on the arm to stop him from saying more and offered Garrett a patient smile. "He really has missed you. We all have."

"I'm sorry I disappointed you," Ryder said. "I thought we were off to a good start in finding out what's going on. I didn't realize you were against coming back to Magnolia."

Now he felt terrible. With a sigh, he said, "I'm the one who's sorry, Ryder. I didn't mean to come off as being ungrateful. This whole situation has just been draining."

Nodding, Ryder stood. "Let me make it up to you."

"No. Really. That's not necessary..."

"No, no. I insist," Ryder pressed on. "Come on. I'm treating everyone to lunch. I'll drive." Both Austin and Mia jumped up and immediately followed, and Garrett had no choice but to go along.

No matter how much he was against it.

"I was going to call Emma..." he said as they were all walking out the door.

"You can call her later," Austin argued lightly. "How long do you think lunch will last?" Then he smacked Garrett upside the head. "And how about being a little nicer to Ryder? He's trying to find Dad for us and hopefully get some answers."

"You're right," he murmured, rubbing his head. "No need to get violent."

They piled into Ryder's car, and this time Garrett rode up front. Ryder told them about some of the plans he was considering for the property, but he wasn't going to jump in with anything just yet. They drove down Main Street and Garrett wondered where they were going. They'd passed

The Sand Bar, Michael's, the café, and were going in the opposite direction of The Mystic Magnolia, so...

A block before the bridge that took them out of town, Ryder made a left and pulled up in front of Doc MacEntyre's clinic.

"I...I don't understand what we're doing here," he said stiffly.

Austin and Mia were already climbing from the car, and Ryder grinned at him. "Just follow me. There's something here you need to see."

Groaning, he got out of the car even though what he wanted was to pitch a damn fit. Like it wasn't enough that he drove three hours to come here for lame news and now he had to go here, of all places?

Slowly, he made his way over to Austin and grabbed him by the collar. "You've done some shitty things to me in my life as my older brother, but this is the worst." And shoving him away, he followed Ryder up to the front entrance of the clinic. Ryder held the door open for him and all Garrett could do was mumble, "Thanks."

He stepped inside and froze.

Ed and Christine were standing there, and there were balloons scattered around the room. Aunt Georgia, Uncle Beau, Mason, Scarlett, his mom, and Doc MacEntyre were all standing there smiling. Looking back at Ryder, he asked, "Is this Doc's retirement party or something?"

"In a way," he replied vaguely before nudging Garrett farther into the room.

He made his way around saying hello to everyone but felt more than a little confused.

Then Emma walked in. She looked so happy and hopeful and beautiful. He no longer cared why they were at the clinic and kicked himself for being a coward for not calling her earlier.

"Hey, you," she said softly as she leaned in and kissed him.

"Hey, yourself." Hugging her close, he asked, "What's going on here?"

Putting some distance between them, she gave him a playful shove toward the group as Ryder came to stand beside her.

"Thank you, everyone, for coming," Ryder said boldly. "It is my pleasure to announce that Doc MacEntyre will be officially retiring since he has sold me this clinic."

"What?!" Garrett cried out and fought the urge to lunge at Ryder.

Lousy, stinking, opportunistic...

As if sensing his thoughts, Ryder held out a hand to stop him. "I never pass up a good opportunity and Magnolia Sound needs this clinic." He stared hard at Garrett. "And this clinic needs you." Reaching into his pocket, he pulled out a set of keys and tossed them to him.

He caught them easily. "What...I mean...what is happening right now?"

Ryder looked at Emma and she nodded.

"It was brought to my attention recently how it's important for me to invest in this community in more of a...selfless way," Ryder explained. "Austin brought this town to my attention a year ago and there's something about it that really speaks to me. And because of that, I want to see it prosper." He paused. "I know a lot about you, Garrett, and I respect you, and that's why I know you are the only person who can run this clinic with the same love and devotion that Doc put into it for the last twenty-five years."

Garrett was pretty sure he was dreaming because stuff like this didn't happen to him.

Ever.

"I know you have a lot of questions and there is a lot to discuss, but you need to know that every person in this room–hell, every person in this town–believes in you. And we're all ready to watch you make this place even more of a success than it already is."

Emma stepped forward and took his hands in hers. "It's a lot to take in, but I hope you know how much love there is in this room for you and how much we all want you to come home." She blushed as she moved closer. "Especially me."

Tears stung his eyes as he looked at her and then around the room where everyone was smiling at him and it was overwhelming. "I...I don't know how this happened..."

"You can thank Emma for that," Ryder explained. "She did it all. Your girl is quite a pistol who knows how to get things done. If she wasn't so settled here in Magnolia, I'd be trying to lure her away to come and work for me. She got more accomplished this week than you can even imagine."

She blushed when he looked at her again. "I've learned a lot since you left."

"It's only been a week..."

But she wasn't listening. "I go after what I want and fight for it." She caressed his jaw. "And I'm going to keep fighting for you because I love you."

Yeah, he was never going to get tired of hearing that.

Ever.

"So what do you say, Garrett?" Ryder asked. "You ready to take this on?"

"I...I..."

Austin stepped up beside him and clapped him on the back. "You can ask all the questions you want later. Right now, you just need to know that Emma drove a hard bargain and she's too good for you," he teased. "You can thank her later, too. Now, how about some champagne to celebrate?"

"Champagne? There's champagne?"

Austin motioned to Christine, who was passing out glasses of champagne. When everyone had one, he raised his glass. "To my little brother, Garrett–the best veterinarian and brother a guy could ask for. Here's to all your success!"

"Here, here!" everyone called out and Garrett still couldn't believe any of this was real.

But Emma wrapped her arms around him and kissed him on the cheek before whispering, "I know we have to stay and socialize and you'll want to talk to Ryder, but I can't wait to go home with you and celebrate. Just the two of us."

Smiling, he said, "Then let's get to socializing because a week away from you was too long."

"What do you say, G? Want a tour of your new offices, Dr. Coleman?" Austin asked.

He downed the rest of his champagne before saying, "Hell, yeah!"

15

THEY STAYED at the clinic for an hour before Garrett insisted that he wanted to be alone with her, and thankfully no one argued.

However, they were all meeting for a celebratory dinner at Austin's later.

The drive back to her place took almost fifteen minutes and she enjoyed listening to him talk about all the things he was going to do once he got settled. Doc MacEntyre was going to work with him for a few more weeks, but Garrett would be fully in charge by the end of the month.

He held her hand when they got to her place and walked to the door, and she was convinced that they were just going to go inside and talk.

Boy, was she wrong.

The front door had barely closed before he had her off her feet, in his arms, kissing her.

Oh, my…

Her back was against the wall, her legs were wrapped around his waist, and it was awkward and perfect at the same time.

"Need you," he murmured against her lips as he rubbed against her.

"Need you too," she panted, and seriously hoped they didn't move from this spot. Hastily, she kicked off her sandals and then forced her arms between them to whip her shirt off. Garrett's mouth instantly found her breast and sucked hard on her nipple.

It was pleasure and pain and oh-so-good.

Raking her hands into his hair, she held him to her and realized she wanted more, but as sexy and wild as sex against the wall sounded, she wasn't coordinated enough to enjoy it.

"Bedroom, Garrett. Please," she begged, and he was on the move before she even finished talking.

Garrett dropped her on the bed and she laughed as she bounced but immediately began undressing—her eyes never leaving him because his body was a thing of beauty.

"One of these days we really are going to finish what we start against a wall," he teased, and then he was gloriously naked and crawling on the bed, covering her body with his. She knew she would get the chance to look at him later, but for now, she just wanted to touch and kiss and feel him with every fiber of her being.

His hands touched her everywhere.

His lips kissed her everywhere.

"I love you, Emmaline," he whispered. And yeah, she felt that everywhere too.

It was fast and frantic and over way too soon, but still worth it.

Now, as they lay tangled up in each other, she sighed contentedly. With her head on his shoulder, she softly asked, "Okay, be honest. Are you upset that I did what I did?"

Garrett kissed the top of her head. "You mean right here in this bed? No. I loved every sweaty minute of it."

"Garrett..."

"Em, how can I possibly be upset? You were bold enough to fight for me when I was too afraid to." Another kiss. "But now I need to know how you made it happen."

She explained the meeting she held in her mother's kitchen and how things fell into place even though they almost went off the rails. "We are going to have to find out what your aunt did and what she has to do with your father. Maybe she can help Ryder's guy figure out what's going on."

Pulling back, he stared at her in disbelief. "Wait...you know about Ryder's guy?"

Smiling, she said, "I feel like I know way too much about Ryder's guy."

"Meaning?"

"Meaning, he's also the guy who found Steven."

Sitting straight up, his eyes went wide. "*What?!* How... when...I was only gone a week! How did all this happen?"

Emma got comfortable against the pillows with a bit of a sigh and pulled the sheet up to cover herself. "After everyone left my mom's last week, Ryder stayed behind so we could hash things out for the clinic. It was amazing how fast he can get things done."

"Uh-huh..." he murmured.

"Anyway, he said he appreciated someone who knows what they want and goes after it and how important that is in business." She chuckled. "He really has offered me a job several times. I'll never take him up on it, but it's nice to be appreciated."

"Em..."

"Okay, okay...so he called his lawyer and started getting

everything put together so he and Doc could get the ball rolling on the clinic, and when that was done, he asked about what was going on with Steven." Pausing, she frowned at him. "I'm not happy that you went and shared that with him."

"Technically, I shared it with Austin and he shared it with Ryder..."

"I wish you hadn't shared it with anyone, but...I guess that's not true. If you hadn't, I wouldn't have gotten the legal help I so desperately needed. His guy–and he really does just call him *guy*–found Steven in less than forty-eight hours. It was crazy. They got him on several things–he's had a bench warrant out for his arrest for over a year! If my lawyer had gone to a judge, they would have known that and we could have potentially gotten some of this cleared up a year ago!"

"Damn, Em. I'm sorry." Reaching out, he gently squeezed her hand. "So what does this all mean?"

"Okay, let me backtrack a minute. So he asked me about Steven, and I told him the situation, and he immediately made the call to his guy. When he hung up, I asked him why he would do that, and he said it was because he believes in justice and likes to help wherever he can. I told him I could never possibly repay him for this–or afford his lawyer's fees–and he said it was his gift to us because he wants us starting our lives together without all this stress hanging over our heads."

"Wow...just...wow."

"I know." She quietly observed him for a moment and wondered what he was thinking. "You know we all only did what we thought was best, right? This deal with Ryder...it's a five-year thing, but if you want to renegotiate it, I'm sure you could."

He let out a long breath before reclining beside her and taking her in his arms again. "I know I've said this probably a hundred times, but...I struggled with not ever feeling like I was good enough for most of my life. I've skated by on my looks and charm, and now that I was ready to work, no one would take me seriously." He gently played with her hair. "When I walked into the clinic today and saw so many faces and knew they were all there because they believed in me, was the greatest gift anyone could have ever given me."

"There will be even more people celebrating with you tonight. I believe Mia told me that almost all of your cousins and their spouses will be there, along with your Aunt Susannah and her husband, Colton. It's going to be huge and everyone is so excited for you."

"It's very humbling, and I guess the only thing I'm struggling with here is...well...it's something my brother said earlier."

"What did he say?"

"That you were too good for me." Pausing, he looked at her sadly. "It's true. You are too good for me, and everything you did this week showed me that I need you more than you need me and...call it pride but...I want you to need me too, Em. Even just a little bit."

Silly man...

Rolling onto her side, she kissed him softly on the lips. "I do need you, Garrett. I need you so much that sometimes it scares me. I didn't realize how much of my life was missing for all these years until you came back. That first night when we went out for pizza was the first time I felt whole in years. You complete me. I need you more than you can ever know. I love you."

It was hard to watch the tears form in his eyes. "I may not be the kind of man who shows it to the world, but you need to know that I would do anything for you. I'd slay any dragon and do my best to be your knight in shining armor. You give me the confidence to do that, Emmaline, and from this moment on, I am going to prove to everyone that I'm worthy of you."

"I don't care what anyone else thinks. It's none of their business. What we have is for us and no one else." She kissed him again just because she could, and it was wonderful. And as he slowly rolled her beneath him, she said a silent prayer of thanks that things were finally going their way.

———

Hours later, Garrett was still more than a little dazed that this was his life.

They were back at Austin and Mia's and there were easily fifty people mingling around and each of them was gushing over his accomplishments and how excited they were for this new venture. It was so good to see everyone, and he knew it was going to be nice to see everyone on a regular basis again. Coming home for an occasional holiday was one thing, but now that he and his cousins were all grown up, he found that they were all good friends as well.

"You having a good time?" his mom said as she came to stand beside him.

Smiling, he hugged her. "I am. How about you? Aunt Georgia's not bugging you, is she?"

"Are you kidding?" Grace said with a small laugh. "I thought I was going to pass out earlier when she came over and apologized to me for bringing your father back into our lives."

"I still can't believe she did that. I mean...it's weird. All these years, she's been openly hostile toward us and never missed an opportunity to put Dad down, and then she reaches out to him and convinces him to come home? Why?"

With a slight shrug, Grace replied, "I think she's starting to realize just how incredibly...um...what's the word I'm looking for...?"

"Bitchy. She's been incredibly bitchy to all of us."

"Okay, I was trying to think of a less potty-mouthed way to say it, but yes. Bitchy. I'm not sure what's behind this big transformation she's going through, but whatever it is, she's been almost pleasant to be around." She paused. "So she apologized and asked if there was anything she could do to help and I told her that we need to know where he is so I can finally get my divorce."

"You're really going to go through with it?"

Her eyes went wide. "Why on earth wouldn't I?"

"Well...the two of you had started getting...you know... close when he was here. We were all beginning to think you were going to take him back."

She didn't immediately deny it, so Garrett knew he wasn't too far off.

"Does she know where he is?" he asked.

"She claims she doesn't and I believe her. But she's promised to help in any way she can, so...we'll see."

He nodded, and they stood in companionable silence as they looked around at all the people there celebrating. "This is good," he said. "Really good. I'm disappointed that my original plans didn't work out, but the more I think about it, the more I realize this is better."

Hugging him, she agreed. "I'm glad you're back home where you belong, Garrett. I never thought any of you boys would move back to Magnolia and now look—I've got two of you here."

"And who knows where Jackson will end up."

"He's got almost another two years left of service. I don't think he knows what he wants to do when he's done and I'm not going to push." She paused. "But maybe seeing that you and Austin have both settled here will encourage him to come home too."

"We'll see."

"Oh, Susannah's waving me over. We're working on plans for a bridal shower for Mia." She kissed him on the cheek before walking away.

"There you are," Emma said as she handed him a piece of cake. "I didn't think you got to have any yet, so I made sure to grab a slice before they were all gone."

"Thanks." Taking a forkful of the chocolate cake, he moaned with pleasure. "If I start going to Henderson's too often, promise you'll stop me."

"Only if you go and don't bring anything home for me," she teased. Looking around the room, she smiled. "You have a massive family, Garrett. I don't think I ever realized how big it was."

"And we're missing a few people."

"Really? Who?"

"My cousins Parker and Peyton aren't here. They're Mason's sisters."

"Oh. They don't live here anymore?"

"Peyton does, but she's at some food show up in New York. She's the one who owns the café in town. As for Parker, I think I heard someone mention that she was temporarily living down in Florida. She's house-sitting for some friends or something."

"Oh, okay. Good for her!"

"She's the traveler in the family, and it seems whenever I'm home, she's got a story to tell about someplace she's recently visited so she is definitely living her dream."

He caught her looking over at his mom.

"Something the matter?"

"Well, I guess your mother and Dominic haven't patched things up yet. I asked her if he was coming and she could barely talk. I hate that things happened the way they did."

"Yeah, me too. But this is what happens when Cash Coleman is around. He stirs up trouble and leaves a big mess in his wake. It's been his M.O. for his whole life. So it doesn't matter if he's dying or not, he refuses to change."

"You think Ryder's guy is going to find him?"

"It really won't matter if he does or doesn't. It's not going to change anything. The damage has been done. Again." He felt himself getting angry again and reminded himself that this was a party in his honor. "Come on. Let's go outside and sit on the beach and watch the sun go down. It's been a while since we've done that."

Together they walked hand in hand out onto the deck and down the steps to the sand. They waved and talked to a few of his cousins along the way, but they were alone again by the time they were near the water.

They sat down and watched the waves crash, and Garrett felt himself relax. "You know things are going to be crazy for the next several weeks, right?"

She nodded.

"I mean, between getting things set up at the clinic and then going back to Norfolk to move out of the apartment, I don't think we're going to have more than a few minutes to breathe."

She nodded again.

"Em, we're looking at probably a solid month of craziness and then we should probably start thinking about moving. Your life's been nice and simple for a while, and I'm complicating it a lot. Are you...?"

Turning, she slapped her hand over his mouth. "Garrett Coleman, if you ask me one more time if I'm sure about anything where you and I are concerned, I swear I'll scream! My life has been staid and boring for far too long. You came back and put life back in my life! So for the last time, I am all in with you and all the craziness and all the complications! Stop worrying so much about me and start believing in us!"

She was right. He was a worrier and planner by nature, and it was hard to break old habits. Emma was going to be good for him, and the thought of planning a future with her was more than he ever thought he'd deserve.

But she was worth it.

They were worth it.

And from this moment forward, he vowed to himself that they weren't ever looking back. There was no more Steven and no more Cash because that was their old lives, and together they were building something new.

Something better.

The sky was growing dimmer, and behind them, voices were getting softer. He hated to get up and move, but he knew they should return to the party. He still wanted to talk with Ryder some more and spend some time with Ed and Christine.

"Come on, beautiful girl. Let's go mingle for a little while longer," he said as he held out his hand to help her stand. They brushed the sand off each other and strolled back up to the house. Almost everyone was gone within an hour, and Ryder asked if they could get together tomorrow because he had some calls to make.

When it was down to just them, Austin and Mia, it seemed like the perfect way to end the day.

"Aren't you glad you returned my call this morning?" Austin asked.

"I can't believe that was only this morning. I feel like I've lived an entire month today."

"That's how I felt this whole week," Emma said, resting her head on his shoulder. "It's crazy how everything fell into place, but it certainly took a lot of work."

"So what's the plan for the two of you now?" Mia asked.

"We are going home and crawling into bed and not getting out of it until we have to meet Ryder for dinner tomorrow night," Garrett said with a grin. "I have a feeling that's going to be the last time for a long while that we'll be able to sleep in like that." He looked at his brother. "Which reminds me, you need to come to Norfolk with me either next weekend or the one after to move my stuff."

"Can't you hire someone to do that?"

"Consider it brotherly bonding time. You know, since you've missed me so much."

Austin threw a plastic cup at him with a laugh. "You're such an ass, but yeah. Whichever weekend is better for you, I'll be there."

"Thanks, man. I appreciate it."

Beside him, Emma yawned, and he took that as the perfect cue for them to leave.

"It really has been a long day and I appreciate you hosting the party for me," he said as he stood and stretched. "This has been amazing. Thank you."

Mia hugged him before Austin walked over and did the same. "I'm proud of you, G. And I'm glad I get to watch you do your thing with the clinic. This town is lucky to have you."

That made him chuckle. "There was a time they didn't particularly think that way."

Austin shrugged. "Who cares? We showed them, huh? We're no longer those wild Coleman boys who wreaked havoc around town. Now we're the ones they call when they need help, so...good on us."

"Absolutely."

Emma yawned again and he tucked her in close to his side and kissed her cheek. "Let's get you home." She thanked Austin and Mia and they made plans to get together for dinner once the move was done.

Out in the car, Garrett got Emma settled in the passenger seat before getting behind the wheel. It wasn't until they pulled out of the driveway that she spoke.

"Thank God you finally took the hint. I don't know how many more fake yawns I could have handled."

"Fake yawns? You mean...?"

"I want to go to bed, Garrett, but I'm not sleepy," she said seductively.

And there had never been a better incentive to get home.

EPILOGUE
THREE MONTHS LATER...

"That has got to be the last of it." Stretching, Emma looked around their new kitchen and smiled. Everything was officially unpacked and put away, and she didn't think this day would ever come.

They were renting a house that was only a few blocks away from the clinic, and it was everything she had ever wanted in a home. Eventually they hoped to buy it, but Ryder–who bought it as an investment and was more than happy to rent it out to them–assured them that he'd help them find someplace even better when they were ready.

And as much as she hated to admit it, he hadn't been wrong on anything they'd discussed with him. Ever.

She cut the final box down, flattened it, and put it out in the garage with the others before walking out to get the mail. It was a beautiful day and it was nice to just walk barefoot to the mailbox while waving to the neighbors.

This is home...

There were just a few items in the mailbox and she flipped through them as she walked back into the house. The last one made her pause. The return address was from

Ryder's lawyer and it was for her, but she had no idea what it could be. He was doing the work pro-bono so it couldn't be a bill, but she also didn't think he'd send a letter about anything happening on her case with Steven. It had been a while since there'd been any progress, so maybe he was just touching base with her.

With a weary sigh, she sat down at the kitchen island and opened the envelope.

It was a check.

"What the...?" She stared at the amount for several minutes and swore she must need glasses because she couldn't possibly be reading it right. With shaky hands, she read the letter that was attached to it.

Dear Ms. Ryan,

Please find enclosed a check in the amount of $85,000.00. Per our discussions, this is half of the amount owed to you...

Her heart was racing and it seemed almost too good to be true. There was more to the letter, she knew that, but she needed to call Garrett and share the news with him because this was huge! Grabbing her phone, she swiped the screen and saw she had a text from him. When she opened it, there was a link to an Instagram post. Her finger was poised to tap it when the phone rang.

Garrett.

"Hey! I just saw your text. What's going on?"

He chuckled. "I've been waiting for you to check that link for almost ten minutes," he said, still laughing. "And you're telling me you haven't even looked at it yet?"

"Um...no. I was unpacking the last of the kitchen stuff and then I went and got the mail. Garrett, you are not going to believe it, but..."

"No! No, no, no...I don't want to hear anything until after you watch the video, so...go watch it and call me back."

"But..."

He hung up.

"Seriously?" she murmured and was about to click the link when her phone dinged with a message from her mother.

"Oh, my goodness! Did you see the video?"

Now her curiosity was piqued.

Another text came in. This one from Mia.

"I'm crying! Please tell me you're on your way!"

Apparently everyone they knew had seen the video because her inbox was exploding with messages. Instead of reading them all, Emma opened Garrett's text and clicked the link.

The video opened on a closeup of his face and she couldn't help but smile.

"Hey, Everyone! It's Dr. Garrett Coleman, and I'm here at Happy Tails in Magnolia Sound, hanging out with some friends." The camera pulled back and she laughed out loud.

He was shirtless.

"It's been a while since I've done one of these videos, but today is a special occasion. You see, I've got someone very special for you to meet." Pausing, he bent down and then there was Axel's little face pressed up against his. "This is Axel. He's a Border Jack mix, and he has been desperately avoiding being adopted." He turned his head and exchanged glances with the dog before looking at the camera again. "Happy Tails is an animal rescue here in Magnolia and they have been saving dogs from kill shelters for almost twenty years. The work Ed and Christine do here is absolutely amazing." The camera panned around to show the property as he explained a little more about what they did.

When the camera was back on him, he was smiling. "But back to my friend here. You see, all these sweet dogs running around behind me are looking for loving homes. Axel has been picked by three different families in the past, but they always brought him back. He's not a bad dog, he just knew the family he was meant to be with hadn't come for him yet." He turned and looked at Axel again. "Your wait is over, little man. Today, your family is bringing you home."

Emma was openly sobbing while trying to figure out just what it was she was supposed to do. Was Garrett coming home? Was she supposed to go to Happy Tails?

The two of them looked like Axel was whispering something in his ear. "What's that?" He paused and pretended to listen. "You think we should do that today?" Another pause, and then he nodded. "I like that plan. Let's do that." He looked at the camera and gave a smile she knew was especially for her. "Emma, we've both waited a lifetime to be a family with you. Won't you come here to us so we can make it official?" Then he winked and the video ended.

"What the...?" She threw her flip-flops on and ran out the door in less than a minute.

Even with the move, she was still several minutes away from Happy Tails and it was like everyone in the world was trying to drive down Main Street. Her frustration made her yell all the bad words, but she forced herself to calm down when she finally turned onto the dirt driveway.

She parked and spotted Garrett standing in the middle of the dog yard, still holding Axel, and surrounded by her family and his.

And he'd put a shirt back on.

Dammit.

Initially, she thought she'd run across the yard to greet them, but now that she was here and it was happening, emotion threatened to overwhelm her, so she walked toward them.

When she got close enough, her brother held up a phone and she knew this was being recorded and possibly happening live, but she didn't care. Her cheeks felt hot and tears were already blurring her vision, but it didn't matter.

Garrett gave her a lopsided grin. "If you think I was going to let all those guys outdo me with their videos, you're crazy," he whispered to her.

In truth, they had more volunteers than they knew what to do with when it came to shirtless social media posts. His cousin Mason did one with a dog in the office with him. His other cousin Sam did a cute one on a riding mower with a puppy. Scarlett's three brothers all did posts—one at the firehouse, one on a construction site, and one in a convertible that were all big hits. And just last week, Austin did one while fishing at the beach.

Clearly Garrett was feeling a little competitive and decided he was going to outdo them all.

"Emma Ryan," he said, his voice strong and confident. "You once told me that you dreamed of moving into a place of your own that had a yard so you could bring this little guy home with you. And since you said we are officially unpacked and completely moved in, it seems only fair that he not wait any longer." He passed the squirming dog to her, and Axel covered her face in puppy kisses while she laughed.

"Oh my goodness! You have no idea how long I've dreamed about this day," she said, kissing the top of his little head while she hugged him tightly. Then she smiled at

Garrett. "This is amazing. I'm so glad we're doing this today."

Her mother stepped forward with a little suitcase and dog bed, and her sisters moved a dog house beside it that looked a lot like the Happy Tails barn.

"Oh! That's one of Scarlett's designs, isn't it?" she said with awe as she crouched down to examine it.

"It is," Garrett replied. "Let him check it out and see what he thinks."

Axel jumped down and immediately went into the little house and sniffed it out, making her laugh. "I think he likes it." When she turned, Garrett was kneeling beside her.

Actually, he was on one knee.

It was all too much. This entire day was just...

"Somebody needs to pinch me," she whispered.

"Um...what?" Garrett asked, confused.

"Pinch me! Someone needs to pinch me!"

"Em...I'm kind of in the middle of something..."

"Then you need to...*ouch!*" Turning her head, she glared at her sister Maddie. "What in the world?"

"What? You said someone needed to pinch you, so..." She grinned and stepped just out of Emma's reach.

Garrett cleared his throat and Emma rubbed her sore arm before facing him. "Sorry."

He grinned. "Okay, Emmaline Ryan..."

Because, of course he needed to use her full name.

"I've been in love with you since I was eight years old. I know this is fast and maybe you think it's too soon, but I want us to start our lives together. You own my heart and there is nothing I want more than to be your husband." He opened the ring box he'd been holding behind his back. "Will you marry me?"

Axel barked before she could answer, and everyone laughed.

Then she was nodding and crying all at once. "Yes," she barely got out before Garrett was kissing her. It took several minutes for them to break apart and then everyone was talking and ushering them to the house for a toast.

Garrett held her back for a minute. "I love you."

She smiled. "I love you too. So much." She kissed him again, and when they broke apart, they started walking toward the house.

"Oh, you started to tell me something on the phone earlier. Did something happen?"

It was right there on the tip of her tongue to tell him her news, but she decided to wait until tomorrow. Today was a big day for him–for them.

And that's what was most important.

"It can wait," she said, hooking her arm through his. "Let's go celebrate."

Please remember to support your local animal rescues.

Xoxo

https://savinggracenc.org/

SNEAK PEEK

Want to know who's coming to Magnolia Sound next??
Here's a sneak peek at the upcoming
NOBODY DOES IT BETTER
Coming October 19th, 2021

Nobody Does it Better

It's James Bond...

Peyton Bishop knew she sometimes romanticized things going on around her, but when the perfect man walks into a room wearing a tuxedo and oozing confidence, it was hard not to think of one of her favorite action heroes.

She pressed herself back against the wall of her café so she'd be in the shadows and could watch this magnificent man with a hint of privacy. He was tall with broad shoulders, dark hair and even darker eyes, and Peyton felt her heart flutter when his lips lifted with a small smile as he looked around.

Like what you see? I know I do.

He might have been smiling as he looked around Café Magnolia, but Peyton only had eyes for him.

They'd been at a handful of events at the same time, the two of them, but they'd never been introduced. Well, people had always wanted to introduce her to him, but Peyton had always run away like a scared schoolgirl–and usually with a nervous giggle–because Ryder Ashford was just like something off a movie screen. He was the epitome of tall, dark, and handsome, and the thought of going anywhere near him intimidated the crap out of her.

But then again, the same thing happened the first time she met author Mia Kingsley, who was now engaged to Peyton's cousin Austin. She had declined an introduction multiple times and when she finally did it, Mia had been an absolute delight and now the two of them were good friends.

Somehow she doubted she'd get the same results from being introduced to Ryder.

Sneaking another glance, she wondered what he was doing here at her little café.

And dressed in a tuxedo.

He was no stranger to Magnolia Sound–he'd already purchased several homes, property, and the veterinary clinic that her cousin Garrett was now running. He'd never come in here before that she knew of. And again, why the tuxedo?

From where she was standing, Peyton admired his strong jaw and the smile on his face as he took in his surroundings. When she had inherited the café several years ago, it had been somewhat outdated. Truth be told, it still was. But she was doing the updates a little at a time so she wouldn't have to shut down for any extended period of time. Basically she'd updated the menu, gotten new tables and chairs, painted the walls, purchased new artwork... it was all cosmetic. The kitchen was next on her list and fortunately she would be able to do it all without disrupting business. This coming weekend the new appliances were being delivered and the work to take out the old ones and install the new ones would be done overnight. She was proud of what she'd done here and her customers loved it.

It was her next endeavor, however, that she was most looking forward to.

Next month, she would finally be able to put in an offer on a small piece of property she'd been eyeing for a while. Her dream was to build a place of her own–literally from the ground up. For years, Peyton had dreamed of what it would look like, what she wanted on the menu, and already had her sign and logo designed.

She was nothing if not thorough.

Out of the corner of her eye, she saw Ryder chatting with her hostess, Dana. Then she saw Dana turn and point in her direction, and damn if Ryder wasn't looking directly at her.

Busted.

Straightening, Peyton willed her heart rate to calm down. This so was not the way she wanted to meet him. She wasn't dressed to impress, but... pretty much there wasn't anything she had in her wardrobe that would wow a guy in what could only be described as a custom made tuxedo. Still, she seriously wished she was dressed in something a little more stylish rather than a pair of navy capris and a white t-shirt. Her hand smoothed up over her sleek ponytail as she sighed. This morning she swore she looked cute. Now? Not so much.

Straightening, she threw her shoulders back and stepped out from behind the large potted Dracaena Marginata with all the confidence she could muster.

"Oh, here she is now," Dana said with a smile. "Peyton, this is Mr. Ashford. He was looking to speak to the owner." She stepped away to seat a party of two that was standing there, leaving Peyton alone with Ryder.

Holding out her hand, she smiled up at him. "It's nice to meet you, Mrs. Ashford. I'm Peyton Bishop. How can I help you?"

His large hand enveloped hers in a gently clasp, but he wasn't smiling.

Not even a little.

Releasing her hand, Ryder cleared his throat. "Are you the manager?"

"Um... no," she replied, confused.

"I was looking for the owner," he said slowly, as if she wouldn't understand.

"Then you've found her," she stated with just a hint of annoyance.

"Do your folks own the place and you're just running it?"

"Excuse me?" Okay, now she was more than a little annoyed.

"It's just..." He looked her up and down–and not in a flattering way. "You don't quite look old enough to own this place."

It didn't matter how many people had said that to her in the past, this time it really bothered her. He said it with just enough condescension to truly rub her the wrong way.

"Trust me, Mr. Ashford, I'm the owner and I'm old enough. Is there something I can do for you?" And yeah, her polite tone and smile were gone.

Not that it mattered. He didn't look the least bit sheepish or apologetic. "I need a dinner catered tonight and I was told this was the place to come to. Austin Coleman recommended you."

Normally she loved a recommendation from her family, but right now she didn't feel like basking in it. "Of course. How many people will be attending?"

"Four."

"Okay. Do you know what you want to order? Have you looked at the menu?" Reaching for one, she held it out for him and was dying to know if they were all going to be in tuxes and evening gowns. It was on the tip of her tongue to suggest he go to the Magnolia Country Club, but figured Austin had to know what he was doing by suggesting her and the café.

"This is a very important dinner and I was told you do custom menus," he replied, ignoring the menu in her hand.

With a serene smile that she totally wasn't feeling, she put the menu down. "With advanced notice we do, but considering it's after three..."

"It's still advanced notice," he interrupted smoothly. "It will need to be delivered promptly at seven and delivered hot. We won't be reheating."

This guy...

Peyton forced herself to mentally count to ten before speaking. "Mr. Ashford, I appreciate your inquiry, but unfortunately we cannot accommodate your request. If you'd like to order something off the menu, then I'd be more than happy to take your order. As for delivering it, I'm afraid we can't accommodate that either."

And just like that, Ryder's expression hardened and Peyton was sure that look caused many a person to fall in line, but so far he'd been condescending and insulting and she wasn't having any more of it. So she met his gaze and waited for whatever insult was coming next.

"Miss Bishop," he began after a moment. "In this day and age, I would think delivery would be an obvious service to offer. Even a small town café..." And he paused to look around with disdain... "should keep up with the current trends. Especially when so many new businesses are coming into the area. Surely you don't want the competition to put you out of business."

Wait... new businesses? What new businesses? And was he threatening her? Seriously?

Her brother Mason worked for the town and always kept her up to date on any new businesses moving in. So if Mason hadn't mentioned it, that meant Ryder was either bluffing to get his way or planning to open someplace himself.

Which made him a major jerk right now.

"I don't see that happening," she told him levelly. And because she was feeling a little extra bold right now, she added, "And I would think if this dinner were so important, you would have made arrangements more than four hours before it begins."

One corner of his mouth lifted slightly. "Touché."

"I wish you luck with your dinner, Mr. Ashford. Have a wonderful day!" Feeling rather proud of herself, she turned and made it all of three steps before he called out to her again.

So close...

Glancing over her shoulder, she replied, "Yes?"

He slowly walked over to her and it was hard not to hum with appreciation. Ryder Ashford in a tux was stunning enough, but Ryder Ashford in motion was almost like watching porn.

Or... so she thought.

"Surely you could help out a friend of your cousin's," he said, his voice low and gruff and damn if she didn't want to promise him whatever he wanted. "You'll be paid handsomely for it." Then he glanced around again. "And from the looks of things, you can use a good infusion of cash."

And that was it. Now she was officially done.

"Thanks, but I'm good," she said and turned and walked away, her heart hammering hard in her chest the entire time. It wasn't until she was in her office with the door closed that Peyton finally let herself breathe. Collapsing in her desk chair, she let out a long breath. "What a jerk!"

Eyeing her phone, she considered calling Austin and telling him just how awful his friend was, but she also considered calling her brother to see if what Ryder had just said was true. Unfortunately, she wasn't sure her heart was up for hearing if it was. She'd already overcome so many obstacles with the café and it finally felt like things were going her way. Why did Mr. Looks Too Sexy in a Tuxedo have to come in and ruin that for her?

Ownership should have been a no-brainer. Café Magnolia was already wildly successful when she inherited it. All she had to do was keep doing what the staff was already doing and she'd be fine. But when you're young and things are handed to you, the critics seemed to take great joy in waiting for you to fail. It didn't matter how her great-grandfather was from the founding family of Magnolia

Sound and it didn't matter that her parents were very prominent in the community.

If anything, that one seemed to work against her.

But she'd persevered and practically killed herself trying to prove to everyone that she was smart enough and more than competent enough to not only continue the café's success, but that she could do it with other places as well. Two years ago, she'd stepped in and helped her brother make a success of the pub he'd inherited from their great-grandfather. After a traumatic fire, she'd helped redesign the space, reworked the menu, and trained the staff of The Mystic Magnolia, and now it was one of the most successful eateries in town. And she took great pride in knowing she'd helped make that happen.

Damn Ryder Ashford for getting in her head like this.

It had been a long time since she'd second-guessed herself and it was an awful feeling.

"Call Austin or call Mason? Call Austin or call Mason?" she murmured as she slowly spun herself around in her chair. A soft knock on the door had her pausing and straightening. "Come in!"

Dana popped her head inside with a nervous smile. "Um... Mr. Ashford placed a rather large order and asked if anyone would be able to deliver it." She hesitated a moment before stepping fully into the office. "Landon offered to do it, but I thought I should check with you and see if it was okay for him to do that."

Peyton took a moment to think on it. "What did he order?"

"Um..."

"Did he order from the menu?"

She nodded. "He ordered a couple of pints of the She-crab soup, four of the Southern loaded sweet potatoes, two orders of the Peach-Chipotle Baby Back Ribs, two orders of the shrimp and cheddar grits, two of the baked catfish specials, two orders of crab cakes, um... an order of the seaside egg rolls, a whole sweet tea cake, a whole pecan pie... and... some cornbread and biscuits."

Nodding, Peyton was mildly impressed. He'd caved and ordered. If he'd simply done that while they were talking, she wouldn't be sitting here thinking negative things about him.

And herself.

Still, she had to wonder what kind of dinner party consisted of grits and tuxes...

"So?" Dana asked, interrupting her thoughts. "Is that all okay with you? Mr. Ashford was insistent that Landon get your approval."

She fought hard to hide her smile. "As long as Landon knows he's off the clock..."

"Oh, yeah. He does. His shift ends at seven and that's what he told Mr. Ashford." She paused and stepped in a little closer to Peyton as she whispered, "And he's paying him fifty bucks to deliver it!"

It seemed Ryder was the kind of person who believed throwing cash at people was the way to get what he wanted rather than simply following the rules. Still, Peyton knew that Landon and his wife had a new baby, so the extra money would probably come in handy. "Tell them both I'm more than fine with it and be sure to thank Mr. Ashford for his business."

"Thanks, Peyton," Dana said with a smile as she walked out of the office.

Once the door was closed, Peyton leaned back in her

chair and sighed. It boggled her mind why some people simply had to be difficult. Would it have killed the man to simply accept the way she did business graciously? Did he have to use veiled threats and intimidation? Is that how he ran his businesses?

"Probably," she murmured before straightening and dealing with some paperwork she'd been putting off.

And wished she could put off some more.

She was tired; exhausted, really. It seemed like her life was consumed with the café, consulting with The Mystic Magnolia, and her plans for the new place. There was very little time left over for... well... a life. It had been a long time since she'd gone out with friends or seen anyone socially except for her family. She missed going to lunch with her sister and her cousin Mallory or going for pedicures and catching up on all the town gossip. It had been a couple of months since she'd done any of that and even longer since she'd gone out on a date.

Groaning, she forced herself to acknowledge what she really missed.

Sex.

Yeah, and thanks to Ryder looking like sex on a stick in his tux, that's what she had on the brain right now.

Hot, sweaty, sex.

Damn him.

"Bills," she blurted out as she booted up her computer. "Pay some bills. There is nothing even remotely sexy about that." And sure enough, an hour later all thoughts of Ryder were pushed aside as she paid the last invoice and pulled up her plans for her new venture. Pretty soon, she'd have a little piece of Magnolia Sound for herself and no one could say she hadn't earned it.

NOBODY DOES IT BETTER
COMING OCTOBER 19th, 2021
BUY IT NOW!!
https://www.chasing-romance.com/nobody-does-it-better

ALSO BY SAMANTHA CHASE

The Magnolia Sound Series:

Sunkissed Days

Remind Me

A Girl Like You

In Case You Didn't Know

All the Befores

And Then One Day

Can't Help Falling in Love

Last Beautiful Girl

The Way the Story Goes

Since You've Been Gone

Meet Me at the Altar:

The Engagement Embargo

With this Cake

You May Kiss the Groomsman

The Enchanted Bridal Series:

The Wedding Season

Friday Night Brides

The Bridal Squad

Glam Squad & Groomsmen

Bride & Seek

The RoadTripping Series:

Drive Me Crazy

Wrong Turn

Test Drive

Head Over Wheels

The Montgomery Brothers Series:

Wait for Me

Trust in Me

Stay with Me

More of Me

Return to You

Meant for You

I'll Be There

Until There Was Us

Suddenly Mine

A Dash of Christmas

The Shaughnessy Brothers Series:

Made for Us

Love Walks In

Always My Girl

This is Our Song

Sky Full of Stars

Holiday Spice

Tangled Up in You

Band on the Run Series:

One More Kiss

One More Promise

One More Moment

The Christmas Cottage Series:

The Christmas Cottage

Ever After

Silver Bell Falls Series:

Christmas in Silver Bell Falls

Christmas On Pointe

A Very Married Christmas

A Christmas Rescue

Christmas Inn Love

The Christmas Plan

Life, Love & Babies Series:

The Baby Arrangement

Baby, Be Mine

Baby, I'm Yours

Preston's Mill Series:

Roommating

Speed Dating

Complicating

The Protectors Series:

Protecting His Best Friend's Sister

Protecting the Enemy

Protecting the Girl Next Door

Protecting the Movie Star

7 Brides for 7 Soldiers

Ford

7 Brides for 7 Blackthornes

Logan

Standalone Novels:

Jordan's Return

Catering to the CEO

In the Eye of the Storm

A Touch of Heaven

Moonlight in Winter Park

Waiting for Midnight

Mistletoe Between Friends

Snowflake Inn

Wildest Dreams (currently unavailable)

Going My Way (currently unavailable)

Going to Be Yours (currently unavailable)

ABOUT SAMANTHA CHASE

Samantha Chase is a *New York Times* and *USA Today* bestseller of contemporary romance that's hotter than sweet, sweeter than hot. She released her debut novel in 2011 and currently has more than sixty titles under her belt – including *THE CHRISTMAS COTTAGE* which was a Hallmark Christmas movie in 2017! When she's not working on a new story, she spends her time reading romances, playing way too many games of Solitaire on Facebook, wearing a tiara while playing with her sassy pug Maylene...oh, and spending time with her husband of 30 years and their two sons in Wake Forest, North Carolina.

Where to Find Me:

Website:
www.chasing-romance.com
Facebook:
www.facebook.com/SamanthaChaseFanClub
Instagram:
https://www.instagram.com/samanthachaseromance/
Twitter:
https://twitter.com/SamanthaChase3
Reader Group:
https://www.facebook.com/groups/1034673493228089/
Sign up for my mailing list and get exclusive content and chances to win members-only prizes!

https://www.chasing-romance.com/newsletter

Made in the USA
Columbia, SC
15 July 2021